Günter Ohnemus, born in 1946, lives in Munich and is a novelist, essayist and translator. He has written three collections of short stories and a best seller for teenagers. He won the Tukan Prize of the city of Munich for his first novel and is well known for his translations of Richard Brautigan and Raymond Carver. *The Russian Passenger* is his first novel to be translated into English.

THE RUSSIAN PASSENGER

Günter Ohnemus

Translated from the German by

John Brownjohn

BITTER LEMON PRESS
LONDON

BITTER LEMON PRESS

First published in the United Kingdom in 2004 by
Bitter Lemon Press, 37 Arundel Gardens, London W11 2LW

www.bitterlemonpress.com

First published in German as *Reise in die Angst* by
Droemersche Verlagsanstalt, Munich in 2002

The publication of this work was sponsored with the help of a grant
from the GOETHE-INSTITUT INTER NATIONES.

A CIP record for this book is available from the British Library

ISBN 1–904738–02–8

Acknowledgement
Permission to use the quotation on pages 29–31 from *A Confederate
General from Big Sur*, © 1964 Richard Brautigan, © renewed 1992
Ianthe Brautigan Swenson, is granted by PFD on behalf of
The Estate of Richard Brautigan.

Typeset by RefineCatch Limited, Broad Street, Bungay, Suffolk
Printed and bound by WS Bookwell, Finland.

For Susannah Timmerman

He stared at the oncoming Frenchmen, and although, only a short time before, he had set off at a gallop with the sole intention of getting to those Frenchmen and cutting them to pieces, he now felt their proximity to be something so terrible that he couldn't believe his eyes. "Who are they? Why are they running? Are they really running towards me? And why? Do they mean to kill me? Me, whom everyone likes so much?" He thought how fond of him his mother, his relations and friends were, and it seemed quite impossible that the enemy could really be intent on killing him.

Leo Tolstoy
War and Peace

In a room that knows your death
A closet freezes like a postage stamp.
A coat, a dress is hanging there.

Text on an old hippy poster
in San Francisco

San Francisco

At fifty the good Buddhist takes to the road, leaving all his belongings behind. His sole possession is a begging bowl. That's fine. That's how it should be, and that's probably how one ought to roam the world for the rest of one's days. My problem was, there were four million dollars in my begging bowl and the Mafia were after me. It was their money. They wanted it back, and they also wanted the girl, the woman, who was with me: Sonia Kovalevskaya.

That was around four months ago. Or four years or four centuries. Or was it five months? Two years ago I abandoned everything I owned. Or almost everything. I moved out of the big flat I'd shared with Ellen, with Ellen and the child, Ellen and our daughter. With Ellen and Jessie. With Ellen. But that had been for only a few years. Thereafter I spent twenty-two years alone in that flat. Until, shortly after my fiftieth birthday, I sold it all: the flat, the books, the furniture, the record collection. Almost everything apart from the things you need when you move into a one-room flat.

I also threw away nearly all my personal stuff, letters, photos and papers. And my birth certificate. Today I couldn't prove that I was ever born at all. I still have my ID, of course, and my passport and some insurance policies and a few other documents. They would probably suffice to prove my existence. I also have my bank papers. I'm not a poor man, even though I don't use

1

the money in my account – or rather, I haven't done so yet. Contacting my bank might prove fatal.

What I found hardest of all was throwing away the letters and photos and taking the books to a dealer. We had a couple of thousand books, Ellen and I, and I'd always thought life without books was impossible. I haven't owned a single one since my fiftieth birthday, even though I've read a great deal these past two years. I often have plenty of time to spare, waiting for a fare. But now, when I'm through with a book, I simply leave it lying in some café or dump it in a dustbin. Sometimes, too, when I've finished a book, I offer it to my passengers. They usually look quite disconcerted. They've just paid for a ride in my cab and given me a tip, large or small, and then I say thanks and hold a book under their nose. It startles them every time. My own reaction would probably be just as disconcerted.

I well remember the young woman I presented with Marcel Proust's *Combray* and *Swann in Love* two years ago. I had first read Proust as a young man of twenty, and now, more than thirty years later, I was giving them to the prettyish, youngish woman I'd just driven from Grünwald to Nymphenburg.

I've never read them, she said, taking the books. She now looked prettier still. Most pretty women don't know they look still prettier when they're holding a copy of *Swann in Love*. But *I* do. I was reading Proust when I met Ellen over thirty years ago. Or was it the other way round, and had I just met Ellen when I started to read Proust? Anyway, it was more or less contemporaneous. I can't recall which came first, but I do know that pretty women look even prettier when they're holding a copy of *Swann in Love*. Even Ellen, who couldn't have been any prettier than she was, looked prettier still. These books, I told the puzzled

2

young woman in the passenger seat beside me, are just as good as they were thirty years ago, when I read them for the first time.

She looked at me and said: You don't look as if you could have read books like these thirty years ago. I mean, you don't look old enough.

Oh, I said, I was an infant prodigy.

She smiled indulgently. Why should I read them? she asked.

You always have to explain to the younger generation precisely why they should do something. Above all, why they ought to read some book or other.

Well, I said, looking at the cover of *Combray*, that's one of the best books ever written.

Maybe, she said, but what was it that appealed to you particularly? Or who?

Oh, I said, the grandmother. And I told her how the grandmother always removed the rose supports when she walked through the garden, to allow the plants to develop naturally. When I'd finished, I said: My grandmother was just the same. She always did that too.

The fact is, my grandmother never did that. Being perpetually worried about the health of every member of the family, she would have found it quite natural to support weak plants of any kind.

I'd told a downright lie. I lie quite often – several times a day, I guess. On the other hand, it wasn't really a lie. One winter, when I was four or five years old, I developed a high temperature and had to be taken to the hospital by ambulance. The hospital was situated in a mountain valley, and the approach road was so steep and icy that the ambulance couldn't make it. One of the ambulance men was about to carry me down, but my grandmother said to let her do it. She

3

took me on her lap, sat down on the frozen road, and slid the last hundred yards. Well, that's not so different from someone who removes the supports from roses.

I like that bit about the rose supports, said the young woman. Plants must grow strong by themselves.

She probably votes for the Greens.

I must read that, she said, like someone who might well have decided not to. *Swann in Love* had a close shave. I mean, if she hadn't taken both books I would probably have chucked it into a refuse bin on some street corner.

The last thing I said to her was: There are plenty more where they came from.

Strange that I should be writing all this. I've now been on the run from the Mafia for weeks and months on end. I don't really have the time, and I'm sometimes scared to death at night. No, I'm scared to death most days – scared if someone in the street gives me more than a passing stranger's cursory glance. My whole body stiffens as if in response to a shrilling alarm bell, even though it probably doesn't show at all on the outside. Yes, it's true, I don't have much time left. I'm running for my life, yet I'm sitting here writing about a chance encounter. About a woman to whom I once gave two books, and who may never have read them and never will.

My time has run out, and that young woman is merely someone from a time that no longer exists, that's been washed away while I sit here writing. It's been washed away by this nothingness that also keeps me on the move through an ocean of time and fear and suspense. There are no more dates, no weeks, no months, no years. There are only these days that still have names – Monday, Tuesday, Wednesday, Thursday – nothing else, and here I sit in this hotel room, in

4

some hotel room in which it's Monday or Wednesday, and tomorrow I'll be sitting in another hotel room in which it may be Friday or Saturday. I sit in these rooms, writing to stave off fear and this ocean of time that will sooner or later wash me away.

Thursday

The young woman may never read the book, and she'll never know, of course, what became of her tip. I'm not entirely like one of those itinerant Buddhist monks who roam around with their begging bowls. I drive my taxi through the city and its environs (and sometimes a bit further, to Vienna or Zurich or Regensburg), but I seldom venture far from Munich, and I live on the money I make from my fares. But I don't keep my tips. Those I always give away to tramps. I know some of them quite well. Where two or three of them are concerned, I sometimes think I'm their most important source of income. Or *was* their most important source of income, because that's all over – permanently. I don't know who gives them his tips these days. The tramps never venture very far from the city either. We were all like stationary itinerant monks waiting for eternity or a miracle. A miracle that would last for ever, or an eternity replete with miracles. But the age of miracles is past, even though I sometimes manage to recapture the *fringe* of that age. I see a girl, a young woman in the street somewhere in the city, and there comes a moment when that young woman is Jessie, and I know that it isn't, that it *can't* be her, yet it is and it isn't, and I protect her like some unseen spirit. Just for a moment. For the space of a breath or two.

Yes, that's what I'd like to be now, an invisible spirit protecting my daughter, or I'd like to be sliding down this long, cold street on someone's lap. That's what

I'm made for, not for protecting Sonia Kovalevskaya and taking on the Mafia.

Sonia has just gone into town because she wanted to see a movie. Ridley Scott's *Gladiator*. I don't like letting her go alone, but she insisted on being alone tonight. She simply wanted to sit there in the dark and breathe easy. Besides, she said, I must improve my accent.

Take care you don't come out speaking Roman English, I said. She laughed, which was good. It's good she can still laugh. Here in San Francisco we always travel by bus or streetcar, so we have to speak to as few people as possible (cabbies, for instance), because Sonia speaks English with a perceptible Russian accent. Not a strong one, but you can hear it all the same. We always buy a Muni Pass, a seven-day ticket for fifteen dollars, so we don't have to speak to the bus drivers. We simply board the bus, show our tickets, say "Hi", and smile. Sonia can say "Hi" without a trace of an accent. We never board a bus together if we can avoid it, but let a few people go between us. We never sit together, either. That lessens the risk of our looking familiar to someone, some European tourist who's seen our pictures in the paper. Because it isn't just the Mafia who are after us. The police are too, though I'm sure no one suspects we're in the States – yet. They're probably still looking for us in France and Italy. Or in Eastern Europe. Hopefully in Eastern Europe.

We never sit together on a bus, nor do we stand together. We usually station ourselves in the rear section of the bus, near the central door, with me behind Sonia and near enough to be able to intervene if anything happens. So far, however, she has only been accosted by a few friendly Americans, and her invariable response has been to smile back and say "Oh", or "Sure", or "How wonderful", or "That's right". Aside

7

from "Hi", those are the things she can say without a trace of an accent. Sometimes she overdoes it a bit and gives people a loud, vivacious "Hi" when a smile would have been enough. When that happens, I'm always afraid her enthusiasm may transmute itself into a Russian accent, and we have to be careful.

She had no accent at all the day I met her in Munich. She was standing on the kerb in Würmtalstrasse with a small rucksack, and she waved when she saw my taxi approaching, and when I pulled up and lowered the window she said: Are you free? She had absolutely no accent in German. She'd spent several years in East Germany, teaching Russian for the KGB, and had learnt good German in the process. Sonia is quite unembarrassed about having worked for the KGB. A few weeks ago she said to me: For us, being a member of the KGB is a bit like you joining a breakdown service – and it's actually quite practical.

It was still pretty early when she hailed me, maybe half past seven, and it must have been a Thursday, because I always drove an old lady to the hospital for her dialysis on Thursdays. If there was time we occasionally had coffee at her place first. Her son collected her from the hospital afterwards. She had to go for dialysis three times a week, but I only took her on Thursdays because I had other regular customers on the other days. So it was definitely a Thursday when I first met Sonia.

I got out and stowed her suitcase in the boot while she was settling herself on the back seat. She was pretty – I mean, she still is, of course, and it's strange that women should interest a man even when he's lost all interest in them. The only women that interested me were Ellen and Jessie, but I naturally noticed how pretty Sonia looked, sitting in the back, and I found that very pleasant. She seemed rather tense.

Just drive on, she said. I have to get to the airport eventually, but just drive. She had no accent, nor did she look Russian. If she'd looked Russian I might have been a bit more wary. More suspicious, too, in which case I would probably have thought her less pretty. I used to drive quite a lot of Russians around, and I found them rather arrogant and insufferable. They also had that wry, knowing Slav smile, as if they knew what makes the world tick. I mean, as if they knew what a *bad* place it is, and as if everyone in it is simply out to cheat and deceive the Russians of this world. As if life is one big con. I don't like that, and I don't like people who think like that.

Sonia took me on quite a tour of the south of Munich – Please turn left here, now turn right – until we were back near the hospital and driving down one of the little side streets. I had to drive very slowly because she seemed interested in one particular house. Then she said: Now we can go to the airport.

She'd spent the whole time looking round. She probably thought she could do so unobtrusively, but you can't look round unobtrusively on the back seat of a car. There's no rear-view mirror, so you have to turn round. I watched her in my own rear-view mirror. She really was extremely edgy, and completely blind to the beauties of the morning.

We drove down Lagerhausstrasse, and as we were passing Wittelsbach Bridge I said: Lovely day, isn't it?

Yes, she said distractedly. She wasn't the only one whose thoughts were elsewhere. If you've lived in a city for a long time, it contains a whole host of sacred places. Places where you've had significant experiences. Good experiences and bad. Munich was full of such places. I wasn't there as a child and didn't grow up there, but when you've lived in a city for over thirty years it's almost as if you'd been there as a child. And my child had been a child there, so I was one too.

When we drove past Wittelsbach Bridge I was pretty indifferent to what Sonia thought of the day as she sat there on the back seat. This was because, for some years now, it had always been a nice day when I passed that bridge. I'd driven across it one summer's day a few years earlier, and two kids were standing roughly in the middle, looking down at the tramps who live there nearly all year round. In fine weather they put out tables and benches, like in a beer garden. Sun umbrellas too.

So there they stood on the bridge, those two kids, looking down at the tramps. I say "kids", but they must have been sixteen or seventeen years old. The girl was extremely pretty. She had a very vivacious face, and although she wasn't smiling in the least, it seemed to wear the smile of someone who knows what makes the world tick. But it wasn't like that Slav smile which knows that the world is a lousy place and refuses to be conned. It was the smile of someone who regards the world with wonderment. And who wants to know everything.

I pulled up a few yards away from the pair and watched them. And, of course, it instantly occurred to me that Jessie could have been that girl. I always think, when I see a girl or young woman who appeals to me, that she could have been Jessie. In the case of the girl on the bridge, though, that was impossible. She was sixteen or seventeen, perhaps, and Jessie would then have been twenty-eight.

While the girl and boy were looking down at the tramps, half a dozen smartly dressed riders approached the bridge at a leisurely trot, wearing hard black riding hats. Suddenly the girl took a camera from her little rucksack – yes, I think she had a rucksack with her – and said to the boy: Hey, now we'll get some really terrific sociocritical pix – members of the upper crust riding past a bunch of tramps with their noses in the air!

The horsemen slowed as they neared the tramps, rode straight up to them, and then reined in. After exchanging a few words, they dismounted and sat down, and the tramps fetched some cans of beer from the River Isar, where they'd been left to cool, and put them down on the table in front of the riders.

Cool! said the girl. Then she said: But this is much harder to photograph. We'll have to come back tomorrow.

I was terribly happy when she said that: *We'll have to come back tomorrow.* Her life still held so many days in store, and there was still so much to discover. Yes. Yes, that girl *was* Jessie even though she couldn't possibly have been, and I stood watching her like a tutelary spirit. I think sheer happiness had made me genuinely invisible – at all events, the pair of them hadn't noticed me. I was like a guardian angel watching over them. They should really have noticed me, and sometimes I think it was all just a dream, and those kids existed as little as Jessie does.

I looked at Sonia in the rear-view mirror when we were a little way beyond Wittelsbach Bridge. Our eyes met, and I half turned to her and said, smiling like a guardian angel: If you're wondering whether we're being followed, we aren't.

How do you know? she said. Anyway, what makes you so sure I think someone's following us?

I go to the cinema from time to time, I told her. I've seen all the relevant films. And I'm a taxi driver, in case you hadn't noticed.

She laughed, completely relaxed for a moment or two. It would never have occurred to me that she could be Russian. And now it's as if that moment in the taxi, when Sonia sat laughing on the back seat and relaxed for a moment or two, was the last thing I remember of Munich. That and the kids on the bridge, who may not – for all I know – have existed at all.

Yes, those two things were the last I saw of Munich, not that I knew it at the time. I didn't know I would never return.

When we'd driven along the autobahn for a while, I asked Sonia: What are you scared of?

I'm not scared, she said.

That's what they all say, I said.

Okay, she said, I'm scared I'm being followed, and that people will find out where I'm flying to.

So where are you flying to?

I could tell she wanted to tell me to mind my own business, but she said: Luxembourg.

Oh, Luxembourg, I said. To withdraw some cash?

Drop it, she said.

If you *fly* there, I said, they can easily find out where you're going. It's all recorded. Had you thought of that?

She didn't answer, and I said nothing more for a while, but I could see in the mirror that she was thinking hard. And that she was very frightened.

When we passed the Garching exit I said: If I drive you to Luxembourg, no one will know where you've gone.

She thought this over. Then she said: Surely it would cost a lot?

12

I said: To someone with so much money she has to go to Luxembourg to withdraw it, a taxi fare is neither here nor there.

She didn't reply.

Okay, I said, I'll drive you to Luxembourg and back for the price of a return ticket.

I don't need a return ticket, she said.

Oh, I said, so it's like that.

I suddenly felt an overwhelming urge to drive to Luxembourg. I can't tell why this was so. I could say it was the memory of those two youngsters on Wittelsbach Bridge, whose guardian angel I was, but I don't know if it's true. I only know I wanted to persuade that young woman to let me drive her to Luxembourg, simply because it was safer. I think my interest in the operation was purely technical. At the Eching exit I said: Well, how about it?

She thought awhile, and I helped her a bit. I'll drive you there for the price of a single ticket, I said.

She thought awhile longer, and we were almost at the interchange when she said: All right, drive me to Luxembourg. I briefly debated whether to drive on in the direction of Nuremberg and then turn west, or whether to take the Stuttgart autobahn. I sometimes find it hard to get my bearings, which is unusual in a taxi driver. We'd almost passed the exit and driven on towards Nuremberg when I pulled off sharply to the right because the Stuttgart route struck me as being shorter after all. We shimmied a bit, and the tyres squealed. A few of the drivers behind us sounded their horns. I saw them gesticulate behind their windscreens.

My God! Sonia exclaimed.

Don't worry, I said, I've seen all the relevant films.

13

When we'd driven on for a few miles and Sonia had calmed down, she said: But shouldn't you get back to your family?

I don't have a family, I said. I don't even have a cat any more. I could absent myself from Munich for a whole year and no one would miss me. When I'm away there's just one less taxi in the city. Otherwise, no change.

I don't have a family either, said Sonia.

So who are you running away from?

She said nothing for a while, then: My name is Kova-levskaya, by the way. Sonia. Sonia Kovalevskaya, I mean, and I *would* be missed. I'm running away from some people who are either missing me right now or won't, with luck, miss me till tomorrow or the day after.

My name's Harry Willemer, I told her. Are you from Poland?

No, she said.

I'd have been surprised, I said. You don't have a trace of a Polish accent.

She laughed. Would you recognize a Polish accent?

Well, I said, I'd recognize a *Slav* accent of any kind.

I was born in Leningrad, she said. I ought by rights to have a Russian accent, but I lived in East Germany as a child. My father was an officer in the Red Army. A general.

Ah, Leningrad, I said, the city of many names. St Petersburg, Petrograd, Leningrad, and now St Petersburg again. Built by a barbarian who tortured his son to death.

She winced when I said the word "tortured": You say that as if you think all Russians are barbarians.

I'm sorry, I said. I didn't mean that.

It doesn't matter, she said. Peter the Great *was* a barbarian who tortured his son to death. Or at least, he

14

watched his son being flogged to death, that's absolutely true, and two hundred thousand labourers died while he was building the city. And sixty years ago a million people died while it was being besieged by some other barbarians.

So now we're quits, I said.

We're quits, she said. It's a wonderful, accursed city.

Even so, I said, you've opted for the German name again. St Petersburg.

She smiled. Unpredictable folk, these Russians.

You went back to St Petersburg after East Germany? I asked.

Yes, she said, after seven years. A few years later I went back to East Germany again.

As a grown-up, you mean, I said.

She laughed. Yes, a grown-up secret agent.

Aha, I said, very frank of you. What do you do in Munich?

I represent a Russian firm.

Import–export?

No, she said, blood and iron. Her big eyes regarded me in the rear-view mirror. Drugs and cigarettes. Counterfeiting and money-laundering. Women and children. Torture and death.

I see, I said. You really are being frank. Then I said: And what's *your* speciality?

I shouldn't have said that. She looked utterly horrified. I've never harmed anyone, she said. Harmed them physically, I mean, and I've never stolen anything either. All I do is handle financial transactions – *minor* financial transactions. The petty cash, as you call it.

This petty cash, I said, doesn't it come from drugs and trafficking in human beings?

Sure, she said, that's why I'm sitting here now. But that's not so interesting. What interests me far more is why *you're* sitting here. You don't look as if you've always done this for a living.

I haven't, I told her. I was a writer before I drove a cab.

She thought it extremely funny that someone should have been a writer before becoming a taxi driver. You used to be a writer and now you drive a taxi, she said. Usually it's the other way round, isn't it? People start out as taxi drivers, janitors, undertaker's assistants or petrol-pump attendants, and then they become writers. You really put the cart before the horse. How did it happen? Weren't you a success?

That wouldn't have mattered so much, I said. There came a time when I found I couldn't write any more.

That sounds very mysterious.

It isn't mysterious, I said. It's private, that's all.

I apologize, she said. Then she smiled. I didn't mean to invade your space.

No need to apologize. It isn't such a private decision, really, becoming a taxi driver. How were you to know it was different for me?

She looked at me with a mistrustful smile – with that mistrustful Russian smile that says: Nothing in this world is the way it looks. You automatically feel like a conman when someone gives you a smile like that. In recent years I've driven Russians around at least once a week, and nearly all of them had the same mistrustful smile. Perhaps it's inevitable when liberation means you've exchanged the KGB for the Mafia. The one Russian I didn't see smile like that was a man of around forty. As one of the quota of Russian Jews imported into Germany by the Kohl government, he was faced with a problem: the Jewish community he wanted to join insisted that he and his two sons should be circumcised. He was genuinely dismayed, because he didn't feel he could ask this of his children. He himself was prepared to be circumcised, but his children? No, they must decide for themselves – after all, they now lived in a free country. He was completely at a loss, but he smiled – except that his smile wasn't a mistrustful Russian smile; it was a forlorn smile. They can't expect it of me, he kept saying. You can't tell two boys of fifteen and sixteen to let someone snip a bit of *that* off. They really can't expect it of me.

The worst of those Russian importees was an oldish, stoutish woman who told me precisely how she planned to get her daughter and granddaughter to follow her. Her son-in-law, who commanded a nuclear submarine, could stay in Russia as far as she was concerned. He was just a burden, she said. They were probably averse to taking him along because he might have been contaminated, and anyway, they wanted to start a new life in Germany. Besides, that would have spared them any circumcision problems. All the time she was outlining her plan to me, she smiled in that insidious, mistrustful way. It's the most repulsive kind of smile there is. If you spend too much time with such people, you can't help smiling mistrustfully yourself.

I don't think you're a Jewess at all, I told the plump woman.

Only God knows that, she said, smirking like someone who has decided exactly how much God is allowed to know – someone who has got it all worked out. They don't even trust their own God. If they have one.

All Sonia has in common with such people is that smile. Nothing else. She doesn't even have a Russian accent in German. All the same, that smile sometimes bothers me a bit. It reminds me of that odious woman who didn't want to take her contaminated son-in-law along. If it had been up to her, he and his submarine would never have surfaced again. Sonia sometimes becomes that woman for an instant. But only for an instant.

Meantime, I kept watching her in the rear-view mirror. Our eyes occasionally met, and we smiled the way one does on such occasions. Sonia has dark brown bobbed hair and eyes verging on black, and that day in my taxi she was wearing a green dress. She looked pretty sexy. Very far removed from someone who leaves her son-in-law to rot aboard a nuclear submarine.

Women didn't interest me any more, and even in the old days I wasn't interested in women more than a few months younger than myself. That's just the way it was. Like a law of nature. But in my taxi that day I enjoyed looking at Sonia, nothing more. Our eyes continued to meet in the mirror.

How old are you? I asked her.

Oh, she said, thirty-eight.

Jessie would then have been thirty-two. Jessie's eyes were grey.

Wouldn't you like to sit up front? I asked, watching her in the mirror.

Why? she said. You can see me far better back here.

We both laughed, and she said: I'm a dangerous Russian, after all.

But it's safer up front, I told her. With the airbags, I mean.

Fine, she said. That's just the kind of safety I need.

I pulled into the next rest area. We stretched our legs for a bit, then she got into the passenger seat. Better like that? she asked. Safer?

Well, yes, I said. At least we got rid of that Russian agent in the back.

When we were out on the autobahn again she asked if I would be driving straight back to Munich or staying overnight. I was planning to spend half a day in Luxembourg because I'd never been there before and wanted to take a look around.

She said: If I pay you the price of a return ticket, not just a single, could you stay a few hours longer and do me a favour?

Her plan was quite simple. She owned a small flat in Luxembourg, and I was to fetch two suitcases from the basement of the block, then meet her in a restaurant on the outskirts of the city and hand them over.

What's in the suitcases? I asked. Drugs? Guns? A nuclear warhead? I wanted no truck with drugs or guns. I'm all in favour of decriminalizing drugs because it would simplify a lot of things, but dealing in them is quite another matter.

The suitcases are empty, she said.

So all I have to do is turn up at this restaurant with two empty suitcases? Why not fetch them yourself?

I can't enter the building, she said. It may be watched. Besides, you'll have to put something in them.

She explained what I would have to do. The suitcases were in the basement storage space of a neighbour who had gone off to Australia for a few months. Sonia, who had promised to keep an eye on her flat, had taken the opportunity to store the suitcases – and the money I was to put in them – in the neighbour's space in case her own was searched. The money was in some dusty old cardboard boxes. While I was stowing it in the suitcases and getting them out of the building, Sonia would go to her bank to distract the attention of anyone who might be watching the bank or the apartment house.

It must be a lot of money if it takes two suitcases to hold it, I said. How much?

How much is beside the point, she said. It'll fit, that's the main thing.

Is it clean? I asked. Not counterfeit, I mean?

No, it's clean, she said. Then she smiled and said: It's even been laundered. And it's *mine*, even though one or two people think it belongs to them. So you won't be doing anything illegal, my dear cabby. You'll simply be helping me to preserve my money from the clutches of some criminals.

That sounded good. Intriguing. Even if a single air fare from Munich to Luxembourg wasn't a very generous fee for an operation that might lead to a head-to-head with some crooks. But Sonia reassured me on that point. She had laid a false trail for the people from the "Firm" – she always called it that. A girlfriend of hers had flown to London for three days, using Sonia's name and passport, so anyone making inquiries would be bound to believe she was in England. No one in the Russian Mafia knew this friend. She had simply flown to London on Sonia's passport and would never use it again.

Which means you're now short of a passport, I said.

She gave me an indulgent smile, reached back and retrieved her little brown rucksack from behind the passenger seat. Then she opened it, took out three passports, and said solemnly, as though reciting a short poem:

One German.
One French.
One Italian.
One burgundy.
One claret.
One chianti.

Gesine Kerckhoff.

Catherine Marchais.

Patrizia Calabrese.

The French and Italian passports were more oxblood than wine-red. Sonia opened them. They're genuine, she said. Three different photographs, but they're all of me. They aren't too similar, though. People never look like their passport photos. Three different names too, of course, and three different dates of birth. Even three different years of birth, although I don't like being made older than I am. The Firm really does allow for everything. Except for the fact that Sonia Kovalevskaya isn't in London. Let's hope they haven't allowed for that.

Great outfit to work for, I said. Do you get a pension as well?

Yes, she said. I'm just about to draw mine.

What makes you so sure I won't run off with the money once I've put the suitcases in the boot?

One can never be a hundred per cent sure, she said, but I'm a pretty good judge of character. You're a romantic. You might run off with a woman, but not – unless I'm very much mistaken – with money. If you did run off with the money I'd have to go back to the Firm. I wouldn't get a pension, that's all.

Beyond Ulm I turned off at the Aichen service area and pulled up in the car park.

What are you doing? Sonia asked.

Relax, I told her. I won't be a minute.

I took an adjustable spanner from the boot and removed the taxi sign from the roof. It only attracts attention, driving around abroad with a taxi sign. The colour of our cabs, that inconspicuous shade of ivory, is conspicuous enough already. Sonia had got out of the car and was watching me.

That's the way we romantics say "yes", I said. The cabbies among us, at any rate.

When we were sitting side by side again, she said: I really do trust you, my romantic cabby. Don't get any wrong ideas, that's all.

Time will tell, I said.

* * *

Sonia had it all worked out. We would spend the night at a hotel, and next morning she would go to the bank, armed only with her little rucksack, and spend at least half an hour talking to her financial adviser. Half an hour before that I would enter her block of flats, make my way down to her neighbour's storage space in the basement, transfer the money from the dusty cardboard boxes to the suitcases, and put them in the boot of my taxi. An old grey Samsonite and a fairly new green lightweight, Sonia told me, neither of them very big, and the keys were inside them. Then I would drive to our restaurant rendezvous and wait for her in the car park.

As far as you're concerned, she said, there's absolutely no risk. This is just a safety measure, in case someone has, after all, discovered that I'm in Luxembourg, not London.

What if someone sees me in the basement? I asked. I'm a total stranger, after all. I might be a burglar.

We'll have to risk that, she said. The building has a high turnover – bank employees, airport staff, nearly all singles. People who work long hours. It's unlikely anyone will go down to the basement at half past nine in the morning.

It occurred to me that I had some dungarees in the boot, a mechanic's outfit for emergencies, in case something went wrong with the car. If I went down to the basement in dungarees, people would take me for a workman.

Hey, said Sonia, good idea. You're developing a genuinely criminal mentality. You'll have to change in the car, though. You can't go waltzing out of the hotel in a mechanic's outfit.

Sonia would turn up at the restaurant in a blue Peugeot 306, to which the suitcases would then be transferred. After that, she would drive on in the direction of France and I would return to Munich.

The Peugeot presents another little problem, she told me.

What, another? I said. It seemed that the Peugeot belonged to the neighbour who owned the storage space where the money was. Sonia wanted me to collect it from the underground garage that evening and leave it at a certain spot in town.

Then you can take a look at the building in advance, she said. You might even pay a quick visit to the basement, so you don't have to spend too long looking tomorrow morning. I've got the keys to the car and the storage space right here.

She really had thought of everything, but she still became more and more nervous as we drove into Luxembourg.

What would you have done, I asked, if you'd turned up here on your own?

I shouldn't have said that. She became even edgier.

I'd have had to run far greater risks, she said.

You mean I've got to run them for you?

There's no risk from your point of view, she said. Now let's head for our hotel. The Christophe Colombe, if there's a vacancy. We'll take a double room, of course.

No, I said.

What do you mean, no? Are you scared of me?

No, I told her, I'm not scared of you – I won't share a double room with you, that's all. I never share my bedroom with a woman.

With a man, then? she said.

Not that either, I told her. But it wouldn't bother me, not for one night.

Very interesting, she said. Very mysterious, too. But we'll have to take a double room. Hotels keep records just like airlines, and you didn't want me to appear on any passenger list, did you? If someone really is looking for me, he'll look for a woman on her own, not a couple. Besides, when hotels ask for some ID, the man's is usually enough for them. Women aren't as important. Italy's the only country where they insist on both. So the hotel register won't list anyone by the name of Sonia Kovalevskaya – or Gesine Kerckhoff, Catherine Marchais, Patrizia Calabrese, or anything else.

She really had thought of everything, but she'd probably been trained to. All right, I told her, we'll take a double room with twin beds. One for you and one for me, with a pathetic little bedside table in between.

Sonia took out her mobile and booked us a room at the Christophe Colombe in my name. It's always better to book in advance, she said. That way, they never ask for your ID.

We drove first past her block of flats and then to the hotel. At the reception desk I alone had to fill in a form with Sonia watching over my shoulder. When I came to the box headed *Madame*, I wrote "Jessie". I did it just like that, without thinking. Who's Jessie? Sonia whispered.

It popped into my head, that's all.

24

Jessie for Jessica?

No, I said. Jessie for Jessie.

I've no idea why I put Jessie's name. It was simply the first name that occurred to me, and I couldn't afford to spend too long wondering what my wife's name was, not at the reception desk. Now, as I write this, it could be said that I wrote Jessie's name in order to give Sonia the protection I couldn't give Jessie, but that would be utterly wrong. I didn't want to protect Sonia, I merely wanted to do her a favour and drive home next day.

Is that your only luggage? the receptionist asked, indicating Sonia's rucksack.

Yes, I said. We weren't intending to remain in Luxembourg overnight. It was a spur-of-the-moment decision.

I don't know why I said that. It was quite superfluous, but I was already, even at that stage, starting to cover myself. To cover myself more than necessary – to supply explanations no one expected of me.

The man behind the desk gave me an understanding smile, and I asked him for a toothbrush and some shaving things.

We had two cappuccinos brought to our room. After that I went alone to Sonia's block of flats and collected the blue Peugeot from the underground garage. First, however, I reconnoitred the basement and located the relevant storage space. I spotted the cardboard boxes and an old grey blanket that presumably concealed the two suitcases. Then I drove the Peugeot to the car park Sonia had specified. I removed the ignition key and sat there in the dark for a few minutes. The moon had risen. Jessie was always the first to see the moon, even in the afternoon, when it was just a pale wraith. She did that even when she was two years old. She would point at the sky and say: Moon. And then she always wanted one of us to kiss her. Ellen, I said softly, I wrote your daughter's name on the registration form. Wouldn't it be nice if it were for real? It's a pretty place, Luxembourg, and we could go off and eat together. I often talk to Ellen, mostly at night but sometimes in the daytime too. I suspect I sometimes talk to her without realizing it, and the people who see me probably think I'm crazy. They're probably right. I think I've been crazy for twenty-four years.

I walked back to the hotel, then dined with Sonia at a small restaurant. She was very edgy. So edgy, she had to have a long, soothing shower when we got back to the hotel.

I lay down on my bed and turned the radio on. They were playing some old French hits. I could hear Sonia nervously humming some tune in the bathroom, something Russian, probably, and I thought of Ellen and Jessie and the fact that I was now, for the first time in twenty-four years, sharing a bedroom with a woman, and of the night when it all ended, my life and Ellen's life and Jessie's life, just because I was so stupid and stubborn and jealous and intent on destroying everything, and simply wouldn't stop. Jessie was sleeping over with a friend that night, and I wouldn't stop destroying everything, and there was absolutely no reason to be jealous, it merely looked that way, and even if there *had* been a reason, that would have been no reason to destroy everything, and that night, at that one instant when Ellen became frightened of me, I was genuinely insane. No, I didn't hit her – I didn't even shove or shake her – but she suddenly became afraid that I might, and I saw the fear in her eyes, that boundless fear, not surprise, just fear and dismay at what might happen, and it lasted only a second or two, no longer, and then it was all over; then Ellen was dead, like someone dead but still moving, and we both knew that it was all over, destroyed, and when Ellen packed her little bag like a ghost we both realized that, from that moment on, our life together was over because it must never happen again, she must never be frightened of me again. We had always known that, although we'd never talked about it, because it was quite impossible – because no two people in the world, no two people in human history, perhaps, had ever been so perfectly suited, and now it was all over, over for good, and I knew I could never again share a bedroom with a woman because I must never again make a woman feel frightened of me. My dear boy, my mother told me once, you were made for women, made for love, and now Ellen was packing her little bag because of me, filled with fear and dismay, and once or twice she glanced at me for a second or two and her eyes said: Why did you do it, even though you did nothing, why have you destroyed our life for ever? You're good at football, my mother had told me, but you're made for women, and we both laughed, and Ellen laughed when I told her that once. You play football pretty badly nowadays, she said, looking at me with big, dead eyes. Her eyes said, Why did you do it, why did you destroy it all for good, and when she'd finished packing her bag, she said, I'm going to fetch Jessie, and her eyes said, I've just died, we've just died, and she said, I'm taking Jessie to a hotel. I'll call you sometime. We'll be needing some clothes. Jessie will need some clothes. And some toys. Toys, too. And her eyes said, Harry, I'm drowning. Harry, the world is ending and I'm drowning. The world died long ago, and I've only been dreaming I'm alive. The world is dead and no one can help me. No doctor, no mother, no father, no God. Nor you either.

Sunday

What is it? What's the matter? Sonia was standing, wet-haired and bathrobed, beside my bed.

I must have been having a nightmare, I said. We all get them sometimes, don't we?

Shall I ask them to send up a bottle of wine?

Yes, I said. That's an excellent idea.

We drank the wine in our twin beds, and eventually Sonia turned out the light between us and said goodnight. A moment or two later she murmured: Jessie, not like Jessica. Jessie like Jessie. Good idea for my next passport.

Goodnight, I said. But don't forget, the name is good for only one night. It's been reserved for ages.

It was a long night for us both. Neither of us could sleep, even though we'd shared a bottle of red wine.

Jessie for Jessie . . . It was really a man's name. When Ellen became pregnant we naturally didn't know whether the baby would be a boy or a girl, or what it would be called. We took our time choosing a name. It wasn't so important. What mattered more was whether the baby would be healthy, because my mother suffered from epilepsy. At some point during her pregnancy Ellen read an American novel about two early hippies living in California at a time when hippies didn't exist yet. When she'd finished three or four chapters she started reading the whole book aloud to me because she thought it was so wonderfully funny, and all at once we had a name for our child. Yesterday in San Francisco, all these many years later, I went to City Lights to find a copy of the book, and read it aloud to Sonia last night. The book came out in 1964, when I was sixteen and living in San Francisco. Like I am now. Not that I knew anything about the book then. It was a long time since Sonia and I had laughed so much, and now, one night later, I'm going to copy out the passage from the book that gave Jessie her name.

When I was at school I often copied out long passages in an exercise book because I couldn't afford the books themselves. We were a well-off family – wealthy, in fact – but I was given no more pocket money than the other children. And now, probably for the last time in my life, I'm going to copy out a longish passage from a book. It's important, after all. It marks the moment when it became clear that someone in our family would bear the name Jessie.

The two hippies in the book are called Lee and Jesse, and they live in a rather decrepit shack in Big Sur, here in California. The pond near the shack is full of frogs that croak all night long. The hippies have just dined on jack mackerel. Jesse describes their effect: They rip your whole organism apart. They've barely reached your stomach when you start to rumble and squeal and flap. Noises made in a haunted house during an earthquake go tearing horizontally across your stomach. Mighty farts and belches burst forth. Your pores almost exude jack mackerel.

It goes on:

* * *

A little while after dinner, to avoid the sound of the frogs that were really laying it in now from the early color of the evening, I decided to take my farts and belches to the privacy of my cabin and read Ecclesiastes.

"I think I'm going to sit here and read frogs," Lee Mellon farted.

"What did you say, Lee? I can't hear you. The frogs. Yell louder," I farted.

Lee Mellon got up and threw a great rock into the pond and screamed, "Campbell's Soup!" The frogs were instantly quiet. That would work for a few moments and then they would start again. Lee Mellon had quite a pile of rocks in the room. The frogs would always begin with one croak, and then the second and then the 7,452nd frog would join in.

Funny thing though, about Lee Mellon's yelling "Campbell's Soup!" at the frogs while he was launching various missiles into the pond. He had yelled every kind of obscenity possible at them, and then he decided to experiment with nonsense syllables to see if they would have any effect, along with a well-aimed rock.

Lee Mellon had an inquiring mind, and by the hit-or-miss method he came upon "Campbell's Soup!" as the phrase that struck the most fear into the frogs. So now, instead of yelling some boring obscenity, he yelled, "Campbell's Soup!" at the top of his voice in the Big Sur night.

"Now what did you say?" I farted.

"I think I'm going to sit here and read frogs. What's wrong, don't you like frogs?" Lee Mellon farted. "That's what I said. Where's your spirit of patriotism? After all, there's a frog on the American flag."

"I'm going to my cabin," I farted. "Read some Ecclesiastes."

"You've been reading a lot of Ecclesiastes lately," Lee Mellon farted. "And as I remember there's not much to read. Better watch yourself, kid."

"Just putting in time," I said.

"I think dynamite's too good for these frogs," Lee Mellon said. "I'm working on something special. Dynamite's too fast. I'm getting a great idea."

* * *

Lee Mellon had tried various ways of silencing the frogs. He had thrown rocks at them. He had beaten the pond with a broom. He had thrown pans full of boiling water on them. He had thrown two gallons of sour red wine into the pond.

For a time he was catching the frogs when they first appeared at twilight and throwing them down the canyon. He caught a dozen or so every evening and vanquished them down the canyon. This went on for a week.

Lee Mellon suddenly got the idea they were crawling back up the canyon again. He said that it took them a couple of days. "God-damn them," he said. "It's a long pull up, but they're making it."

He'd gotten so mad that the next frog he threw into the fireplace. The frog became black and stringy and then the frog became not at all. I looked at Lee Mellon. He looked at me. "You're right. I'll try something else."

He took a couple dozen rocks and spent an afternoon tying pieces of string to them, and then that evening when he caught the frogs, he tied them to the rocks and threw them down the canyon. "That ought to slow them down a little bit. Make it a little harder to get back up here," he said, but it did not work out for there were just too many frogs to fight effectively, and after another week he grew tired of this and went back to throwing rocks at the pond and shouting "Campbell's Soup!"

At least we never saw any frogs in the pond with rocks tied to their backs. That would have been too much.

There were a couple of little water snakes in the pond, but they could only eat a frog or two every day or so.

31

The snakes weren't very much help. We needed anacondas. The snakes we had were more ornamental than functional.

*   *   *

"Well, I'll leave you to your frogs," I farted. The first one had just croaked and now they would all start up again and hell would come forth from that pond.

"Mark my words, Jesse. I got a plan going." Lee Mellon farted and then tapped his head in the fashion people do to see if a watermelon is ripe. It was. A shiver traveled down my spine.

"Good-night," I farted.

"Yes, indeed," Lee Mellon farted.

*   *   *

Sonia and I laughed the way Ellen and I had laughed. There were times when Ellen couldn't read on for laughing, and I'd say: Stop laughing, it could be bad for the baby – too much jolting around. And Ellen, still laughing, retorted: It can't be worse than spending nine months in the tummy of an epileptic.

Neither of us could sleep that night, and Ellen suddenly said in the darkness: What did you say, Jesse? And a bit later she said: If we have a daughter we'll call her Jesse, but with "ie" at the end. Then everyone will think it comes from Jessica, and they won't question it. From that night on, whenever we couldn't hear what one of the others had said, we'd say: What did you say, Jesse? We always called it out quite loud, as if to drown the croaking of frogs. We must have said it a few thousand times in our lives, and before long, when Jessie was older and could talk, she too was calling: *What did*

you say, Jesse? So sometimes all three of us were Jesse!
Or Jessie.

* * *

Cycling with Jessie on the child's seat in front of me.
It's raining, and we're going quite fast. She's three or
four years old. She hasn't caught what I've just said to
her, so she yells into the rain: What did you say, Jessie?
Then she calls across to her mother on the other bike:
What did you say, Jessie? And Ellen laughs and calls
back: What did you say, Jessie?

Tuesday

Jessie, who was always the first to see the moon. She wasn't sick. I mean, she never had even a trace of an epileptic fit, any more than I have. As far as one could tell, my mother was the only epileptic in our family's recent history. She took a keen interest in Buddhism, and sometimes she used to laugh and say: I'm an epileptic Buddhist – if that's not a contradiction in terms. It's a great combination. Still, where Buddhism's concerned, we Westerners are all more or less, well . . . epileptic.

And once she told me: At fifty the good Buddhist leaves all his possessions behind and goes roaming. *We* won't do that, though. You won't because you'll have children and are made for love. A man like you couldn't take a begging bowl and roam the world on his own. As for me, I won't see fifty. You'd better get used to the idea.

My mother was a fiery, energetic woman, even though her fits sometimes left her utterly drained. No one in our family could simply float and be happy. Only Ellen could. And sometimes I could too, in her company and for brief moments. For a brief instant, never longer. Ellen thought I was always looking for a fight, even though I pretended it was a game. I think she was absolutely right. I'm at my happiest when under pressure and compelled to fight – when I've almost lost. Then comes the moment when I'm utterly calm and happy, simultaneously indifferent and blissful. I probably get it from my mother. That's my theory, at least. If it's true that our long months in the maternal amniotic sac betoken the perfect security to which we always long to return – and when I consider that I was jolted while in that perfect security, heaven alone knows how often, by epileptic fits – then it seems pretty clear that, for me, security and physical shocks go together. For me, happiness is almost inseparable from such convulsions.

Yes, it's true what Ellen once told me: You're always on the lookout for adversaries, for enemies. Your world is teeming with enemies, and if there's no enemy around you manufacture one. It's the only time you're happy.

Well, I ought to be superlatively happy now, because my world really is teeming with enemies. They could be anywhere. I ought to be genuinely happy now. I've nothing to lose, either – I haven't had for a long time. But I'm scared and I'm running away. I'm scared I won't make it.

Friday

We were feeling pretty shattered, Sonia and I, when we awoke in our room at the Christophe Colombe the next morning. Shattered but excited at the same time. In the breakfast room Sonia suggested we switch to the informal mode of address. English speakers have it a whole lot easier, I often think. No *Du* and *Sie*, *tu* and *vous*, just plain "you", whether you're talking to the queen or a road sweeper. We won't see each other again after today, Sonia said, but I think we should. After all, we're going to collect my pension. You don't doublecross someone you're on familiar terms with – not that I think you'll run off with my money, you romantic.

She laughed as she said it, and I laughed too.

It was half past nine when I rose from the breakfast table, picked up her rucksack, and said: See you at the restaurant at eleven.

Half past at the latest, she said with a nervous smile.

We had arranged to check in at the Campanile, the airport hotel, if anything went wrong. I couldn't simply hang around in a café or a restaurant, not with two suitcases. A hotel would be safer.

It'll all go like clockwork, I told her. Unless you raid the bank.

Yes, she said, still smiling nervously. It'll all go like clockwork.

And it did, too. I didn't park outside Sonia's block of flats, although I could have, but drove into the underground garage and left the car in a vacant slot. I took my blue dungarees from the boot and put them on. Then I made my way to her neighbour's storage section, removed the suitcases from under the blanket, which I used to dust off the cardboard boxes, and proceeded to transfer the money. It was all in bundles of hundred-dollar bills. The bills were neither particularly old nor particularly new – they'd been laundered really well. I roughly calculated how much money there was, and a voice inside me suddenly said, in an undertone: Man, oh man, it must be several million!

A young woman was just getting out of her car when I returned to the underground garage with the suitcases. We had to pass one another, and I gave her a friendly nod. She smiled and said good morning. A wholly unexceptional occurrence in an underground garage.

I drove into the restaurant car park shortly after half past ten. I got out and walked up and down for bit to calm my nerves. When you've got that amount of cash with you, the temptation is to sit on it – to remain in permanent physical contact. Suddenly, everyone you see is a potential thief. You'd like the money to become invisible. Best of all, you'd probably like to swallow it. But I forced myself to walk out on to the pavement and watch the traffic, and something made me peer into passing cars to see if anyone inside them looked Russian.

It was a long time before Sonia showed up. I was just beginning to worry when I spotted a slim figure coming towards me a few hundred yards along the street. When it drew nearer I saw it was Sonia. She was walking pretty fast.

What's happened? I asked when she reached me. She was looking rather distraught.

That damned Peugeot wouldn't start, she said. I tried umpteen times.

I suggested driving back into town. I could try to get it going again. Or we could tow it to a garage.

She thought about this briefly. No, she said, it would take too long. I must get out of here. Then something occurred to her: You have got the money, haven't you? And nobody saw you?

I said nothing, just nodded. She looked at me. Can you stay with me for another day? she asked.

I waited awhile, then I said: I'd have to buy myself a change of underpants in the next town. And some shaving kit.

You're very methodical for a romantic, she said.

Yes, I said. German romantics are renowned for changing their underpants every day. And for always being clean-shaven.

* * *

We headed towards Sedan. It wasn't a very pleasant drive because there were a lot of trucks on the road. On the way I told Sonia: I'm not interested in your money, but I do think I'm being a bit underpaid.

We stopped at a small town and parked near the church. Sonia stayed in the car while I went off and acquired two pairs of underpants and some shaving things. Then we drove on.

After about twenty minutes Sonia said: Do you see what I see?

No, I said. She was referring to a green BMW that had overtaken several trucks but not the one immediately behind us, although it could have done so long before.

Okay, let's see if you're right, I said, and overtook the truck ahead of us. Two minutes later the BMW pulled out and tucked itself in behind the truck we'd just overtaken. We drove on like that for ten minutes. The BMW made no move to overtake the truck behind us. Very odd.

You could be right, I said. Villains always drive Mercedes or BMWs. "Bad Man's Wagon" – that's what the blacks call them in the States.

I don't feel like laughing, said Sonia.

Shall I lose it?

On the open road? A BMW?

I'll have a go.

I overtook the truck ahead of us, then several cars and another truck. The BMW maintained its distance. If they really were after us, they either felt very sure of themselves or didn't want to arouse suspicion.

We were passing a longish stretch of woodland when I spotted a track that led off into the trees and ended in a small clearing. I slowed, turned off, and coasted towards the clearing. The BMW drove past, travelling at the same speed as the car ahead of it. No one looked out of the window. They didn't appear to have noticed. Sonia was trembling all over. I put my arms round her and held her tight. We remained sitting there like that.

All at once the BMW reappeared, coming the other way. It turned off and drove a little way along the track, then backed until it was blocking the exit with its bonnet pointing towards Luxembourg. We couldn't see the licence plates. The driver switched off, but no one got out.

Police? I whispered, as if there was some reason for whispering.

Have you ever seen a French policeman in a BMW? Sonia whispered back.

The car stood there for at least fifteen minutes, and still no one got out. They really were trying to throw a scare into us. There was no way out of the clearing, just a narrow path leading back to the road.

Have you got a gun? I whispered.

Sonia shook her head.

I could ram them, I said. We might get lucky.

All we'd get is an airbag in the face, she said.

You're right, but maybe I should try it.

Then we saw the passenger door slowly open. A man in a dark brown suit got out and walked the few yards back to the road, so at first we only saw him from behind. He looked up and down the road, then turned and walked back to the BMW. Propping his chin on the roof of the car, he stared in our direction. His movements were those of someone with all the time in the world to spare.

That's Dmitry, Sonia whispered. Aliosha's brother.

Who's Aliosha? I whispered back.

Aliosha is my husband.

A few minutes later a man emerged from the back of the BMW and stationed himself beside Dmitry.

That's Viktor, said Sonia. One of Dmitry's hit men.

What'll they do to us?

To me, nothing, Sonia said. It would be against orders. They'll take me back to Aliosha.

What about me?

I'll tell them you don't know a thing. You're just a common or garden cabby.

Thanks, I said. And who's the type behind the wheel?

I can't tell, said Sonia. Another hit man, probably.

Dmitry and the man named Viktor left the BMW and strolled towards us. I felt terrified. Sonia wasn't the only one trembling now. We got out and positioned ourselves so my car was between us and the two mafiosi.

They stopped about five yards away. Sonia said something to Dmitry in Russian, and he stared at me. He was a good-looking man, well over six feet tall and pretty broad-shouldered. Whatever he said to Sonia, it sounded angry. Then he went to the boot of my car and opened it. His expression changed to one of amusement. He tried to open one of the suitcases, then held out his hand imperiously. He wanted Sonia to give him the keys. The silly thing was, she didn't have them. I did. I took the keys from my pocket and tossed them to him. He grinned triumphantly. No one on earth would entrust an innocent cabby with the keys to two suitcases stuffed with dollar bills.

He opened one of the suitcases and grinned still more triumphantly when he saw the contents. Then he got angry again – absolutely furious, in fact. He yelled something in Russian and lunged at Sonia, but I darted between them. He simply pushed me over, but that gave her time to say something to him. All I caught was Aliosha's name. He'd already raised his fist, but he didn't hit her. By the time I'd scrambled to my feet the man named Viktor was prodding my back with an automatic.

Sonia was now talking heatedly to Dmitry. He stood there, stiff and motionless, merely glancing at me from time to time.

I've said they're not to harm you, Sonia told me. They're to bind and gag you, but that's all.

Viktor transferred his gun to my ribs, gripped my neck with his other hand, said Come!, and propelled me into the trees. Sonia was crying.

When we were a little way into the wood and couldn't see the cars any longer, Viktor said: On your knees! I was trembling all over now. Hands behind your back! There were two possibilities: I could kneel down and wait for the inevitable, or I could defend myself. Viktor wasn't carrying anything he could bind and gag me with, so his intention was clear. I was in pretty good shape, and not just for someone over fifty. I was in good shape, period, and suddenly I felt quite calm. I made as if to kneel, clenched my right fist, gripped it with my left hand, spun round, and lashed out. I was in luck. My fist caught Viktor full in the throat. It must have felt like a bomb going off. He dropped the gun and clutched his throat with both hands. I kicked him in the stomach and he went down. Everything in me exulted, but I had no time for exultation. I saw the automatic lying on the ground and hurled myself at it. When I straightened up Viktor was taking a second gun from his jacket. Hearing the click of the safety catch, I didn't waste time aiming. I simply pointed the gun in his direction and fired.

An instant later I heard Sonia cry out. She yelled something in Russian, yelled like a maniac. She must have thought Viktor had shot me, because she broke away from Dmitry and dashed to the spot in the wood where Viktor and I had disappeared from view. I ran back to the clearing.

I was nearly there when I saw her running across the grass towards me. I also saw Dmitry, who had drawn his gun and was aiming at her. I shouted something, I can't remember what, but I wanted her to hit the ground. She did so just as Dmitry fired. Then he saw me. He raised his automatic and I raised mine. I simply walked towards him and pulled the trigger. Stop it, stop it! I shouted, and the tears ran down my cheeks and I went on firing. *So this is what it's like*, I thought. *This is what it's like to kill a man. You shout and yell and weep, and you're filled with sorrow and compassion, and you walk towards him firing again and again.*

This must also be what it's like to go permanently insane. I fired at the face on the driver's side of the BMW, which started up and drove out on to the main road.

I went over to Sonia, who was lying on the grass, sobbing. She wasn't hurt, just in shock. I knelt down beside her and took her head on my lap. She looked up at me. My God, she said, you're weeping.

So are you, Sonia, I said. We're both weeping. He meant to kill you, though.

I know, she said, Dmitry's unpredictable. But he wouldn't have survived in any case. If he'd shot me Aliosha would have killed him.

His own brother? I said.

It makes no difference, she said. Aliosha is the only one entitled to kill me. That's how it is in the Firm.

We had to get away fast. We couldn't afford to be seen, and the driver of the BMW might be going for reinforcements. I collected the dead men's guns, put Dmitry's into Sonia's rucksack and shoved the other two under the front seat. Then we drove on towards France. We didn't speak for a long time.

Suddenly Sonia said: You realize what this means? They'll hunt you down for evermore. They'll never give up until they get you. You've killed the boss's son. His eldest, first-born son. Even if you'd only killed Viktor, they would still keep after you until they find you. Anyone who crosses the Mafia, the way you have, can never rest easy again. The same goes for me. She gave a sudden smile: I guess we'll be buying plenty more underpants before we're through.

Let's hope so, I said.

I had fired at a human being for the first time in my life – two human beings, and I'd killed them. I would never have believed it possible. I know a bit about guns and I'm a pretty good shot, but I'd never aimed at anyone before, even in fun – except, of course, when playing cops and robbers as a boy. I'd never even killed an animal. I'd always considered myself incapable of doing so and found that very comforting.

Ellen's best friend lived in Scotland. We often spent holidays there, and one summer night I went shooting with five other men. One of them owned a pheasantry which was always being raided by a fox. The six of us piled into a big station wagon and set off to shoot the fox with our pockets full of shotgun cartridges. In summer the daylight takes a long time to fade up north. We spread out and concealed ourselves behind the dry-stone walls surrounding the property. The cows continued to graze peacefully nearby. We waited and waited, and I became more and more impatient. I'd come to shoot a fox with my pockets full of cartridges. I could hardly endure the suspense. After two hours my trigger finger was so itchy, I felt like putting a charge of shot into the nearest cow's backside.

The fox was too smart for us, and we eventually gave up. Because we were all infected with the same blood-lust, however, the others decided to go rabbit-hunting instead. They knew where rabbits were to be found, so the six of us lay down on the grass and waited for them to appear. The first of them emerged from their holes a few minutes later. Shortly afterwards the guns to the left and right of me went off. I sighted a rabbit that should have been mine, but I couldn't fire. I simply couldn't pull the trigger.

The others collected their rabbits and we walked back to the car. It was strange. I'd been so gun-happy, I could have pumped a charge of shot into a cow, but then, when it came to killing, I couldn't pull the trigger. I was consoled and reassured by the fact that we obviously have some inhibition that prevents us from killing. Yes, Ellen said at the time, one person out of six has it.

She was right. Five had opened fire and one hadn't, but I wouldn't have bet on that one either.

Saturday

Sonia and I debated what to do. We had to make for some largish city where we wouldn't be too conspicuous. That meant Rheims. We found a medium-sized hotel on the outskirts and I parked the car so it couldn't be seen from the street. Then we took a bus into town. I got some money from a cash dispenser and we bought a few things to wear. After dinner we asked for a bottle of wine and two glasses and went up to our room. We'd been in a kind of trance ever since leaving that clearing. We did everything quite automatically, like robots. We were both suffering from shock. It only relaxed its grip, and then only gradually, during the meal.

We lay on our beds and watched the news on television. Dmitry and Viktor had not been found yet, it seemed. That was something at least.

What'll happen now? I asked. What will your people do? What comes next?

Aliosha will come, said Sonia. He'll come looking for me, and when he finds me he'll kill me.

Me too, I said.

I'm so sorry, Harry, she said. This is awful. Terrible.

Sonia felt sure that Aliosha would come on his own, not with a couple of hit men. This was something that concerned him alone. His wife had decamped, cheating him out of several million dollars, and her new lover (he was bound to think that) had killed his eldest brother. It was quite clear what Aliosha had to do.

Aliosha was the youngest of three brothers. In addition to Dmitry there was Ivan. Outwardly, Ivan was the boss of the Firm in direct charge of its four divisions: drug dealing, prostitution, political contacts, and enforcement. He came immediately below his father, but Dmitry and Aliosha were senior to him. Responsible to their father alone, they had to ensure that no one in the lower ranks became too powerful. Not even Ivan was allowed to become too powerful. Sonia said it was rare for a "firm" to be controlled by one family, but that's how it was in this case. It's almost Italian, she said. *La famiglia.*

But Aliosha was a suspicious character. He didn't even trust his family completely. He trusted Sonia, and Sonia, in addition to the Luxembourg bank accounts she managed as a "bookkeeper", had opened one for herself and Aliosha alone. An emergency reserve, as she put it. Not even Aliosha had access to that account, only Sonia. Its purpose was precautionary, in case the Firm collapsed or Aliosha was imprisoned or killed, and if Sonia and Aliosha ever had to make a run for it, they would not lack for funds. There were other accounts in other countries, but only Aliosha had access to those.

So it's *my* money, as you see, said Sonia. And it's in my name alone. I kept my parents' name when we married. It's my money, and only mine. No one else has any claim to it.

How much is it? I asked.

Almost exactly four million dollars.

She took a passport from her rucksack and handed it to me. It was an American passport. Opening it, I saw the photo of a man in early middle age. Hair dark, features lean and slightly tanned. A hesitant, passport-photo smile. Not unappealing. The name was given as Colin Herrick, born 1956 in Denver, Colorado.

The Russians had trained Aliosha for espionage operations in the United States. He and his fellow trainees had lived in the Soviet Union like Americans. They spoke nothing but English, read nothing but American newspapers, watched American TV programmes and films. Nothing but baseball, basketball, American bestsellers, American drinks, and so on. Before the collapse of the Soviet Union, Sonia told me with a smile, they had everything most other Russians still don't have. Aliosha is indistinguishable from an American.

I returned the passport. Sonia said: I loved him very much. It was like a genuine Russian novel. Aliosha was the whole wide world to me.

But he had less and less time for her. When the Soviet Union collapsed, he poured all his energies into building up the Firm. That wasn't Sonia's problem, because she also had plenty to do. Her problem had started the year before, when she found out that Aliosha had tortured a man. His methods were so frightful, and he'd set to work with such enthusiasm, that Sonia had decided to leave him – and the Firm. She visited Luxembourg at least twice a month, so it was quite easy for her to syphon off the four million dollars little by little.

Aliosha, Sonia told me, had begun by torturing the man with an electric cattle prod. I knew what she meant. I once saw a TV documentary on transporting cattle in the Lebanon. One scene showed an ox that had broken its leg in transit and couldn't stand. Someone applied a cattle prod, and the poor beast lurched to its feet in agony. I almost vomited in front of the television set. I could well imagine what it must be like for a human being to be tortured with something of the kind. Sonia had never slept with Aliosha after that.

I didn't know why she was telling me all this. Perhaps she simply wanted to convey what we had to be prepared for – what form of revenge. She told me that the Brooklyn Mafia had once punished a man by killing his wife. When she was dead the killers ripped out her eyes because they believed that a murderer's image remains imprinted on his victim's retinas. No eyes, no evidence.

Typically Russian, I said. Disgusting. The height of superstition and brutality.

You're wrong! she said. It *isn't* typically Russian!

Of course it is! I positively bellowed the words in her face. Still at the top of my voice, I told her how an old Berlin couple, who'd been returning home from the theatre one night, had been brutally beaten up by two men. For no reason. The wife died and her husband was badly injured.

And I knew right away they were from the East, I shouted. Russians or Yugoslavs. No one else would have been as brutal!

Stop it! Sonia shouted back. You guessed right for once, that's all!

And your Aliosha – what will *he* do to us? Torture us with a cattle prod till our brains spurt out of our ears! Then he'll shoot us and gouge our eyes out. It won't hurt by then, but that's the worst thing of all.

Stop it! Stop it! Aliosha isn't a killer. He isn't superstitious either!

No, of course not! I shouted. Aliosha isn't a killer, he's only planning to kill us. Hurrah for the fine distinction!

Later, when we'd calmed down and were lying on our beds in the dark, Sonia said: People are the same everywhere. There's no difference. They're all capable of the best and the worst. Everyone everywhere. You Germans are no better than us. As for being superstitious, in World War Two the Americans believed the Japanese were unsuited to air warfare because their slit eyes were a handicap when flying. That was before Japanese planes sank the American fleet in Pearl Harbor.

*   *   *

It was on the news the following afternoon. A lumberjack had spotted Dmitry's body in the clearing, and when the police searched the area they found Viktor among the trees. The authorities assumed them to be victims of an internal dispute between members of a crime syndicate. There was no mention of us or my car, only of tyre tracks that still had to be investigated.

We learned from the late news that the same weapon had been used both times, but that cartridge cases of two different calibres had been found at the scene. Again no mention of us or the car, so we still had time. No one knew that some of the tyre tracks were mine. No one knew what make of car I drove. No one knew who had been driving it. No one knew I'd shot the two men. No one but Aliosha.

The driver of the green BMW was bound to have made a note of my number, and even if he wasn't familiar with my car, a Citroën XM, the Mafia would find it child's play to discover my identity from the taxi call centre in Munich or the police database. Or from automobile insurance records.

Sunday

The night it all ended – the night Ellen went to fetch Jessie – I walked the streets without knowing where I was. All I kept seeing were Ellen's eyes. *Harry, I'm drowning. Harry, the world is ending and I'm drowning. The world died long ago, and I've only been dreaming I'm alive. The world is dead and no one can help me. No doctor, no mother, no father, no God. Nor you either.*

It was the night my life ended, even though I've already outlived that night by so many years. Three days later Ellen took Jessie and set off by car for her parents' place in northern Germany. We put everything they wanted to take with them in the boot. Jessie said: Mummy says it'll all come right again.

Yes, I said, it'll all come right again, we need a little time, that's all. What else could one tell a child? At that moment I may really have thought that all we needed was a little time, but I simultaneously realized that the time we needed would expand for ever like the universe – that it would never end because Ellen must never again be frightened of me, never again get that look of fear in her eyes. There mustn't be the slightest chance of its happening again.

It wasn't raining the night it happened. There was very little traffic in the area – there never is much. For some unaccountable reason the car left the road and hurtled down a grassy slope. It glanced off a tree, inflating the airbags, turned over a couple of times, and came to a stop the right way up. They were both

51

unmarked. Not a scratch, not a graze. Ellen didn't even have concussion. The people who found them thought they were both dead, they were sitting so still. But only Jessie was.

It's odd that I see airbags inflate whenever I think of it, as I do now, while writing this. There weren't any airbags in 1976, but for many years I've seen them inflate when the car glances off the tree in that field. They inflate very slowly, all soft and yielding.

Four days later everyone came to Munich for the funeral. Ellen, Jessie, and Ellen's parents. Jessie came in a hearse. She arrived first. Ellen was still stiff and absent, like a ghost. She stood between her parents all the time. After the burial she rested her hands on their shoulders, turned, and walked off. And I kept walking along beside her.

We walked the streets all day like two mute ghosts, never uttering a word. I noticed people turning to look at us. Once, Ellen went into an ice-cream parlour and sat down on a chair, just like that. When the waiter came to our table I ordered two banana splits. At some stage Ellen went to the ladies' room, and when she returned she made straight for the exit. But then she lingered in the doorway, irresolutely, as if waiting for me. We walked on through the streets, two mute ghosts condemned to roam for evermore.

It wasn't a romantic tour of the city. Nor a commemoration of the dead. We didn't visit any of the places that had been important to Jessie or us, we simply walked. When you walk through a void, a leaden waste, that's the way it has to be. We were two dead people walking through a dead world.

When it got dark we went into the park near our flat. Ellen came to a halt. She simply halted as mechanically as she had walked all day long. The park was entirely deserted and dark. We stood like that for a long time, side by side, and suddenly Ellen said something – murmured something I didn't catch. And then she said, quite loudly: What did you say, Jessie? And the tears ran down her cheeks. Her whole body seemed to stream with tears and she sank to her knees. It was as if she had nothing on, as if tears were all she wore. She was all tears, just tears. Her grief was so great, so searing, I thought the ground beneath her would melt and engulf her, and all I thought was: *She mustn't lose her mind. She mustn't, not now.*

Much later I picked her up and carried her home. I sat beside her bed all night. She slept very soundly. It was the last night we ever spent together.

Tuesday

From now on, said Sonia, we shouldn't withdraw any more money from cash dispensers. They must have identified you by now, and they'll have your credit card numbers. Aliosha has good connections with the authorities and the private sector, so no more cash dispensers. I've got ten thousand marks' worth of French francs. That'll be enough for the time being. There's a hilarious story about a Ukrainian named Balagula whose girlfriend used a credit card in his name, so the KGB were able to trace his route perfectly. It's a stock joke.

I started to say something.

You were going to say "typically Russian", right?

Yes. Sorry.

Aliosha's good connections also meant that we couldn't rent a less conspicuous car. But Sonia felt pretty sure that Aliosha would suspect we were in Paris, or not, at least, so close to Luxembourg and the scene of the crime. The Mafia are everywhere, she said, but they can't look everywhere. Not even they have men enough for that.

We changed hotels even so, and parked the car in another district, away from the hotel.

Wednesday

Ellen stayed with her parents for nearly six months. Then she went off to Switzerland for a year. To Geneva. She took her mother's maiden name. We weren't married, which meant that she dropped her father's name, not mine, and adopted the other one. Perhaps she simply wanted to make the past disappear. I don't know.

What I did know, after that last night, was that I couldn't be a writer any longer. You can't be a writer if you don't love anyone any more. If you've lost all hope. If you've done what I had. If you've seen what I had seen: the end of the world in Ellen's eyes. I was twenty-eight years old, and in Ellen's eyes the world had ended. Because of me. I wasn't *entitled* to be a writer any more.

I could still have written book reviews, of course. As a reviewer you don't have to love anyone or anything. Nor do you need to have hope. You have only to turn out your little pieces and need only write about literature, nothing else. I've read millions of those pompous, broken-backed sentences that crawl across the pages of the Sunday supplements in the guise of literary criticism. It must be a strange life, spending your days writing that kind of stuff, just being a sausage machine. Tess would have disapproved. You aren't here on earth to do that, she would have said. You didn't become my son for that. When Tess read book reviews she often quoted an American author on the subject. In America, young journalists who weren't capable of turning out adequate reports on sporting events would be handed a book and told: Here, write something about that. Tess said that so often, I remember it as being one of her maxims, like her invariable follow-up: My dear boy, if you want to become a writer, you'll have to reckon with the direct and indirect descendants of those people. There's no escaping those who write daft things about you.

The best that can happen is that what you write will encourage people to buy a book. But what mattered to me wasn't just that people bought a book when I wrote about it. I also wanted them to read what I wrote because it was good and interesting. Because they could gain something from it, not because I was advising them on what to read.

I wanted to kill myself, of course. It was the only solution, in fact, and if Jessie had survived I would probably have done so. But I didn't want to leave Ellen alone in the world, even though we would never see each other again. Till doomsday, we always said when we got to know each other. That was clear from the start. Ellen also said: At least for the next fifty years. She's a great realist. We always made bets as to which of us would die first because each of us wanted to die first, sometime in the next fifty years. We usually ended by agreeing to die together.

Then, one August, there was that cycling accident. Jessie was with her grandparents at the time, and Ellen and I were pedalling pretty fast along the river bank. It was raining, and the road was deserted. We were riding some ten or twelve yards apart, and all at once we both came to grief. Quite independently of each other. As I hit the ground I thought: Damn it, that was my head, but my head was quite unscathed. It was Ellen who had hit her head. She had a cut on her forehead and was slightly concussed, and our left thighs turned green, red, blue, and black. The bruises lasted for weeks. It was a curious accident. Afterwards, when we got home, Ellen said with a smile: If it hadn't been a stupid accident – if it hadn't been something negative – you could say it was a miracle. The two of us at the same time and quite independently of each other. Perhaps we'll both go the same way one day.

* * *

No, I wasn't going to write any book reviews and I wanted to go on living. I had to go on living. Till doomsday. Instead of killing myself I got my cabby's licence.

That was it. That was my life. I drove a taxi. There had to be taxis and I drove one. That was a sufficient *raison d'être*. That has long been my function among the living: I'm a taxi driver.

After her year in Geneva Ellen moved to Scotland. That was the first time we talked at any length on the phone. Do you know what it said on the door of the office where I had to register with the police? she said. "Aliens & Firearms." Two extremely dangerous things behind one and the same door. Speaking of xenophobia, I'm an alien. What do you think of that?

You can laugh again, I said.

Yes, she said, I can. Occasionally. One can laugh again in the end. Somebody once said: It's awful that it isn't awful enough.

I'd always like to know where you are, I said. That's all.

Yes, she said.

* * *

57

I called her once a year, usually on her birthday. I'm living in a wonderful street called Lover's Walk, she told me the year she moved into the flat where she lived from then on. I paid a visit to Munich, to Jessie's grave. But I didn't want to call you.

No, she told me once, she wasn't lonely. She was very busy and knew a lot of people.

Is there, I asked, I mean, is there anyone –

Are there any men around, you mean? Yes, several, and it's not good for a person to be alone. But I don't need any man. Why should I? It was you I needed, Harry. Only you. I don't need just any man.

A few years later I asked her: That time . . . I mean, did you mean to . . .

Suicide isn't an option for me, she said. You ought to know that.

One can never tell.

But Harry, I would never have killed my own child.

Who would have looked after your child if you'd really killed yourself?

You, she said.

Me? I said. Me, of all people?

Yes, you. I can't conceive of a better father. I simply can't. But forget it.

Friday

I think we should get rid of your car, said Sonia, two days and two hotels later.

I didn't want to get rid of my car, so I debated what to do. The taxi colour wasn't paint, it was plastic film. A lot of cabbies get that done to their taxis because it makes them easier to sell later on. Applying a film of that kind costs around a thousand marks. Maybe a bit more by now. My car was really dark blue, and a dark blue Citroën wouldn't stand out in France, even with German number plates. Or not so much, and I might be able to organize some new plates. But I didn't know how to remove the film. It had to be subjected to heat, that was all I knew, but how could I heat up a car in the street in the middle of France?

It was a real shame, but it couldn't be done. If only I had a gigantic hairdryer, I said to Sonia. But we can't go on driving around in this colour.

No, she said. That inconspicuous shade of ivory stands out like a sore thumb.

The evening news gave a description of my car, together with the licence number and my name. A German taxi driver by the name of Harry Willemer was strongly suspected of the murders. He was thought to be in the Paris area, probably accompanied by a woman.

The late night news showed a photograph of me, probably obtained from the passport office. It looked very much like my passport photo.

59

Sonia said: Aliosha's using the police to trace us.

How do you mean?

Think, she said. No one saw us in that clearing. No one registered the make of your car, still less made a note of the number. The only person who could have done so is the driver of the green BMW. Aliosha has failed to find us for three whole days. The Mafia may be everywhere, but they can't look everywhere at once. The police can, so Aliosha is using them to look for us.

Although the "Wanted" photo wasn't a very good one, that meant we had to quit our hotel as soon as possible. We couldn't use my taxi either, of course. It would be found the next day at latest, and then the police and Aliosha would be looking for us in Rheims.

It was almost midnight. If I stole a car now, it wouldn't be missed for at least six hours. Possibly longer.

Where shall we go? Sonia asked.

Luxembourg, I said. Your neighbour's blue Peugeot is still there. Nobody knows it, nobody's looking for it. Besides, driving back to Luxembourg is the last thing Aliosha will think we've done.

You really are developing a criminal mentality.

I'll be back in an hour at most. Pack our things.

The night porter was behind the reception desk. I told him we unfortunately had to leave right away and settled the bill.

A quarter of an hour later I was outside the hotel with an old red Golf, and ten minutes after that we were on our way to Luxembourg. We'd spent a couple of minutes chatting casually to the night porter in case he got any unwelcome ideas.

We reached Luxembourg by six a.m. and parked a few streets away from the blue Peugeot. Sonia got in behind the wheel of the Golf and I made for the

Peugeot on foot. It was child's play. The petrol feed had become detached.

When we were sitting side by side in the Peugeot, Sonia looked at me enquiringly: What now?

I don't know, I said. You're the mafioso's girlfriend.

Stop that! she said.

It won't be long before they find the Golf here in Luxembourg, which means they'll think we've returned to Germany. So we ought to do the exact opposite and drive back to France.

The *police* will think that, Sonia said. Aliosha won't. Aliosha will expect us to do exactly what you suggest and drive back to France.

So?

So we'll make for Germany. Aliosha is far more dangerous than the police. Incidentally, maybe you should stop shaving.

I'd look like a criminal.

You *are* a criminal. You stole a car last night, remember?

Russian humour, I said.

Yes, she said.

What about this Peugeot? I said. It's stolen too, isn't it?

Not really, said Sonia. She had drawn out fifty thousand dollars and mailed them to her neighbour's address in a Jiffy bag. So you see, she said, she can easily buy *two* Peugeots for that.

Instead of going to ground in a big city, we made for as unlikely a destination as possible: a holiday area. To be more precise, an area in the Black Forest south of Freiburg. It was called the Markgräfler Land, and I'd never heard of it. This was Sonia's idea. Staufen, Müllheim, Sulzburg, Badenweiler. The only place I'd heard of was Badenweiler. Sonia thought we

61

could use a few days' holiday to unwind. We might even take the waters there, she suggested with a smile. Apparently, Badenweiler was an old Russian stamping ground.

The Markgräfler Land was a brilliant idea. I doubted if the Mafia had heard of it any more than I had. We drove there via Metz, Strasbourg and Colmar, never using the autobahn, and were lucky enough to find a room in a converted farmhouse that catered for tourists. We had a meal and went straight to bed. A perfectly normal end to a holidaymaker's day. Except that now we always carried our guns.

Naturally we were afraid of being recognized. Holidaymakers tend to have plenty of time to read the newspapers. Time to scrutinize those around them, too, but so did other people. We wouldn't be truly safe anywhere, but we were probably safest as tourists.

The next day we got up late and drove into Badenweiler. We immediately bought some German newspapers, but there was nothing new in them. Because we had very little German currency left, Sonia changed some of her French francs into marks. The cashier asked for some ID, so she slid the Catherine Marchais passport across the counter.

We bought ourselves some bathing gear and went to the local swimming baths. Afterwards we had a so-called Roman massage. Together with about twenty other people, we wound up swathed in white sheets and reclining on slabs like Roman senators. Or cadavers in a morgue.

Later, over dinner, Sonia talked about Anton Chekhov, who had died in Badenweiler around the beginning of the twentieth century. Chekhov is one of her favourite authors. In his last letter he stated that he'd never seen a single well-dressed German woman;

German women's lack of taste was depressing. Sonia told me that with a hint of satisfaction.

Rather out of place in a farewell letter, I said.

No, Harry, by Chekhov's standards it was a perfect farewell letter. He was a seeker after beauty. What I like best in women is beauty, he said once. As for humanity in general, he thought its most important attribute was civilization as manifested in carpets, well-sprung carriages, and perspicacity.

That I can't deny, I said, and she went on to describe his last moments. The doctor sent for some champagne to assist the dying man's breathing. Chekhov sat up in bed and announced, in German: I'm dying. Then he picked up his glass, smiled at his wife, and said: It's a long time since I drank champagne. He drained the glass, lay back, and died. The room was absolutely silent except for a huge moth that kept colliding with the light bulbs. Then, all at once, the cork flew out of the half-empty champagne bottle with a loud pop.

What a death, said Sonia. The pop of a champagne cork. Suddenly she turned serious. While we're on the subject of Germans, is there anyone you should warn?

How do you mean?

If Aliosha doesn't find us soon he may abduct someone. Someone who means a lot to you. He'll try to lure you out into the open.

Ellen! Ellen, I thought. My whole body started to hurt. But then I thought again. They couldn't find Ellen. Ellen lived in Scotland. She had a different name, not even the name of her parents, and there was no document on which we both appeared apart from Jessie's birth certificate, and Ellen had that. Besides, I couldn't remember if my name really did appear on it. It was a long time since we – or I, at least – had been touch with any of our old friends, and none of the people I'd met in the last twenty-four years knew anything about Ellen. It wasn't good for a person to be alone – Ellen was right – but I had no friends. There was no one Aliosha could abduct in order to lure me out. I played squash with a dentist, a chemist and another taxi driver, and I occasionally had a meal with them. I also belonged to a shooting club – air pistols only – and worked out at a gym once or sometimes twice a week, but no one there knew me well. My only contacts were male, which was the way I wanted it, and even they were pretty limited. Sport and an occasional beer. And I went jogging because it's an aid to marksmanship. You can control your breathing better, keep it nice and shallow.

Such was my world, if you could call it that. *You were made for women, my dear boy*, my mother had said, *You were made for love*, and now, for more than two decades, my only acquaintances had been men. I always steered clear of women. Or nearly always. But there were many faces in the street that reminded me of Jessie. No, reminded is wrong, but I often *imagined* they were Jessie, or could be. Jessie would now have been three years older than Ellen and I were. Once more the car left the road, glanced off the tree, inflating the airbags, turned over several times, righted itself, and came to a stop.

No, there was no one Aliosha could abduct in order to coax me into the open. My flat contained almost nothing of a personal nature – I had my address book with me – and certainly no clue to Ellen's existence. Anyone searching the place would find nothing.

But Ellen would have to be told. I would have to tell her, reassure her. It might occur to her that someone would use her to trace me.

It was late when we left the restaurant in Baden-weiler. I went to a phone booth and called Scotland. Ellen's answering machine cut in and I hung up. No, there was no reason to worry. She was out, that's all.

Next morning I called the firm where she worked. Ellen was in Hamburg, they told me. I said I was her uncle and they gave me her number.

Harry, she said. Harry.

You know what's happened?

Of course, she said. The papers are full of it. Everyone's looking for you. Who's this woman?

A customer, I told her. It's all down to bad luck. I got mixed up in this in the craziest way.

Yes, she said. Of course you couldn't help it and it's all a big mistake, right? Of course you didn't kill those two mafiosi. Of course you're entirely innocent. You're quite incapable of killing anyone.

No need to be sarcastic, I said. It all happened just the way it says in the papers. I simply wanted to tell you not to worry. No one can find you. There's nothing to connect us. If they search my flat they won't find any clues to your existence.

I see, she said, and her tone was still sarcastic. No clues to my existence.

They're all in my head and my body, if you want to know, I said. I sometimes feel like one big, open wound.

Yes, she said.

We hung up.

I'd left the phone booth and taken a few steps when I turned back. It had occurred to me that there was one other person I ought to call. My hairdresser. I like the man. He's one of the old school, incredibly polite and obliging. A bit obsequious at times, but utterly sincere for all that. Utterly. He could easily have cut my hair in half an hour, but I always sat there for an hour or more. Sometimes I told him cabby's anecdotes. We talked about the weather and politics and growing older and recipes. I used to describe the big parties I went to with my friends and what we got to eat there. I lied and lied until his mouth started watering, and after a few years we reached the stage where I put together Christmas menus for his family. I used to enjoy cooking when my life was still a life, so these Christmas menus – menus concocted for a family of strangers – became my way of sharing Christmas dinner with someone. They were absolutely thrilled, he would tell me when I turned up for my first post-Christmas haircut, and he always paid me special compliments, like: My wife almost swooned with pleasure.

I had given up cooking and never ate at home unless I was ill, which didn't happen often. You go to the dogs if you eat on your own. I only ate in restaurants.

He answered the phone at once, of course, being alone in the salon.

Harry Willemer here, I said, and without giving him time to reply I told him I wouldn't be able to come again for the time being, he could guess why.

It's incredible the rubbish they print in the papers, he said. I don't believe a word of it.

Quite right too, I said. It's all balls. Just a big misunderstanding.

* * *

Our stay in the Markgräfler Land was uneventful, although I was always looking over my shoulder to see if anyone was behaving oddly or watching us too closely in restaurants or elsewhere. Sonia was the same, I could tell. She used to talk in her sleep. Once she woke me up and said: Take it easy, no need to shout. Everything's all right.

The day after we arrived it was announced on TV that my car had been found in Rheims. Nothing more about us after that, but there was a press report that my flat had been ransacked. The red Golf had also been found in Luxembourg. That's a trick, said Sonia. Aliosha must have had your flat searched the day he discovered your identity. They're bound to have left everything the way it was. They can work very neatly when they want to. Now they've turned the whole place over as if they were conducting a thorough search. Aliosha is simply trying to unnerve you.

I called Ellen again. She already knew about the flat. There are no clues, I repeated. You're quite safe. As safe as anyone can be in this world.

Yes, she said, as safe as anyone can be. Then she said: I'm afraid, Harry.

There's no need, I told her. You're quite safe.

No, she said, I'm afraid for *you*.

You've no need to be afraid on my account.

Will they kill you? she asked. *They'll hunt you down for evermore*, Sonia had said. *They'll never give up until they get you.*

Will they kill you? Ellen asked again.

They'll try to, I said.

* * *

But our days in the Markgräfler Land were peaceful. I started to shave again. I only have a few grey hairs on my head, but my beard is very grizzled. I didn't like that, so I started shaving again. We behaved like tourists, sat on the terrace, walked to Staufen, bought ourselves some clothes in Müllheim, went to a barbecue

67

given by our landlords. I can really recommend this area, Sonia said with a smile.

To die in? I said.

Not until the champagne cork goes pop, she said, still smiling.

At a restaurant one night I had to go to the men's room. A few moments later a man came in but paused just inside the door. He was probably staring at my back. I began to tremble slightly. I was utterly defenceless. It was an unpleasant notion, being killed while peeing. The man didn't come right in. He retraced his steps to the washroom and turned a tap on. The water went on running and running and I waited and waited, and when I opened the door to the washroom all was quiet and deserted. Except that the tap kept on running.

I couldn't sleep that night. Lying beside Sonia, I felt my hatred of Aliosha steadily mounting. I was sorry about Dmitry and Viktor. The nightmares in which I relived that long moment in the clearing when I walked towards Dmitry, gun in hand, firing again and again, were filled with anguish. Anguish and compassion and tears. And horror at having acted as I had.

It was different with Aliosha. Aliosha wasn't someone whose path I'd crossed by chance, and who was trying to kill me. Aliosha was death. Chance didn't come into it. Aliosha was as much my destiny as death itself. He was after me, just as death is after us all, and he would not give up for years, decades, a lifetime, not for all eternity, until he had caught up with us.

Aliosha was death, and I hated him without knowing him. I feared him, and I felt this boundless rage welling up inside me. A rage so immense that it outweighed my fear. I sat up in bed. What does this goddamned Russian killer think he's up to? I bellowed into the darkness. What does this torturer think he can do to me, the dirty bastard? What kind of people are you, you goddamned Russians?

Harry! Harry! Sonia turned the light on. Hush, people will hear you!

When we were lying side by side again in the dark, I noticed she was weeping. Why do you hate us so much, Harry? So terribly? All that hatred and contempt of yours. Why do you hate us so much?

We lay side by side in the darkness, the way she had lain beside her grandmother as a child, and she talked and talked the way her grandmother had, recounting the terrible story of the siege of Leningrad. Nine hundred days, Harry – they besieged and bombed and shelled the city for nine hundred days. A million people died, six hundred thousand of them from cold and starvation. The German gunners often ceased fire for half an hour, and then, when they could count on people having ventured out into the streets again, they opened fire once more. Do you know what it's like when you think you've escaped death, only to go out into the street and encounter it after all? Do you know what it's like to be shelled continuously, day and night? And do you know what it's like to starve? To be so hungry that your body starts to devour itself, and it hurts, it hurts all the time, and the only antidote to your pain and despair is death? Do you know what it's like? No, you don't, and neither do I. I wasn't born until many years later, but my grandmother knew what it's like and so did my parents – they all knew, the living and the dead and the dogs and the cats and the trees and stones. But the dogs and the cats didn't know it for long because people were so hungry they ate them.

In the end Leningrad was almost denuded of dogs and cats, and there's the story of this old man – there were many who did what he did, but his is the story everyone knows, the old folk still tell it – the awful story of how he strangled his cat and ate it, and he felt so terrible afterwards, he hanged himself, but the rope gave way and he fell to the ground and broke his leg and couldn't get up, so he froze to death instead. You, Harry, would no doubt call that a typically Russian story, full of brutality and inefficiency, but it only looks that way. Brutality and inefficiency had nothing to do with it, just utter despair and weakness. My grandmother understood that. She knew it all and understood it, both then and afterwards.

Yes, my grandmother knew what you and I don't know. Do you know what people did when their hunger became too great, when the city was stripped bare of anything alive to eat? They took straps and belts, leather belts, and boiled them till they were soft, and then they ate them. How many calories in an old leather belt? Tell me! How many stomachs can it fill?

And then something happened which my grandmother didn't tell me about. She never spoke of it, no one did, they were all too ashamed, and I won't tell you either. I'll only tell you what someone once said about the worst period of the siege: Leningrad was in the hands of cannibals. Nobody knew what went on in people's homes. I'll say no more about it, Harry, but that's what you Germans drove us to – not you, Harry, and not me, the Germans didn't drive us to those lengths, we weren't even born – and at some stage, in the winter of 1941–2, even the rats abandoned the city, or so it was said. I don't believe it myself, but people said so.

In winter everything was transported on children's sledges – food, corpses, everything. There were hardly any cars left. The city was silent, eerily silent, my grandmother said, as if God himself had died, and people lay starving in their beds and dreamed of caviar, and the frozen corpses were so stiff they made a metallic sound when thrown into the back of a truck, but my grandmother didn't tell me that, not about that sound, but she did tell me how people went to the hospital and simply died in the waiting room because they were beyond help, no one could help them – no doctor, no mother or father or God – and she told me the story of the little boy who took his family's last reserves, a few crumbs in a biscuit tin, and fed them to a mouse because the animal's hunger meant as much to him as his own. Why hasn't anyone written a story about that boy, I wonder?

My grandmother told me that, but she didn't tell me another story – not, at least, when I was still a child and lying in bed beside her. But she told it to me later on – told me how a little boy found his grandmother dead one night. He ran off to tell his mother, who was lying in bed with her overcoat on and a few blankets over her, it was so cold. She's dead, he told his mother. Yes, my son, said his mother, she's better off than we are. No one can escape death. We all have to die in the end, don't be frightened.

That's how to console a child, Harry: We all have to die in the end, don't be frightened.

That's what they made us do – made us console our children with the thought of death. I wasn't consoled like that – I wasn't alive then, Harry, and neither were you, but that's how it was. That's what they did to us.

And don't tell me the besiegers didn't know what havoc they were creating inside the city. You sit in a plane and drop a bomb, you serve a gun and pull some lever or whatever you have to do to fire a shell – how can you know what happens at the other end? Don't say it, don't tell me they couldn't have known.

71

But you could know it, Harry. You were born later. You know so much about Peter the Great, the barbarian who civilized a barbaric country, you know how appallingly brutal he was. You know all that, but you know nothing about Leningrad, only that it was besieged during the war. How could the besiegers have known what was happening in the city when they themselves weren't there? They had maps, Harry – maps marking targets for the artillery. A school, a hospital, a maternity home, the Hermitage, a block of flats. Those were *targets*, so don't tell me the besiegers couldn't have known. You let yourselves be governed by barbarians – not you but the people before you – by barbarians who loudly proclaimed what they thought. I learnt one of their barbarous maxims by heart, so I wouldn't forget it: Whether or not ten thousand Russian women drop dead from exhaustion while digging an anti-tank ditch is of interest only insofar as they complete that anti-tank ditch for Germany. I'm one of those Russian women, or could have been, and my mother and grandmother were two of those women who didn't matter.

So don't tell me the besiegers couldn't have known. They were killing people all the time. In Minsk in March 1942 – I know it was Minsk – they transported five thousand Jews from the ghetto to a freshly dug pit outside the city and mowed them down with machine guns. In the children's case – there were several hundred of them – ammunition was considered too good to waste on them. They were thrown into the pit and buried alive. Many of the men who did that may have kissed and cuddled children of their own back home. I'm not pleading for those children's lives, but why, I ask you – why did they think ammunition was too good to waste on them?

You allowed barbarians to rule you and became barbarians yourselves – not you, Harry, not you but the people before you. Many of them. And the barbarian who said those Russian women didn't matter said something else: The Germans, he publicly declared in the course of a speech, were the only people in the world with a decent attitude towards animals, and they would adopt a decent attitude towards these human animals as well.

"These human animals" were us, the Russians. The Allies would have done better to deprive you of all your animals after the war. Dogs, cats, horses, chickens – all of them, mice and rats included. That would have been the right kind of dismantling programme, so you didn't overdo your decent attitude towards them. I wouldn't like to be the dog of someone who buries children alive.

Yes, Harry, and here I am, lying beside you, a Russian female and human animal. Russian animal and human female.

* * *

We lay there in silence for a long time, maybe an hour. I was holding Sonia in my arms. Suddenly I sensed that she was smiling. Then she said: When two people who love one another, or think they do – two people who are living together or think they are – I mean, when there has been something so violent between two people, like between us just now, that "quarrel" is a pale description of it, they often make love afterwards. East or west, there's no difference. I've never regarded that as a bourgeois form of reconciliation – at least, not often. It doesn't really have anything to do with sex. It's just a huge explosion, and sex is merely the vehicle for it.

Why say that now? I asked.

Because it just occurred to me, and because I wouldn't be averse. But it would be obscene, for all that. Too many people died tonight in Petersburg, Petrograd, Leningrad. In Petersburg. In my head.

People are always dying, I said. All the time. Throughout our lives.

We aren't in love, nor do we think we are, Sonia said, and we don't think we're living together and we aren't, and if it weren't obscene I would do with you what we won't do together, or may do after all, and we'll do it because it's utterly pointless and absolutely essential and unstoppable in any case, because thunderstorms are unstoppable. But don't forget: Tomorrow is another day.

* * *

We clung to each other, held each other tight so as not to be carried away by the storm that was ourselves, but carried away we were, ever further and deeper and further and more powerfully, and the next morning, which was the same morning but another day, Sonia went out on to the terrace and looked up at the sky, which was blue and cloudless. It's difficult to say anything after a night like that. We weren't in love, after all, nor did we think we were, but Sonia did just the right thing. She turned to me and said, through the open door: I bet it's ages since they've had a storm like that here.

Then, leaning forward with both hands braced against the door frame, she put her head into the room and said: How's your sex life, taxi driver? I mean, if you leave a city behind and nobody misses you, it can't have been up to much, can it? She smiled derisively. But then, as you yourself said, you never share your bedroom with women.

I don't share my bedroom with women but I'm sharing one with you. The reason has a name: Aliosha. End of story.

Thanks, she said.

Ellen – that was the name of the reason I didn't share my bedroom with women. I hadn't slept in the same room as a woman since the night I saw that terrible fear in Ellen's eyes. The fear whose cause was myself. *Harry, I'm drowning. Harry, the world is ending and I'm drowning. The world died long ago, and I've only been dreaming I'm alive. The world is dead and no one can help me. No doctor, no mother, no father, no God. Nor you either.*

Ellen, who had never been afraid of anything, who never let anything – even a moral standard – intimidate her. She was the first person who told me that women don't want to go to bed with men as often as men do with women. That wasn't easy at a time when everyone believed they were in the thick of a sexual revolution, and anyone who didn't fuck like a rabbit was frigid. And it wasn't easy to say that to a young man who believed that what love meant to him meant the same, and in equal measure, to the other party.

I was hurt. Furious. Disconcerted. It took a long time to sink in properly. Women simply don't enjoy fucking as much, let alone as often, as men do, Ellen told me. With the possible exception of nymphomaniacs, that despised breed, but have you ever met a nymphomaniac? I haven't – apart, of course, from nearly all the men I know. Nearly all men are . . . well . . . nymphomaniacs. There doesn't seem to be an equivalent term for men. Sex maniacs, perhaps?

Once, when we were driving past a brothel a few years later, I said – just for fun – that it might be interesting for me to try one.

Yes, you do that, said Ellen. Otherwise you may wind up regretting it at the age of eighty. And by then it could be too late.

She wasn't joking. Sex is sex, Harry. It's all well and good – very good, sometimes – but it's only sex. There's nothing personal about it. It doesn't matter to me who you sleep with, but it would be bad if you loved someone else. That would be really bad, even though I couldn't do anything about it. The worst thing of all is when someone pretends to love someone because they know it's the only way of getting them into bed. That's obscene in the true sense.

Ellen knew all this long before I did. Men and women are governed by a terrible fact – a brutal, mechanical, wholly biological fact. Any man would in principle have sex with any woman, and any woman would in principle build a nest with any man provided he could protect and maintain that nest. All this is irrespective of the persons concerned. And that seems profoundly insulting or "offensive", as those who specialize in being offended would say. The sole difference is that men, when they've found a woman, soon want to have sex with other women, whereas most women, when they've built a nest, remain in it and love their children. Once again, irrespective of the persons concerned.

* * *

And that's how it was when everything ended. That's how it was. I could no longer be an author and wrote no more books, and I no longer wanted to share my

76

bed with a woman, nor did I. And sex was just sex. Something utterly anonymous, and when it was really anonymous it could be like a drug. I discovered – only a few times, not often – that anonymous sex can be just as potent as sex with someone very close to you: total dissolution. Ellen disliked phrases such as "total dissolution". Oh yes, she said once, like an Alka-Seltzer in a glass of water.

And there were other times, in the street, in the subway, on an escalator somewhere. All at once, in the crowd, a face in which I suddenly immersed myself. For a few moments I immersed myself in that face or that face immersed itself in me. It can happen when you catch sight of someone breathtakingly beautiful. You enter that person like a door, or perhaps it's the other way round and the woman on the escalator enters you like a door, and at that instant when something melts inside you, she moulds your face and your body in her image. You're as beautiful as she is. For a moment. For a second or two. For a second or two you *are* that woman.

For a second or two. Or for ever. The first time I saw Ellen I was like a door through which she passed. Like a door that would preserve her form for ever. That was how it was and still is. A door for ever. All that remains is that door. At least it still exists.

That's how it had been these past twenty-four years – the brothels of Western Europe, occasional anonymous sex and total dissolution, and sometimes this self-immersion in a stranger's face. And I never shared my bed with anyone – I was always alone. But then, it's probably true that the most frequent form of sexual gratification, throughout the world, is masturbation.

One night on television a few months ago there was an interview with a suffragan bishop. I'm not sure what

77

a suffragan bishop is, or whether there's more than one in a diocese. I'd been channel-hopping, but I stayed with this programme because two people were talking and I wanted to hear some human voices in my flat. I nearly always watch programmes in which people talk to each other, even if they're talking nonsense. Anyway, I took to this suffragan bishop. He must have been seventy or thereabouts, and at one point, needless to say, the interviewer asked him about celibacy. He positively smacked his lips as he set this time-honoured trap for a Catholic priest. The bishop smiled at him and said: Well, I used to be a young man myself. I was no stranger to women, but there came a time when I resolved to become a priest, and not to marry or go to bed with them. The decision to become a priest is an experiment. A lifelong experiment of uncertain outcome. And now, he said with a faint smile – now the temptation grows weaker every day. It was a wonderful smile, that smile of his, and he was absolutely right.

That would have appealed to my mother. Tess liked people with a sense of humour. She also liked religious people. Although Buddhism was very important to her, and although she despised monotheistic religions, she liked religious people even when they were Christians. I'm an epileptic Buddhist, my boy, but I'm also a Buddhistic Catholic. I've a Catholic childhood behind me, and you never entirely get over that. I'm a fast talker, too. That above all.

She not only despised monotheistic religions, she was sometimes filled with hatred of them. She particularly disliked Abraham and those who regarded him as an important figure. Abraham was someone she really despised. Honestly, my boy, Abraham was a peculiarly repulsive character, a man so subservient to his god that he was ready to slaughter Isaac, his own son, simply because that jealous deity had demanded it of him. The fact that he didn't do so is no credit to him or his god. He *would* have done so, and his god had demanded it of him, and both things were unforgivable, and this man Abraham, this terrible parent, was the founding father of three religions. To crown everything, it's said that all the nations on earth have been blessed by his seed. That's a phrase that often occurs in the Bible, but in this context it has a disgusting aftertaste. Isaac would have had far more reason to kill his father than poor Oedipus, who had no reason at all. He was merely the victim of a combination of unfortunate circumstances.

It was fate, pure and simple, my mother used to say in her dry way, but the god of the monotheists sets store by such things. For him they represent a system. If the Jehovah's Witnesses alone had this god – a god who issues orders to kill – one would have serious misgivings about the merits of religious freedom.

Look at the monotheists' churches and synagogues and mosques. Listen to their hymns and prayers. They know what pain is, they know the meaning of death and joy and happiness and that crazy presentiment which may or may not be just our imagination. And because they also possess and know these things, we have to tolerate them. We don't have to tolerate religions simply because they're religions. There are no grounds for tolerating a religion that preaches murder and war, as religions often have. But there *are* grounds for tolerating them because they know and possess something: pain and joy and that intimation of eternity.

And all at once Tess was there again, thoroughly present and preoccupied with the things of this world.

I doubt if your father would have made a particularly good father, she told me. He was a macho of the biblical kind, but even he would have laughed to scorn a god who demanded that he slaughter his own son.

Thursday

Sonia and I spent four more days in the Markgräfler Land. Or was it five? We were beginning to feel a little too safe. But every night I thought of Aliosha, and every night I became more tense and uneasy.

We've got to do something, I told Sonia. We can't stay here for ever.

We could, she said. We've got enough money. We could buy ourselves a small hotel or boarding house and live on the takings.

We both laughed, but I couldn't endure this sensation of being hunted. I kept thinking of the man in the toilets who hadn't come in for a pee. I kept seeing the water gushing from the tap in the deserted washroom. Water running for someone with no reason to wash his hands. Ever since then I've always gone into a cubicle when using a public lavatory.

It was an immense strain, covertly eyeing everyone we saw for signs that he might be a spy or a hit man. I was nearing the end of my tether, and Sonia knew it because the tension was wearing her down too.

After those four or five days we decided to do something.

Let's go to another tourist area, I said. Then we have to do something about Aliosha.

That won't be much use, Sonia said. Whatever we do about him, it won't be much use.

Well, we've got to do *something*, I said, or we'll both go insane.

Harry, she said, you saved my life, even if you only did it to save yours. You shot Dmitry when he was about to shoot me.

And now we're running away from Aliosha, I said.

We won't get very far.

But we must try.

All right, she said, where shall we go? Have you given it any thought?

Yes, I told her. I think we should go east to Passau, right over on the Austrian border.

Do you know the place?

Some, I said. I once spent a lovely long summer there as a child.

She looked at me. Her eyes widened. It's where you were born, right?

I nodded.

Let's go there, then. I'd like to see where you were born.

* * *

We took the longer route via Regensburg because I didn't want to go anywhere near Munich, let alone drive through it. On the long drive to Passau I explained my plan to Sonia. I had to challenge Aliosha – set a trap for him. I had it all worked out.

We would check into two hotels, but we'd spend the first two days in only one of them. Officially, I alone would be staying there. I also knew which hotel it should be. It wasn't far from the station, and I'd quite often spent the night there. Once every two or three years. I always spent the night at that hotel because I no longer knew anyone in the town. Tess and I had moved to Munich when I was fifteen. When I visited Passau I occasionally saw a face light up with something akin to

82

a flash of recognition. Somewhere in my face or walk there must still have been some vestige of the youngster I was at seven, twelve or fifteen, but I no longer knew anyone in the town and no one knew me. They didn't know me at the hotel either, but they had my name in their computer, as well as those of all their other guests. Once you were in the computer you didn't have to fill in any forms. Above all, you didn't have to produce any ID.

The hotel had another advantage: There was no need to pass the reception desk when you went up to your room. You simply got into a lift in the courtyard and pressed the button. The reception desk was on the first floor, so you could bypass it on your way up. Just what we needed.

I called the hotel on the way and asked if they had a single room. It was the holiday season, after all. Have you stayed here before? asked a man's voice.

Yes, I said. My name is Dieter Müller.

I had to risk that. I couldn't be a hundred per cent certain, of course, but Dieter Müller was a pretty common name. They *did* have a Dieter Müller. Two of them, in fact.

Herr Müller from Sonthofen or from Nuremberg? asked the voice on the phone.

Sonthofen, I said quickly. They had a double room vacant but were prepared to charge me for a single. Very good.

The voice said: It's been quite a while since your last visit.

Saturday

It's been quite a while since your last visit, the receptionist said when she'd located me in the computer.

Yes, I said, more's the pity. I always enjoy staying here.

Having parked in the courtyard, I took our bags upstairs. Then I went to fetch Sonia, who was waiting for me at a café. We returned to the hotel and went up in the lift together. I showed Sonia my room. The bed was a double, so it wouldn't be too noticeable if two people slept in it.

Herr Müller from Sonthofen is staying here on his own, I told her. Dieter Müller. Nobody knows a woman is staying here too.

So this is our unofficial room?

Yes, I said. We won't move into the official one till tomorrow.

After we'd showered and had a bit of a rest we went for a stroll. Sonia was delighted with Passau. It may be small, she said, but I could walk around here for ever. It's pretty and romantic and Italianate, and it's something else as well. I'm not sure, but I think it smells of you.

Darkness had fallen by the time we sat down at one of the tables outside an Italian restaurant in Residenzplatz. It was still warm, and we were very tired and untalkative. I felt like dissolving into the warm summer air. A stranger would probably have taken us for a couple of long standing.

Sonia said: Maybe *this* is where we ought to buy a hotel or a boarding house.

No, I told her. Only people travelling under false names stay here.

We slept extremely well in Dieter Müller's room. The next morning we breakfasted at a café, so that we would be seen in the hotel by as few people as possible. After that we bought two largish holdalls, one of which would easily fit inside the other. Then we walked to the station, took a taxi back into town, and checked into our official hotel. Later we took one of the bags back to the first hotel.

Sonia had called the day before and booked the room in the name of Calabrese, Patrizia Calabrese being the name on her Italian passport.

She filled in the form for both of us.

Oh, she said, the single room beside ours – could you reserve it? Our friend Signore Schmitz may not get here until late tonight. We can take the key with us and have a look at the room. It'll be paid for come what may.

The man at the reception desk gave us a friendly smile. We rode the lift up to the third floor and inspected both rooms, then deposited our empty bags in the double room. It was around eleven in the morning by now. I went into the single room and called Aliosha's mobile number.

A man's voice answered, naturally. I said I wanted to speak to Aliosha.

Who is it?

A friend of Sonia's, I said.

Aliosha isn't here, said the voice.

Oh, I said. You mean he's lent his mobile to someone?

No answer.

All right, I said, I'll call again in half an hour.

Half an hour later the same voice answered.

Aliosha? I said.

Speaking.

I'm a friend of Sonia's.

So I already gathered.

You can have all the money if you let us go, Sonia and me.

How much money are we talking about?

Almost exactly four million dollars.

And how do I get hold of it? he asked.

I suggested we meet in Passau the following night.

Ah, a frontier town, he said. There was a note of triumph in his voice. From the sound of it, he'd just had a bright idea.

Tomorrow evening at half past seven, I said. The rowing club beside the Inn. In the car park of the club, and come alone. We'll both come alone.

I explained how to get there and we hung up. I rejoined Sonia in the double room. Half past seven tomorrow evening, I told her. We've got masses of time.

It was a fine, warm day. Sonia and I strolled through the town like two tourists with plenty of time to spare. We really did have plenty of time. We were also plenty scared, but we could hardly wait for something to happen. I wondered if I'd called Aliosha too soon and enabled him to be too well-prepared, but Sonia said he would never have agreed to an earlier meeting. My only fear was that he or some of his people would get to Passau early and spot us somewhere.

In that case, said Sonia, we'll simply drive out into the countryside tomorrow. Till the balloon goes up.

She was pretty sure Aliosha wouldn't come alone. He would bring a driver at the very least, in case they had to make a quick getaway, and he would probably have the exit roads watched. Mainly the roads into Austria and, of course, the B12, which leads to the Czech Republic. Still, said Sonia, what does it matter? They won't assign more than one car to each route. The traffic here is heavy, and they don't know what sort of car we're driving. In my mind's eye I saw a long convoy of green BMWs making for southern Germany.

We went into the cathedral and spent a long time sitting side by side in a pew. I saw that Sonia was praying. Strange, I thought. A mafiosa praying before the showdown. Her expression was very grave, but she smiled when she noticed I was watching her. We're the good guys, she said, and later, when we were outside: It must be nice to grow up in a town like this. Romantic and adventurous.

It was more adventurous in the old days, I said.

And romantic? she said. I bet you knew a lot of girls.

Not as many as all that, I told her. For romance I went to America. They sent me to the States for that. I made a perfect knight errant.

Sonia laughed, but what I'd said was true. Fate had ordained that I should go to America at the age of sixteen – that I should meet Susannah Timmerman and then, a few years later, Ellen. I didn't realize that until later on, when I was already living with Ellen, because one probably only ever sees these things after the event. I was surrounded by an invisible cordon that only other people saw or sensed. I myself was unaware of it. When we were between twelve and fifteen my friends took care not to tell any dirty jokes in my hearing (I heard them just the same), and they never willingly lent me the smutty books that passed from hand to hand. It was as if I were some kind of Parzival who had to be protected from certain things. I still managed to get hold of the smutty books, of course, and I found them quite arousing.

The books and dirty jokes penetrated this invisible cordon, but the cordon persisted. I could do things no one else could, and I never stopped to think whether I could afford to do them or not. When we were twelve or thirteen we went off to Scout camp during the summer holidays. By train. Standing there on the platform with all the other boys, I felt incredibly happy because I was going away on my own for the very first time, and because I would be spending four whole weeks with my best friend, an ocean of time so boundless that the end was out of sight, and all at once I turned round – in front of all those boys on the platform – and gave my friend a kiss. He was pretty embarrassed, no doubt, and may even have blushed. I don't remember, but I do know that no one said a word. None of the boys on the platform looked shocked or tittered. Those youngsters, who could detect some gay connotation in a pencil point, found it quite natural that I should kiss my best friend in public. It probably never even occurred to them that there was anything exceptional about it. All they sensed was that cordon I myself was never aware of and never sensed, whose existence is apparent to me only now.

Later on, when we were doing play-reading at school, I always had to take the female parts because there were no girls in our class. I had a pretty good speaking voice. I played Juliet and Maria Stuart and Elektra and Emilia Galotti, and when the teacher was dishing out parts a few boys would always say my name when a female role came up. I kept mum and never put my hand up. I knew I would get the parts anyway, and I wanted to get them because I thought the women far more interesting than the men. It wasn't that I found the women's roles so exceptionally interesting, I simply found it exciting to be a woman for an hour or two. Or half a woman. Only female roles penetrated my cordon. When we were fifteen my friends and I did boxing for a while, maybe nine months or so. It surprised us all that you could punch a friend in the face, even if you were wearing boxing gloves – that you could be hell bent on knocking him out but afterwards you'd drape an arm round his shoulders and everything was the way it had been before. That applied to everyone except my best friend. I didn't want him to lose, least of all to me, but I didn't want to be thrashed by him either, so I often gave up and lost by a technical KO. He soon caught on, so after that we lost in turn, always by a technical KO, and we managed it so cleverly that the others didn't notice. We never talked about it. We simply lost in accordance with some indeterminate arrangement, each time by a technical KO.

Monday

You must tell me about it sometime, said Sonia. I'm sure it makes an interesting story, your adventures as a knight errant in America.

We went into a small church belonging to a school. A girls' school. It now takes boys as well, I think, but it used to be for girls only. My grandmother went to it, and so did Tess. My grandmother always travelled there by horse-drawn carriage when the holidays were over, and when term was over and the next holidays began she was collected the same way. Whenever I pass the school (and I pass it whenever I'm in the town), I see my grandmother getting out of the carriage. She's all light and airy, almost invisible, and the carriage and horses are also light and airy, but I always see them, clear as can be, and my grandmother getting out of the carriage. She was at the school nearly a hundred years ago, but she still turns up there. I stand on the corner, and the carriage drives up, and everything is the way it was a hundred years ago.

Yes, I always pass that school and I always go into that little church. It's almost oriental, Sonia whispered when we were standing inside. Syrian, perhaps. Or like a church in Jerusalem. We stood there and became all slender and white and light and cool, like the church. Suddenly Sonia said: Hey, there's a Russian story here.

Affixed to the grille that separated the choir from the nave was a sheet of cardboard bearing photographs of a group of children taking their first Communion. One of the girls was black. Beneath the photographs was this Russian story. Sonia read it to me in a low voice. It was about hell and heaven, and it went something like this: A rabbi once asked God to show him hell, and God ushered him into a room full of tables laden with delicious food, and the people in the room were trying to eat it with very long spoons. But the spoons were too long, so they couldn't eat all this wonderful fare. They couldn't get the spoons into their mouths. That was hell. Then God escorted the rabbi to heaven. It looked exactly like hell. The same food and the same long, useless spoons. The only difference was, the people in heaven were feeding each other.

Socialist realism, I said to Sonia as we emerged from the church.

Later we sat under a sun umbrella outside an ice-cream parlour and consumed ices with long-handled spoons. Suddenly Sonia held out her spoon and I licked it clean. Then I fed her some ice cream with my own spoon. Then it was her turn again, and so it went on until each of us had finished off the other's ice. The people who saw us must have thought we were a courting couple.

Socialist realism, Sonia said.

Quite right, I said. There's no ice in hell.

Late that afternoon we went to the cemetery. I'd really wanted to go alone, but Sonia insisted on coming too. We belong together, Harry, she said. Whether you like it or not, we're in this business together. Your business is my business, and vice versa.

We stood beside my family plot for a long time. Three people lay buried there. My grandfather. My grandmother. My mother. Three of the people who had made me – people without whom I would have been quite a different person. The same went for another three. Susannah. Ellen. Jessie. Three women and only one man. *You were made for women, my dear boy,* my mother had told me. *You were made for love,* and now I was standing there beside Sonia, for whom I hadn't been made. We weren't in love, nor did we think we were, but we were in this business together.

In a low voice, Sonia read out my mother's name and what was written beneath it: Tessa Willemer. Born 4 July 1922. Died 2 December 1968.

It was cold then, she said. Hard digging, right?

Yes, I said.

She wasn't old. Forty-six, said Sonia. Was she ill?

Yes, I said, and a voice inside my head said: *What do you think of me now, Tess? I've killed two men and I may well kill another, or he me. What do you think of me now?*

Tess wasn't the kind of mother who blackmails her children with the imminence of her death and demands constant consideration and affection. She had only once said she wouldn't make fifty. That had been many years ago, when she told me that at fifty a good Buddhist leaves all his belongings behind and goes roaming. And now I was fifty-two, two, six years older than Tess had been, and I *had* gone roaming, though not in the way we'd envisioned.

I only had one really big row with Tess, and that was when I was due to do my national service. Tess intervened with the draft board because she wanted to stop me going into the air force. My ambition was to be a pilot, a Starfighter pilot, but Tess sent the board some medical certificates which stated that I might have an epileptic fit at any moment.

I was furious when she told me. I yelled at her, but she said, very quietly: I don't want my child shooting other people. Anyway, so many Starfighters are crashing, they won't risk having one of their expensive planes downed by an epileptic fit. The damned disease must be good for something.

I didn't speak to her for a week. And now I was standing over her grave and I'd shot two men.

That was the only time Tess interfered in my life. She wasn't one of those mothers for whom the Oedipus complex was invented, not one of those mother-animals who forge so close a bond with their children, especially their sons and more especially their first-born and only sons, that the poor things don't stand a chance. They inevitably grow up into machos who hate and despise women – all women except, of course, for protective mother-animals. Those mothers strive, through their sons, to gain that control over the world which the fathers deny them. The unfortunate sons not only have to keep their fathers in check but may not grant any other woman a place in their life – apart, perhaps, with certain limitations, from the next mother. Your own mother and the mother of your children, no one else.

Tess knew all this. She had studied the people round her – studied them closely throughout her short, dis-eased life. One night at a party she indicated a very good-looking blonde with a sardonic little jerk of her chin. She said: That woman over there told me recently that her son was the kind of man she'd always dreamed of having for a lover. He's only just turned twelve. What a shame.

Tuesday

Your father? Sonia asked me at the cemetery.

Dead, I said.

You said that as if he'd never been alive.

It's true, more or less.

Your father, Tess told me once, was one of those men who think their wife's problems, their wife's *life*, can be dealt with in five minutes flat. He married the wrong woman, that's all. He was made for someone more stupid. There are as many stupid women as men. It's just that they don't always get together, which is a pity. It was practical, of course, marrying a wealthy heiress. I paid him off when you were a year old. He got a good deal, in my opinion.

That was *almost* all my mother ever told me about my father.

Harry, Sonia said at the cemetery, why did you come to this town? Because you want to die here?

Because I'd like to be buried here, I said. It's more practical. Not so far to go on Judgement Day.

She laughed.

Besides, I said, we're going to beat Aliosha.

How will that help us? she said, and her eyes said: *We all have to die in the end, don't be frightened.*

That night we again had dinner in Residenzplatz. Water splashed in the fountain and the sky resembled a vast, dark blue tent sheltering the entire world. We sat there for a long time after the meal, drinking wine.

I like you, Sonia Kovalevskaya, I said at some stage. I

mean, I like you quite a lot because we aren't in love and don't think we are.

That's a very pleasant thought, she said, and her eyes said: *What will have happened by this time tomorrow?*

On the way back Sonia paused outside a building in the old quarter of the town. Not a particularly beautiful building or a particularly beautiful façade. The door was its only striking feature. I think Sonia lingered outside because of the door, not the building itself. It was an old, round-arched iron door. The metal was pitted, possibly centuries old, and looked rusty, although one couldn't see for sure in the gloom. We stood there for a minute, perhaps, and were about to walk on when I grasped the handle and turned it. The door swung open.

We found ourselves in a dark passage. I pressed a switch. The dim light was really just another form of darkness. We walked along the passage and across a big, oblong trapdoor to some stairs. Looking up, we saw a stairwell enclosed by arches and, on one side, the huge round-arched window that must have illuminated it in the daytime.

Sonia said: These iron banisters look as if they were gilded at one time. They must have been very wealthy people. Very powerful people.

We climbed the stairs until we came to a white grille. That was as far as we ventured. Back downstairs again we walked further along the passage, deeper and deeper into the building. We passed some large latticework gates beyond which lay storerooms of some kind. At one point we came across a refuse bin with spiral fly-papers suspended above it. We looked down into a dark courtyard, then pressed another switch and climbed another flight of stairs. There were doors and passages everywhere, all leading to other doors.

95

The entire building was a town in its own right. It was silent as the grave, too – not a sound to be heard. Sonia took my hand and whispered what she'd been whispering all the time: This is wonderful. I've never seen anything like it. It's a whole town you could get lost in!

As children we had often gone into buildings in the old quarter and snooped around, simultaneously scared and fascinated by their labyrinthine passages. When grown-ups came and asked what we were doing there, we always said we were looking for Herr Zlatobek. It was hard, sometimes, to explain why we should be looking for Herr Zlatobek in the cellar, of all places. Our forays continued for a long time, till we were thirteen or fourteen. The town was a jungle full of mysteries, but I had never been in this particular building before. We never went into buildings that housed shops. Too much activity, too many employees who could have spotted us.

Holding hands, Sonia and I slowly and cautiously descended the stairs until we found a light switch. Before the light came on she whispered: Did someone say "Alice"?

Again we negotiated the stairwell with the wonderful banisters Sonia thought had once been gilded.

What happened to all the gold on them? she asked.

All the banisters in the town used to be gilded, I improvised. The gold was scraped off by children. When they hadn't any money but wanted a carousel ride or a cinema ticket, they simply went and scraped some gold off the banisters. In the course of centuries they stripped the gold off all the banisters in town. That's how it happened.

Sonia smiled. Oh, she said, so that's how it happened.

When we were out in the street again she paused in front of the building and said: Did you have a ferry here?

We had two, I told her. A little motor ferry across the Danube and a cable ferry across the Inn.

She scraped a flake of rust off the front door and put it on her tongue. Not gold, she said. Rust. Metal tastes like blood. Or blood tastes like metal. Let's hope we won't be taking another ferry across another river tomorrow.

She looked at me sadly, and I said: Know what we'll do?

Yes, she said. If things go wrong tomorrow – if we get separated for some reason – we'll meet up here. No one will look for us or find us here. All we have to do is keep walking round this building and no one will ever find us.

We went to our "official" hotel because we had to show our faces there. We mussed up the bed in our double room. Then we went to the hotel where we slept.

* * *

The next morning we had breakfast at the same café as before. Afterwards Sonia changed the rest of her francs at one bank and $5000 at another, using her false passports. Normally, she told me, one didn't have to show any ID for sums up to 30,000 marks, but every bank had its own regulations. Using the passports that day presented no risk. We felt sure the police knew nothing about them, or the names would long ago have appeared in the press. And anyway, the Mafia knew we were here.

After that we drove out into the countryside. The Bavarian Forest. I showed Sonia a few of the towns and places I had often been to as a boy. We sat beside a stream, more or less at the spot where I'd sat with a friend many years ago. That's to say, we'd spent most of the time standing in the stream and fishing for trout, but now I sat with Sonia in the meadow through which the stream flowed, and I told her about the meadow and the stream, and how, before we started fishing, we used to catch a few dozen grasshoppers for bait. That didn't take as long as you might think – maybe five or ten minutes to catch four or five dozen grasshoppers. The place was teeming with them. Every time you combed the grass with your fingers they came out holding a grasshopper. I reckon that meadow was only two or three grasshoppers short of a plague of locusts. By combing the grass for grasshoppers and popping them into old cigar boxes, my friend and I may have been contributing to the area's ecological balance, who knows?

We needed all those grasshoppers because the stream was full of trout. There were almost as many trout in the stream as grasshoppers in the meadow. We took our rods and stationed ourselves in the water, which was quite shallow – thigh-deep at the most. Then we baited our hooks with grasshoppers and looked around for one of the innumerable trout. Once you'd spotted one it was all very easy. You simply cast your grasshopper so it landed in front of the trout's nose, and it struck. That would have been the end of the trout if we'd been fishing seriously, but we only wanted to catch fish, not kill them.

So we landed our fish and removed the hooks from their jaws like expert orthopaedic surgeons. We were anglers, not murderers. I doubt if we could have brought ourselves to kill a trout. It was a bit different with smaller creatures. The only ones we killed when fishing were grasshoppers, and they were really killed by the trout. Sometimes, when we removed the hook from a trout's jaws, the grasshopper would still be attached to it. Then, if it was still alive, we used it to catch another trout.

I want to go swimming with you right now, said Sonia, in your trout-stream paradise. So we had a long swim together. We were *almost* happy. Skin against skin, body against body, and water everywhere, little eddies all around us. We were children, children in the water, even though we didn't do childish things. No one watching us would have guessed what lay ahead of us that day. We wanted to forget about it, blot it out, but I kept hearing Sonia's voice in my head: *We all have to die in the end, don't be frightened.*

Later we passed the house where our tailor used to live. We got all our clothes from him apart from socks and underwear. Nothing off-the-peg. Tess wasn't terribly bothered, but my grandparents attached great importance to it. Nothing off-the-peg and no margarine. Only tailor-made clothes and butter. Those were their only dogmas, but margarine and off-the-peg were anathema.

Sonia laughed. Have you perpetuated the tradition?

Only partly, I told her. I still don't eat margarine.

I drove to the house that had once been the home of my Uncle Philipp. It was empty now and would probably be demolished before long. It seemed to symbolize the decline of our family. Or of part of our family. Philipp was the capable and prosperous son of capable and prosperous parents. He was a cousin of my mother's, and what fascinated me about him was that two fingers of his right hand were missing. It felt strange when you shook hands with him. Not unpleasant, but invariably surprising.

I'm a pretty naive person. I was a naive child, too (unless all children are naive), and it was years before I grasped why Uncle Philipp had lost two fingers on his right hand.

At first there was the story of a wood-chopping accident. Uncle Philipp was right-handed. It seemed odd that a right-hander would chop off two fingers of his right hand, but it was possible that he always used his left hand for chopping wood. I never queried this as a boy, nor were any questions expected of me. It had simply been an accident.

A few years later, maybe eight or nine years after the war, the truth became a little clearer: he had chopped off the two fingers because he didn't want to go to war. He didn't want to die. He had absolutely no wish to do so and was afraid of dying, and because it would have raised a lot of unpleasant questions if a right-hander had chopped off two fingers of his right hand, he asked a friend, his best friend, to chop them off for him. Without your middle finger and index finger, especially the latter, you can't fire a gun.

As a boy I often wondered if I could do it. Chop off two of my friend's fingers, I mean, or get him to chop off my middle and index fingers. But it had to be like that, I suppose. Even if you really did use your left hand for chopping wood, it wouldn't have been easy to convince a draft board that a right-hander used his left hand for that purpose. So his best friend had to chop off the fingers for him. Someone who would never give him away. Two friends were chopping wood together and there was a terrible accident – that was the story.

After another few years the story became clearer still. To me, at least. The rest of the family had probably known it for ages. Uncle Philipp was a homosexual. That was his main reason for not wanting to go into the army. It would have been difficult for a homosexual to remain undiscovered in the army, and Uncle Philipp was a very sociable and amusing person who always attracted a lot of hangers-on. He didn't want to go to war, still less to a concentration camp, so his best friend had to chop off his fingers.

After the war he did what many homosexuals did in the old days – he got married. His wife was an extremely vivacious woman. Very far from homosexual herself, always amiable and good for a laugh, even though she ended by ruining the firm, which many members of the family construed as an act of revenge. She had a boy and a girl, cousins of mine, and at some stage during the fifties Uncle Philipp was sent to prison. Something to do with young trainees in the family firm. "Sexual abuse by a person in authority." Or was it "unnatural offences"? That was serious, even if sexual abuse by a person in authority is a pretty fair description of what the husband gets up to in a middle-class marriage.

I was forbidden to visit Uncle Philipp's house even before he went to prison, but I went anyway. I went and played with my cousins because I couldn't see any reason for the ban and my mother declined to explain. All she said one day was: All right, go. Uncle Philipp is sick. No, he's not really sick, he's perfectly well, in fact. Anyway, it isn't catching, so go. But make sure you're never left alone with him.

I think I was eighteen or nineteen before I knew the full story. Everyone visited Philipp regularly in prison, and when he was released he resumed his visits to us and was as amusing and entertaining as ever. He was my mother's favourite cousin, and his handshake continued to startle me every time. Years later, when the firm had ceased to exist, he died in prison, where he

101

was a universal favourite. He'd been sent down again. In the end, prison may have been the only place he wanted to be, and there weren't any children or youngsters there. He probably died a happy man. He'd sacrificed two fingers so as not to have to die before his time.

I'm slow to spot things, it's true – far slower than most people. There are a lot of names in our family that are Jewish or could be. Süss, Roth, Zimmermann, Berlinger . . . In the States those would all be Jewish names, but I was well into my twenties before it ever occurred to me. Our family isn't Jewish, in fact, like many of the immigrants from Russia in the nineties who are Jewish in name only. My grandmother was a Süss. She had eight brothers and sisters, and she often recalled what it was like in 1940, when the film *Jew Süss* came out in the Third Reich. We girls were all married by then, she used to say, but the boys and their families didn't have a very nice time. Two of them didn't, at least. The other two had emigrated to America long before.

For some years in the early 1950s we often received visits from a woman who looked very beautiful and smelt very nice. In appearance she could have been my mother's sister and my grandmother's daughter. She had been a family friend before the war, and had come back from America because her husband was dying. Her name was Leykauf. I find it hard to admit this now – admit it to myself, I mean – but I was forty-eight when it first occurred to me that Leykauf was a Jewish name. It's just about as inconspicuous as Rothschild, but I never noticed. To me she was just a very beautiful woman who had once been deserted by her husband and had returned to keep him company at his life's end. Before he died he said: I've only ever had one love, and that's my wife. My grandmother often repeated those words in the years that followed – as often as she quoted the German classics – and always gave my grandfather a challenging look as she did so. My grandfather, who was very fond of them both, the husband and the wife, once commented in his sceptical way: They all say that in the end. But a good end doesn't imply that everything else was good as well.

It was decades before I grasped the true significance of this story. Having married a Jewess, the man had probably been presented with a choice: Your wife or your business. He had evidently opted in favour of his business, and now, after all those years of treachery, she had returned so he didn't have to die alone. Completely destitute by this time, he was living in the attic of a large department store. The building had once belonged to him, and in the good old days the attic had housed his enormous electric train set, which had been disposed of long since. He was the first dead person I ever saw. The room smelt of oranges and cut flowers and something else that will always be associated in my mind with his lifeless face and thin, aquiline nose. And invisible, non-existent trains were running through the room. You could only *hear* them.

That's all I know about the woman, except that she drove a snappy little DKW which also smelt very nice, and that she always wore pale, embroidered gloves when driving, and once in the Austrian mountains, when she took me and Tess away for the weekend, we came to a warning sign beside the road with a black death's head in the centre, which meant you had to drive with great care.

Now that I've grasped all these things and pondered them repeatedly, I've often wondered what would have happened to Uncle Philipp if he hadn't had those fingers chopped off. His surname was Süss, so the concentration camp authorities would have looked askance at it. Then they might have had two reasons for killing him. Homosexuality and Jewishness, pink triangle and yellow star. Philipp would have been king of the concentration camp.

Sonia listened to my account of the Leykauf woman and Uncle Philipp with a quiet smile. You're like a child when you talk about these things, she said. You're the way you were in the stream, when we were like children, children in the water, even though we didn't do childish things.

* * *

Then the time for childish things was over. We drove back into town, filled up the car and left it in the car park of my hotel. We showered and packed most of our things, and I took the lift down and stowed everything in the boot. The money remained in the room, of course. Then we checked our guns. Mine was Dmitry's automatic, which had only one round missing from the magazine.

Don't forget, Sonia told me, Aliosha may be carrying a gun capable of firing a lot of bullets. It comes from Yugoslavia. I've never seen the thing, but the magazine is supposed to hold fifty or sixty rounds.

We had to do what must be done. We had no choice. Aliosha would either kill us right away or torture us and then kill us. Alternatively, I would kill him.

No, we had no choice. I looked at Sonia. We could always forget about it, I said. We could still get out of here.

What do you mean?

I mean he's your husband. If everything goes according to plan, I'll be killing your husband.

You know what husbands are like, she said. If they have to choose between their wives and the firm, they opt for the firm. Well, I'm opting for myself. And for you. For life. Or survival, at least to begin with.

I took two blankets from the wardrobe, stuffed them into one of the holdalls we'd bought, and zipped it up. It was just before seven. At half past eight, I said, I'll arrive here by taxi. You're to emerge from the restaurant opposite as soon as I get out. They must see us going into the hotel together.

I walked to the door.

Harry?

Yes?

It's silly to say this, but take care. He's a dangerous man.

Now you know, Sonia – it can take me half a lifetime to recognize a Jewish name, but now I know everything about the world. I'm a dangerous man too.

Good.

I kissed her on the forehead. Then I took her hand.

I feel like a little girl, she said.

That's the ideal feeling. For another few hours. Then you mustn't be a little girl any more. Wait for me. If I don't show up, just take off. You've got enough money.

*   *   *

I took the bag containing the blankets and walked to our official hotel. It was only a few minutes away. I asked for Signore Schmitz's key. Once upstairs I sluiced my face with cold water. Then I went into Signore Schmitz's room, drew the curtains, turned the light on, locked the door behind me, took the lift down to reception, and put the bag in the cubbyhole where hotel guests can deposit their baggage when they've vacated their rooms but aren't leaving yet. I left a message for Signore Schmitz at reception and told the porter that we might have to leave very early the next day, but that Signore Schmitz would definitely be arriving that night.

Then I went to the taxi rank roughly midway between our two hotels. I got in, telling the driver that this was my first visit to Passau for twenty years, so I simply wanted him to drive me around for a bit. Along the Inn to the Neuburg Forest, for example.

It was twenty past seven. We drove along Nikolas-trasse and then out on to the road beside the Inn. As we passed the cemetery landing stage I looked across the river and suddenly felt quite calm. Utterly calm. We drove past the university buildings, a market garden, and the hospital. It occurred to me when we were already past the hospital that the Russian cemetery used to be out there when we were children. We always played football beside the cemetery. It was surrounded by tall bushes, and I don't think there were any graves, just a stretch of grass that looked exactly like the one we played football on. I've no idea who the dead Russians were. Prisoners of war or labour conscripts, perhaps. Strange that I should have remembered the Russian cemetery now, when I was setting a trap for Aliosha! Then we passed the derelict shirt factory, which was no longer even derelict. It simply wasn't there any more. All I could see was part of the gateway. The rest was overgrown with shrubs and bushes. We got to the rowing club soon afterwards. A few cars were parked outside, none of them occupied. We drove to the edge of the forest, then into it until we reached a

106

hotel or restaurant, I don't remember exactly. There was no traffic.

Aliosha hadn't shown up, just as we expected. Just the way we wanted.

We turned round at the hotel or restaurant and drove slowly back to Passau. A road runs down the hill beside the derelict shirt factory, and we hadn't gone far when a big black Lancia – not a Mercedes or a BMW! – turned off it and started following us.

We drove across Ludwigsplatz and over the Danube, then up the Ries to the castle. The black Lancia was still behind us. It disappeared from view occasionally, but it was still there. In the castle car park I got out and walked the hundred yards or so to the viewing point. My driver also got out but stood beside his taxi smoking a cigarette. The Lancia had pulled up beside the kerb about two hundred yards away. While I was admiring the view it drove slowly past the taxi, then back down the road and out of sight.

Sonia! They'd wanted to see if Sonia was in the taxi. It didn't surprise me that they'd driven off. There was only one route back into town. The road to Ilzstadt was closed to traffic.

We drove back, then on past Ilzstadt to Hals. The cabby waited below while I walked up to the ruins to stretch my legs a little. I got to the hotel just after half past eight, and at that moment Sonia came out of the restaurant and walked across the street towards me. She said hello and gave my driver a nod and a smile. I paid him and told him to drive round the corner into the next street, where the underground garage emerged. My wife had to get something from our car, which was parked there, I told him. She would join him in a minute, then he could take her on.

Sonia and I went into the hotel. I fetched the holdall from the cubbyhole and gave it to her. We hugged each other. I'll call you, I told her. From now on we must be grown-ups, not children. They're driving a black Lancia, so keep your eyes peeled.

Sonia went down to the underground garage. In two minutes she would get into the taxi, which was waiting for her at the exit. Everything was going perfectly. I asked for the keys to both rooms and went upstairs.

In our room the first thing I did was draw the curtains and turn on the bedside lights. It was ten to nine. I wondered if our plan had really allowed for every contingency. Half an hour later I called Sonia at the other hotel on my mobile. Everything had gone smoothly. She had got the cabby to drop her at the station and returned to the hotel on foot.

At half past eleven I paid a brief visit to Signore Schmitz's room and turned the light out. Shortly before one I checked my automatic again and turned out the bedside lights in the double room. Having hung the please-do-not-disturb sign on the door handle, I returned to Signore Schmitz's darkened room. The street lamps shed enough light, even through the curtains, for me to get my bearings.

I sat down in an armchair, put the gun on the table beside me, and waited for Aliosha.

My entire body and brain had never been so tense. I heard the blood roaring in my ears and kept rapping my head with my knuckles to get rid of the noise. I didn't dare go to the bathroom to cool my burning face, I couldn't risk it. I sat there and waited. The slightest sound made me flinch as if I'd had an electric shock. I was so wound up, I continued to hear it for minutes afterwards, until the roaring in my ears took over again.

Aliosha turned up just after two. I heard a faint foot-fall on the stairs, then the sound of someone at work on the door of our room. It was almost inaudible. No one in the entire building could have heard it apart from me. I didn't know whether Aliosha would simply walk in and fire at our beds, or whether he wanted us alive. Then I heard the door click open. All at once I felt completely calm. I stood behind my own door, gun in hand, and slowly opened it. Just then I heard some dull thuds that might well have been shots from a gun with a silencer. Then, after an infinitely long moment, I heard muffled curses. Moments later the door was closed from the inside. Aliosha was in the trap. Every-thing had gone according to plan. I had only to wait until he came out again. I aimed my gun at the door.

Then, through the door, came a faint whispering sound. I couldn't account for it at first, but then it dawned on me: he was phoning someone. He had a mobile with him! We hadn't thought of that. He was probably calling the driver of the black Lancia. The car must be parked somewhere near the hotel or in one of the side streets. But Aliosha couldn't risk a shoot-out. What was he planning?

I heard him make another call. His voice sounded different this time, louder and more distinct, almost normal. Then I caught a word: *Fire!* He was calling the fire brigade! That was a really shrewd move. If the fire brigade called back it might only be another minute before the hotel was alerted, but I doubted if the fire brigade called back when there was a fire somewhere – they probably set off at once. Aliosha could always call the night porter, who would naturally raise the alarm. Within seconds the hotel corridors would be swarming with agitated guests, and Aliosha would be able to escape in the confusion. Before that happened *I* had to make *my* escape. I raced down the stairs and out of the hotel.

The hotel fire alarm sounded just as I emerged. At the same time I heard sirens, but they were quite a long way off – you could hear them only if you knew what to listen for. I had to find the black Lancia. I wondered where it could be. Or rather, I didn't stop to wonder, I simply ran to the spot where I myself would have parked a car if I'd had to wait for someone leaving the hotel in need of a quick getaway, and that was in the little side street with the entrance to the underground garage. And there it was.

The Lancia was standing with its back to me, and when the driver saw me in the rear-view mirror he probably mistook me for Aliosha. In any case, he started the engine, leant over, and opened the passenger door as far as it would go. At that moment a shadowy figure emerged from behind some parked cars. With both arms extended, it crouched down on the pavement beside the open passenger door. It was Sonia!

She was holding a gun. The driver switched off the engine and slowly got out. The sound of the sirens was quite close now. I relieved the driver of his gun and his mobile and forced him to lie down in the boot. There was barely room for him, but I didn't know what else to do with the man. Just as I was closing the boot Sonia whispered something urgently. I didn't catch what she said, but I turned and saw someone coming towards us. It had to be Aliosha.

At the same moment Aliosha spotted that something was up and came to a halt. I shut the lid of the boot and drew my gun, which I'd stuck in my waistband.

Aliosha drew his own gun and fired at once. I'd been expecting that, or something or someone inside me had. At all events, I dived between two parked cars and heard two or three bullets slam into the boot.

Then Sonia opened fire. She'd dodged back into the shadows behind the parked cars. As soon as I heard the shot I jumped up and saw Aliosha take aim at her with his gun in both hands. I yelled his name and he spun round to face me. I was quite calm, in fact I felt almost happy. I pulled the trigger, I don't know many times. Subsequent news reports stated that he'd been hit by five bullets from two different guns.

Come on! Sonia called, and it was only then that I heard the sirens again, together with a lot of confused shouting. We left the side street in a hurry.

What now? I said. Where shall we go?

To the other hotel, the way we planned. Everyone will think we've skipped town. Besides, our money's there.

Why didn't you stay there?

She stared at me wide-eyed. Because I was worried about you. I simply couldn't stand it any longer. I hung around here until Aliosha turned up, then I waited to see what would happen. He wouldn't have got away from us. I waited for him in case you didn't make it.

He called the fire brigade, I said.

Sonia smiled. We never thought of that.

* * *

Back in our hotel room we flopped down on the bed and lay there for a long time without speaking. At some stage Sonia took my hand. I thought it would be best if we stayed another two days. No one would look for us in Passau. They might check the hotels for suspicious residents, but I was a long-established guest: Dieter Müller from Sonthofen. Everyone including the police and the Mafia would think we'd crossed the frontier into Austria – or that we intended to do so. The roads were bound to be watched for the next few days, so it would be better to stay put. The only thing we couldn't afford to do was walk the streets. Passau was a small place, and we might be spotted by some employee from the other hotel. We'd always have to take the car; we could never go around on foot, nor should we spend long driving through the town.

Sonia said: Aliosha is dead. He must be.

Yes.

When you shot Dmitry and Viktor I told you we were done for. I said we'd never have another moment's peace – they would never rest until they'd caught up with us, remember? I said they'd hunt us down for all eternity. Do you remember that? Well, now we've lost eternity as well.

* * *

It was on the six a.m. news. A hoax call to the fire brigade. One dead Russian, one badly wounded man in the boot of a black Lancia. Six cartridge cases had been found in our hotel room. The police suspected an act of revenge by members of the Russian Mafia. They had some rough descriptions, but our names were not mentioned.

I went down to the breakfast room at eight. I had to show my face, make sure I didn't arouse suspicion.

Did you hear? asked the young waitress who brought my breakfast. A shoot-out in the street, right in the middle of town. One man dead, one badly wounded, and two people vanished without trace. They're bound to catch them soon, though.

The weather was very warm. At eleven we drove to a swimming pool a little way out of Passau but still within the city limits, because we didn't want to run into a roadblock. Sonia had breakfast at a bakery on the way. We spent nearly all day beside the pool. Who would look for a Mafia killer in a swimming pool? Sonia swam one length after another in the hundred and fifty-foot pool, I went in off the diving platform a couple of times. I'm not a keen swimmer. At some point we went to the restaurant and had a bite to eat.

On the evening news they knew a bit more, not just that Aliosha had been hit by five bullets from two different guns. The six shots fired at our beds (At us, Sonia! I said. At us!) had come from Aliosha's gun, like those fired at the man in the boot of the Lancia. The police weren't sure what this implied.

By the time the late news came on they'd discovered that one of the five bullets in Aliosha's body was from the gun with which Viktor and Dmitry had been killed, and now my name cropped up. The police assumed that I was the hotel guest Aliosha had intended to shoot while asleep, and that my female companion was the woman who had been seen with me in France.

In the course of the next few days it transpired that the cartridge cases of the four other rounds in Aliosha's body were very probably from the same weapon as those found near Dmitry's body.

Forensics had really done their homework. I had indeed used Dmitry's gun, just as Sonia had used Viktor's, the one with which I'd shot him and Dmitry. And now, for the first time, Sonia's name was mentioned. My female companion, they said, was very probably a German citizen of Russian origin named Sonia Kovalevskaya, who also travelled under the names Gesine Kerckhoff, Catherine Marchais, and

113

Patrizia Calabrese. A woman named Calabrese had booked the two hotel rooms. Moreover, two banks in Passau had changed some US dollars and French francs for a woman who gave her name as Patrizia Calabrese and Catherine Marchais respectively.

They must have got that from the Mafia, said Sonia. All my names.

The late news gave more details supplied by the Mafia. It appeared that Sonia had been married to the victim of the shooting, so the whole affair was probably attributable to a *crime passionnel* rather than an outbreak of hostilities within the ranks of organized crime. A TV commentator told the studio audience that organized crime ought to work off its outbursts of emotion like everyone else, and not in the street. He used the expression "civilized society" at least four times.

Sonia kept waking up during the night. Either that or I woke up first and woke her because I was awake.

Now we're all alone in the world, she said. There's nowhere we can go.

We do have one advantage, I told her. The police won't bust a gut looking for us. All the dead belonged to the Mafia. No cop is going to risk getting a bullet in the face at a roadblock for the sake of a few mafiosi.

A few dead *Russian* mafiosi, you mean.

No, Sonia, I mean a few dead mafiosi, period. Quite right too, in my opinion. No point in risking your life for a bunch of killers.

So where do we go now?

We'll go to Italy.

We both knew that you always had to produce some ID when staying anywhere in Italy. The particulars would then be faxed to the Carabinieri. And we no longer had any ID fit to produce. I could tell that

114

something was going through Sonia's mind – something that had just occurred to her. After a while she said: We could always turn ourselves in.

I've no wish to go to prison, I said.

They'd acquit us. The case mightn't even go to trial. You acted in self-defence, after all. *We* acted in self-defence.

I doubt if the police would see it that way. I set a trap for Aliosha because I meant to kill him. I wouldn't exactly call that self-defence.

But you set a trap for him because he would have killed *you*. It was *force majeure*, so to speak.

I don't want to go to prison, I repeated. I don't even want to be remanded for questioning. Besides, the Mafia would find it child's play to bump us off inside.

No, she said. Our people always like going to prison in Germany. German prisons are secure. No one can kill them there. You Germans have always been good at that. When you build prisons and camps in which people are meant to be killed, they're killed, and when you build prisons in which people aren't meant to be killed, they aren't. We Russians have never managed that. With us, you can never be sure of getting out alive.

I didn't comment. I simply said I wasn't going to be locked up, even for questioning.

Just picture it, Sonia. Picture our release after being remanded in custody. We walk to freedom, and there, just outside the prison gates, the people from the Mafia are waiting for us. Plus a bunch of journalists and camera crews. No, I won't do it. I'm not in favour of the death penalty.

So it's Italy, is it? Where would we stay?

* * *

There was someone in Italy who didn't like me but would always put us up for a few days, possibly longer: Luigi Scalisi, my old foe from university and the streets. My favourite enemy. We had been at university together in the 1960s and had dropped out in the spring of 1969, after a few semesters of German and English language and literature. Luigi because he wanted to join the Underground, I because I aspired to be a writer but found that university could teach me none of the things I needed. I learned nothing there I wanted to know. And Jessie was born in the spring of sixty-nine. On 16 April.

I not only quit university, I deserted the group to which Luigi and I belonged. They were filled with hatred of their parents and the system and the rich and the United States. I could never hate anyone for long. Despise, yes, but not hate. Besides, I knew plenty of rich people I liked as well as plenty I didn't. They were just like anyone else. I had no reason to hate the wealthy. My mother was one of the first employers to introduce Christmas bonuses, holiday pay, and thirteen months' salary per annum. She installed a crèche at the factory, too. My left-wing friends thought it was all eyewash – a cosmetic operation on the part of the system. I didn't, and I would never have planted a bomb outside the front door of anyone like my mother. I wouldn't have done that to anyone I knew, whether I liked them or not.

You're a daddy now, Luigi said at the time. A class enemy as cowardly as any Italian. He was one of the few members of the group who didn't stop speaking to me or arguing with me. There were some who no longer greeted me when we passed each other, and who sometimes, when they felt too embarrassed, crossed over to the other side of the street. They were just as bourgeois as the bourgeois parents they despised so heartily.

A few years later Luigi took refuge in our flat because the police were after him. I'm safest with you, he told us. No one will ever look for me here. He stayed for six weeks or so. We often took Jessie to the playground or to a beer garden, or down to the Isar. It was excellent camouflage. Ellen and I learnt cooking from him, and *à la Luigi* became one of our stock phrases. It was strange, someone cooking so serenely while the police were after him. Luigi made spaghetti, all the risottos he knew, monkfish in white wine, carré d'agneau, roast venison, osso bucco, scaloppine al Marsala – all those things. For an anarchist he really was a very good cook. He was a very good cook, period. And a very good anarchist. And he was absolutely captivated by Ellen. What a woman! What a woman! he kept saying. Sometimes he said it when she was there, and she would say: What a cook! It was part of their game that he always looked downcast until she smiled and said: What a Luigi! And sometimes he said: Life here with you is almost the way it was meant to be. Except that the distribution of capital should be a bit fairer. And the division of labour. And the police shouldn't be after me. Then Ellen would fetch her purse and sit on it. *That's* the problem, said Luigi.

You're a kind of friend of mine, he said once. And a kind of enemy. I like you and I can't stand you. I can't stand you *politically*, but there's something that'll always be in your favour, both politically and personally: the fact that you're with Ellen. Or rather, that she's with you. It doesn't help much that you refrain from using the money you've inherited. That's just a handsome gesture on the part of someone who can afford such a luxury, but one forgets it when Ellen's around.

117

He wasn't saddened or dismayed when he heard, many years later, that Jessie was dead. Not to begin with, at least. Jessie, Jessie, Jessie . . . How old would she be now? Twenty-one? Twenty-two? Around the age we were when she was born. I always promised to take her dancing when she grew up, and now? What am I to do now? Tell me! And what about *you*, now that Ellen isn't there any more? What's left of you, Harry? How can you go on living?

I'm not living, Luigi, I'm waiting, that's all. I don't know why I'm waiting, but I am.

* * *

By then he was already living in this house in Italy. At some stage in the eighties he'd abandoned the struggle and returned full-time to Italy, where he grew vines and stopped reading the newspapers. He withdrew to a gloomy little old house in a little wood. He made a living from selling his wine and writing skits for two Italian TV channels. He still lived in that little wood. The house was near a little factory. I didn't know what they manufactured there, but everything in that little wood was little. Little and rather spooky.

Yes, Luigi would put us up. If he was there.

* * *

He wasn't. We spent the night in the car and the following day beside the sea. When we returned that evening the front door was open and Luigi was at home.

Of course you can stay, he said, eyeing Sonia suspiciously. Sure I can get you a new car, he said later, when darkness had fallen and we were sitting over the remains of supper. Sure I can change a few thousand dollars into lire. I may even be able to get you some new passports, but they'll have to be paid for in dollars. I can also dispose of that blue Peugeot. It'll look like a condolence card for a Peugeot by the time they're through with it – flat enough to go through the slit in a mailbox.

Sonia had already gone to bed. It was completely dark outside, except for the stars. What about Ellen? Luigi asked. What's she doing these days?

Ellen's safe.

Good. What do you plan to do now?

I don't know yet. Maybe we should stay a while with you to begin with, if you've no objection and if we're safe here. And if we aren't endangering *you*. We must wait until the police, at least, have stopped looking for us.

We were both smoking. I hadn't smoked a cigarette for over ten years.

They'll find you sooner or later, Harry. The Mafia will, I mean, even here. They're damned good at finding people and they've got infinite patience. So maybe you shouldn't stay here too long.

Isn't it funny, Luigi, me hiding here with you the way you hid at our place?

Yes, except that there isn't a little girl around.

Luigi put his hand on mine in the darkness, and once more the car tore down the slope, glanced off the tree, inflating the airbags, turned over several times, righted itself, and came to a stop.

This woman, this Russian – Sonia, I mean – have you known her long?

She was a passenger of mine. It's all a crazy coincidence.

Are you sleeping with her?

119

I don't sleep with my fares.

Luigi laughed in the darkness. That's no answer.

No, I said, it isn't.

Well?

None of your business. It's nothing to do with sex. It's something . . . existential.

Oh, is that what it's called? What about you and Ellen? That was something *non*-existential, I suppose?

Sex is sex, Luigi. Usually, at least. Usually. A firework. A childish game. A great, long leap. A long laugh in the night. But it's still sex, and sometimes, not very often, it's more than that. The only word I can find for it is religion. Eternity, if you like. That's how it was with me and Ellen. Often. Sometimes. Sometimes is pretty often.

And with Sonia?

Once a gigantic release of energy that had no connection with sex. And once a childish game. A cool stream and two naked children, two children in the water. It was the day we set the trap for Aliosha, when we didn't know if we'd survive the night, Luigi. But for a few moments we were like children. Death was something that didn't exist. That was only a few days ago.

Religion, I'd said. The word had simply slipped out. Total dissolution, and I could hear Ellen's ironical voice: Oh yes, total dissolution, like Alka-Seltzer in a glass of water. But it's true. I've never understood why sex and violence are supposed to go together. For me it had always been sex and dissolution. You were there one minute and somewhere completely different the next. The boys and girls in our Sunday supplements are always talking about the dark, menacing aspects of sex – always blathering about instinctual ambivalence and the potential violence of sexuality. It's the perpetual, toothless mumbling of people who aren't old enough to have lost their teeth. They never say what they really mean – if they know, which they probably don't. For me, sex had never been associated with violence. I was familiar with the converse, though. The moments before a fight, a fierce confrontation, an argument, had always been arousing. Sexually arousing. When I'd walked towards Dmitry in that clearing in France I had shouted and wept, filled with sorrow and compassion, but just before that my body had tensed with excitement. It was lust. Or lustful anticipation. But it had always been like that: violence can be sexually arousing, but for me sex and violence had never gone together. It was a one-way street only.

Luigi and I went on sitting there for a long time, smoking and drinking red wine. Two pet enemies. Once, Luigi rested his hand on mine again. What happened with you and Ellen, Harry? You were so completely different from all the other couples I knew. Everyone noticed it. What the hell happened?

That's just between Ellen and me.

And Jessie.

Yes, and Jessie.

Friday

The next day Luigi drove off in our blue Peugeot. That evening I drove his Honda Civic into La Pesta, the local town, and picked him up. The day after that he came back with a black Fiat Tipo. Three years old, he said. I got it for ten million lire. The papers and everything are absolutely kosher.

Luigi took our photographs, and four days later we had two Italian passports. Fifteen hundred dollars each, my friend. That's cheap, but they aren't that good. You shouldn't use them in Italy, but they're probably fine for anywhere else. I couldn't buy you any better ones or the Mafia might have got to hear of it. There are driving licences to go with the passports, but they're pretty useless. Steer clear of checkpoints with those things – the police would hear at once you aren't Italian. Tell them you're deaf and dumb.

Most days, Sonia and I went swimming in the sea while Luigi worked at home. He also went into town and bought us some underclothes. Of course, he said, I bought them from two different shops. I know the ropes, being a former member of the Underground. Where I got yours, Sonia, I asked the proprietress to recommend something for my daughter. They're all in feminist lilac. I hope you like them.

On our way home in the evening we would stop off at a pavement café in La Pesta. There was a jukebox outside, and we always picked out a few numbers at 300 lire each. Santana, Hanson, Britney Spears . . .

The café was right on the street, and we'd sit there watching the traffic go by. Usually we were the only customers. The place seemed absolutely deserted as it slumbered in the sunshine, almost like a café in a 1950s French existentialist film. Or a thriller. I noticed that Sonia stiffened, just as I did, whenever a BMW or Mercedes drove past. Most of them had German licence plates. There were plenty of Lancias in Italy, we discovered, but very few of them were black.

One Thursday Sonia and I decided to drive to Gavorrano for dinner. The little wood was becoming a little too cramped for us. Luigi didn't feel like coming, but he lent us his mobile. Just in case, he said. If you aren't back by one in the morning, I'll start to worry.

Gavorrano is a small town perched on a hill. It's not particularly beautiful and probably very poor, but I'd been there a couple of times in the old days, and I knew that it takes on a special charm when darkness falls and the townsfolk have already eaten. The lanes and alleyways are usually quite empty, and all at once that charm is there. The whole town becomes infused with a spirit of adventure. You're a child again, a child in some poor little town, waiting for something quite fantastic to happen.

Before dinner we paid a visit to the main square, which doubles as a car park. Looking over a low wall, we saw a bunch of youngsters playing football on a pitted expanse of asphalt. Above them, leaning against the wall beside us, a few fathers were watching their sons chasing the ball. They resembled generals observing and commenting on the progress of a battle. After we'd watched the boys for a while, Sonia said: You would have liked a son, wouldn't you?

Yes, I said. And a daughter.

Do you have any children?

No, I said, and she gave me one of her sidelong, mistrustful Russian smiles. A smile that meant: Nothing in this world is the way it looks.

Then she said: You must tell me more about that sometime.

After dinner we went for a stroll. It was pretty dark by now, but the air was very warm. As warm as our bodies. The narrow streets were deserted. We traversed an empty square, probably the town-hall square, then lost ourselves in the narrow streets again. On one occasion an old woman passed us, and some time later a black immigrant. A girl went into a house which blared out loud rock music when she opened the front door. They were probably dancing inside. Those were the only three people we saw. No one else was about. We were all alone in the town and the darkness.

I took Sonia's hand. This is a forbidden city, I whispered.

In this city, she whispered back, nothing is forbidden. And suddenly it was like a wild explosion: shameless, uninhibited, tremulous. In my memory it's as if we had sex all over the town, as if we'd run through the narrow streets pursued by lust, panting hard as we pressed up against the rough, sun-warmed walls, disappearing into doorways, always on the move, always on the run, yet fucking incessantly. Our bodies knew no bounds. They dissolved, and the town and time and the night dissolved just as we ourselves did.

In the end we sat down on some stone steps. We were utterly exhausted. Dissolved. Completely dissolved. *Almost* completely dissolved. Happy. Permeated by the night and the air. We *were* the night and the air. There was no difference any longer, no separation. Sonia said: Tell me, who pays you for this?

I might ask you the same question, I said. But then, you're paid by the Mafia.

She suddenly turned serious. All the people from the Mafia who might have paid me are dead. Either that, or they're trying to kill me.

*   *   *

When we got back to the Tipo I sat down in the passenger seat, took Luigi's mobile from the glove compartment, and called him. I said we wouldn't be back before one. Sonia was sitting behind the wheel, but she didn't start the car.

Phew, she said. Gavorrano! What a place! What would life be like now if the two of us were . . . innocent. Young. If we still had our lives before us.

We sat in the car for a long time without speaking. Both the doors were open. The air was still very warm, and we were a part of the air and the night. Then I said something after all. I can't understand it, I said, looking out into the darkness. I was very interested in sixteen-year-old girls when I was sixteen and very interested in eighteen-year-old girls when I was eighteen, but I've never once been interested in younger women. It simply never happened. And you're fourteen years younger than me. Why on earth should I be interested in you?

She looked at me wide-eyed. Because we're going to die together.

I said nothing.

But it's quite likely, isn't it? she said. It's pretty certain we'll die together. They're going to kill us both.

Saturday

The next afternoon we were in a small town. It was a very hot day, and we went into a church. We lit two candles. One for the dead and one for the living, said Sonia. There was a fresco on one wall, an Annunciation. I'd seen it somewhere before. Mary kneels on a stool with the angel facing her, both in pink robes. A man, a monk or saint, is standing beside a column on the left-hand side. There's nothing else to be seen, only the arched roof of a vault and, beyond Mary, the suggestion of a door. It's a very luminous, airy scene.

Sonia and I sat in a pew and looked at the fresco. We looked at it for a long time – so long that I forgot I was looking at it. The shadow cast by Mary's figure suddenly became airborne. She had an innocent, open face like that of someone who knows that something new is happening because something always is. She was just a girl with slightly flushed cheeks. Just someone waiting – waiting in the knowledge that the future is about to commence. I gazed at her shadow on the wall, her vague but determinate shadow, which resembled an aperture on the point of closing or opening, as if someone had just disappeared through the wall or was about to emerge from it. I accompanied the shadow through the wall and disappeared.

Later, I don't know how much later, Sonia took my hand. We got up and made our way to the exit. Five or six Italian youths of eighteen or nineteen, perhaps, came strolling along the aisle licking ice-cream cones.

I went up to them and told them in English to take their ices outside. One of them gave me a supercilious smile and said: This isn't your country. And I said: No, but it's my religion.

Strange I should have said that, not being a Christian. It was like Tess calling herself a Buddhistic Catholic. I was a non-Christian Catholic. A Catholic heathen.

Sonia glared at me when we got outside. You must never do that again! What would have happened if they'd beaten you up? If the police had come or identified you in the hospital? After all, they have our fingerprints. We must never get involved in anything like that again.

Besides, she said with a smile, besides, driving people from the temple should be left to the experts.

A young man in pastel chinos and a striped T-shirt was walking across the square, whistling *Jingle Bells*. In the middle of summer, in this heat, said Sonia. You see? Licking ices in church isn't all they do.

Sunday

We've got four million dollars, Harry. We can't spend them here in Italy. America's the only place where we can really do anything with them.

How are we going to get there without passports? We can't leave Italy with the ones we've got – it's too risky.

* * *

We discussed the problem with Luigi over supper. He also thought the States a good idea. But you mustn't take a scheduled flight, he said. A charter flight full of tourists would be best. No one would suspect you of smuggling Mafia money out of the country on a charter flight. I'll see what I can do.

Then he looked at Sonia. Yes, I reckon the dollars would be safest in their place of origin. Does the cash in your bags come from the States? I mean, the bills weren't printed here in Europe, were they?

The money has been laundered, Sonia told him. Laundered twice over, in fact. I drew it out of a bank in Luxembourg, little by little.

Good, said Luigi. Some Russian counterfeiters printed vast quantities of dollar bills in Germany. I don't know what the quality was like, but the gang was busted in the end.

I can imagine, I said.

Sonia gave me an angry look. In Germany even the treasury's official printers botch things up, she said. A few years ago a Munich firm produced a series of hundred-mark notes with no printing on the back. They even got into circulation. You Germans are so stinking rich, you didn't even notice.

Luigi laughed. I did too.

Maybe we'd better take a close look at those dollars of yours, Luigi said.

Still, he went on, turning serious, the passports are a problem. You shouldn't have any trouble in the States with the ones you've got. Italy could be difficult, though. I'll see what can be done.

* * *

Three days later I thought of a way of getting hold of some passports. We were having dinner in a restaurant and got into conversation with an American couple at the next table. They were very nice people with plenty to say for themselves. After dinner they invited us for a drink in the bar of their hotel. It was their last night. Next day they were flying back to the States via Florence and London. They'd had a wonderful time in Italy. When we said goodbye they gave us a book that had served them well – *Under the Tuscan Sun* by someone called Frances Mayes. We brought it with us, the husband said, but I doubt if we'll ever come back to Italy. The same went for me and Sonia.

On the way back to Luigi's place I said to Sonia: I know how to get hold of some passports. *American* passports. We'll steal some, that's all.

Steal them from those nice people, you mean?

No, not from *them*, from some other nice people.

Your criminal mentality is coming on nicely.

It wasn't such a dumb idea, stealing some American passports. When tourists came to Italy they had to show

129

their passports at the border or airport and then at their hotel. After that they didn't need them. They paid in cash or by credit card, so they didn't need them while staying at a hotel for a week or two and probably wouldn't notice their disappearance. Traveller's cheques might be the only problem. Certain shops and restaurants insisted on proof of identity when customers paid with traveller's cheques, but this was rare. We would have to risk it.

If we stole the passports of two people who wouldn't be leaving Italy for another few days, we could use them to travel to the States. As US citizens landing at some airport in America (no matter where) we wouldn't be checked as carefully as a couple of foreigners. Once in the States we could spend the first night at a tourist hotel. Thereafter we could travel on our Italian passports. All we had to do was find two Americans who bore a reasonable resemblance to us.

And how do you steal a passport? asked Sonia.

We'll have to practise, I said. In any case, it's too soon to steal the passports we'll be flying with.

Let's get practising, then, you identity thief.

*   *   *

Okay, get practising. Luigi laughed. You can start with me.

He and Sonia sat up half the night, talking about the Mafia. I just sat there drinking wine and saying little. For someone who hadn't read a newspaper in years, Luigi was remarkably well-informed about the Russian Mafia. In the early 1990s they'd once pulled off a coup with forged letters of credit which, if it hadn't been detected in time, would almost have wrecked the Russian monetary system. This was news to me. I wouldn't have thought Russia had a monetary system to wreck.

They spoke of the evasion of petrol tax and of a Russian bank that had changed a debt of four billion roubles into foreign currency and transferred it abroad. Sonia's voice became more subdued when Luigi made some reference to corrupt Russian generals stationed in East Germany, and they changed the subject. He said that more and more Russian Mafia gangs in Germany were organizing themselves on ethnic lines to avoid being infiltrated by German undercover agents.

I wasn't particularly interested in all this stuff. My thoughts were more of how we could get hold of some passports.

* * *

The next evening Sonia and I drove into La Pesta. On the pretence that we were looking for someone, we sauntered through various restaurants, scanning the customers and keeping our ears open for English speakers. Seated at table in the fourth restaurant were a husband and wife who looked American and bore a vague resemblance to us. They were speaking English with an American accent and had their children with them, two boys around eight and ten. We sat up at the bar, sipped a Campari, and waited for the table beside them to become free.

The wife can't be more than thirty, Sonia said in an undertone, but the husband is about your age. Incredible the way these old guys insist on siring children.

It's the fashion nowadays, I said. All over the world. Men marry women who could be their daughters and father kids who could be their grandchildren. I can't understand it.

Thank God I'm thirty-eight, said Sonia.

I wouldn't marry you anyway. I'd never get involved with a Russian woman.

How about an American?

I might.

Sonia laughed.

When the American family's immediate neighbours got up and left we asked the waiter whether we could have their table. He cleared and relaid it, and we sat down, smiling at the Americans as we did so. The Americans smiled back. They were a very nice family.

We enquired what they had been eating. They rhapsodized about their monkfish and the mushroom risotto, so we ordered the monkfish and the mushroom risotto. No, nothing to start with, we weren't very hungry. They lived in Iowa but hailed from elsewhere: Baton Rouge, Louisiana, and Austin, Texas. We told them we came from Switzerland. Sonia said she was a tennis coach who had emigrated there from Czechoslovakia, a great explanation for her Russian-sounding English. This was the Americans' third day in Italy, and they'd just shaken off their jet lag. They were delighted with the favourable rate of exchange. We joined in their delight, and I asked whether they paid mainly with credit cards or in cash. Traveller's cheques? No traveller's cheques. They were an ideal couple from our point of view. Bill told us about their farm in Iowa, and Jeannie opened her handbag and showed us some photos of the farm, her and Bill's "folks", and the whole family seated beneath the Christmas tree. Jeannie was a high school teacher, and I caught sight of the passport in her handbag. I saw that Sonia had seen it too. The boys asked how big our Christmas trees were, so I stood up, put the younger of the two, Dylan, on my shoulder, looked up at him, and said: This big. Then I looked at his brother, Keith, put Dylan down, swapped them over, and said: No, *this* big. No, said Sonia, that's too big, so I put Dylan back on my shoulder. We did this a couple of times in succession and everyone laughed. Jeannie replaced the photos in her handbag with the passport and Bill ordered grappas all round.

At one point Sonia went to the ladies' room. Jeannie went with her, taking her handbag. When they returned Sonia lingered in the background for a moment. She gave me a warning look and a slight, almost imperceptible shake of the head. *No*, it said, *these people are far too nice.* Bill ordered another round of grappas, after which I ordered a round of espressos and some ices for the boys. Bill asked if we'd like to join him on a tour of the area the next day and do a bit of wine tasting. We could visit three or four vineyards and sample their wines. Jeannie wasn't keen on wine and the children would find it too boring. We could meet them later at the beach and go out to dinner in the evening.

I pronounced this an excellent idea, and Sonia smiled enthusiastically. We all had another espresso. Then the four of them returned to their hotel and we drove back to Luigi's in the Tipo.

Why did you make a date with them? Sonia asked when we were sitting in the car. We're not going to touch their passports – they're far too nice. I could easily have pinched hers in the ladies' room, but I didn't have the heart. We can't do it, Harry, so why bother with them? Why this wine tasting?

For one thing I'm interested in wine, I said. For another, Bill is very pleasant company, and so are Jeannie and the kids. Also they're very friendly people.

They'll soon chum up with some other Americans. So will we. Tonight was just a practice run, but in a week or two we'll have to do it for real. By then, thanks to Bill and Jeannie, we'll probably have got to know plenty of Americans who'll be here when we really need those passports. Could take a couple of weeks, could take a month. Some people will go home and others will take their place, but we'll always be members of a loose-knit group. We'll be passed from one American hand to another – we'll belong, so to speak. We won't have to keep combing the restaurants for people speaking English with an American accent. Who knows, maybe we'll run into some American couple who are thoroughly *un*pleasant. Who *deserve* to have their passports stolen.

Sonia stared at me in surprise. You really are thinking more and more like a criminal.

I know, I said. I'm beginning to feel like a con artist.

You *are* a con artist, my dear Harry.

A few minutes later she said: How nice it would be. I mean, if it were all on the level. The wine tasting, the beach, dinner with Bill and Jeannie tomorrow night. I'd enjoy it so much. You made a wonderful Christmas tree back there. I felt like whistling *Jingle Bells*. Yes, you made a great Christmas tree.

A bogus Christmas tree.

Yes, that's what you are, a bogus Christmas tree.

* * *

The next morning I got up early, made breakfast, and took it out on to the veranda. The other two were still asleep. Luigi had bought us a German newspaper. I read it at the breakfast table. President Putin had decreed national mourning for the crew of the *Kursk*, the nuclear submarine that had sunk some ten days earlier. There was nothing about us. Further on I came to a report about three young ethnic Germans from Russia who had brutally murdered a taxi driver one night on the outskirts of Fürth. They were between eighteen and twenty years old, and had planned the murder carefully. They needed money, but they not only intended to rob the driver, they had planned to murder him from the outset. The youth sitting behind him was to throttle him with the cord from some track-suit trousers, and he did so with such violence that he partly severed the man's neck muscles. The second assailant smashed him in the face and the third drove a knife into his lungs and heart. The taxi driver was fifty-two. My age exactly.

I had a shower after breakfast, and Sonia was sitting at the table when I came out again. The newspaper was lying open beside her. She glared at me.

Why did you leave this on the breakfast table? she demanded.

It just happens to be there, I said.

Typical Russian brutality, eh?

They were ethnic Germans from Russia, Sonia, and I didn't leave it there on purpose. Still, it could have been me. A taxi driver my age.

Don't hold *me* responsible for them! she snapped. Just because you want to court popularity, you reuni-fied Germans, you import a bunch of pit bulls and leave them more or less to their own devices – and they turn rabid. Am *I* responsible for what they get up to?

Monday

It was a very enjoyable day even so. Jeannie took the children to the beach at Punta Ala while the rest of us toured three vineyards and sampled their wines. Sonia drove. Bill expressed surprise at our Italian licence plates, so I told him our car had broken down and the Fiat belonged to the Italian friends we were staying with.

In the afternoon we drove to the beach, where we and the boys played beach tennis with those hard wooden rackets. Then we had to play Christmas trees again. Bill with Dylan and I with Keith and the other way round, then Jeannie with Keith and Sonia with Dylan and Bill with Jeannie and I with Sonia and Bill with Sonia and I with Jeannie. We were a forest of ever-changing Christmas trees. In the evening we drove to their hotel. They let us shower in their bathroom so we didn't have to return to Luigi's before going out to dinner. It would have been all too easy to steal their passports. Bill and Jeannie showered first and waited for us downstairs in the foyer. We could have cleaned out the whole room.

We had dinner with them again the next night. This time they were accompanied by an American couple from San Diego whom they had met at breakfast in their hotel. Sonia gave me an admiring look. We're founding an American colony in Italy, she whispered to me when no one was listening. To the Americans we were Martina and Gerd. Jeannie introduced us to the couple from San Diego. All Czech tennis players are called Martina, Sonia told them with a wry smile. Once upon a time you couldn't leave the country if your name was Martina. Actually, my name is Sonia.

Russian humour.

*   *   *

I can see how things are shaping, Luigi told us a few days later. You'll never get those passports if you go on this way. These Americans are just too nice. Some members of the Underground you are! I mean, you *need* those passports. Your *lives* are at stake. You're in really great danger, but you don't take their passports because you think they're too nice. You simply aren't scared enough yet – you think you're on holiday here. Ellen would thoroughly approve. She'd think it very moral of you not to pinch their passports. I don't. It's very moral, sure, but it's not good.

Who's Ellen? Sonia asked.

Oh, said Luigi. He glanced at me in surprise. Then he looked at Sonia and back at me. Ellen is a friend of ours from the old days, he said offhand. A very good friend.

You also had a friend called Jessie, didn't you? said Sonia, looking Luigi casually in the eye. Luigi returned her gaze just as casually. Casually but unwaveringly. Jessie is another friend from way back, he said. We all belonged to the same political group.

Oh, I see, said Sonia, and Luigi went on: But to revert to you two. He gave us an artful grin. I've got a suggestion for you. It could be months or years before two suitable Americans turn up here – Americans you dislike, I mean, and they'll probably carry their passports around in a bum bag the whole time. They'll

137

probably sleep on them and take them to the toilet. They may even keep them on while fucking – his passport fucks hers and hers fucks his, and it's oh, so good! So here's my suggestion: When the time comes I'll fly to the States with you. At your expense, of course. Anyway, I haven't been there for ages.

We must have looked bewildered, because he grinned even more artfully. This is what we'll do, he went on. When the time comes, and it could be any day now, you'll get hold of two American passports. I mean, you'll rob some terribly nice American couple of their terribly nice, authentic US passports. Then we'll fly to the States together. A cheap charter flight. It won't be too expensive – you're broke, after all. And the next day I'll fly home and the terribly nice American couple will get their passports back. So you won't have stolen their passports, only borrowed them.

Luigi, you're a genius, said Sonia. She kissed him on the nose.

Yes, he said, and an experienced member of the Underground. But there's another point. Two stolen passports fly to America without their legitimate owners. They'll naturally be registered. If the passports have been stolen it means there are two people in Europe who haven't used their own passports to return to America. The United States is a big country. It's not very likely the Mafia will associate you with those particular people, but it's possible. The way things stand now, it won't be long before it occurs to them that you may be in America. It's possible, of course, that the couple will have problems when they really return home, because they'll appear to have done so already, but the US authorities will attribute that to a mix-up or assume that the first passports were forged and wait for them to turn up somewhere in the States – which they won't because they don't exist. So you'll be pretty safe.

Know something? said Sonia. I'm inviting you both to dinner. You're two immensely intelligent men.

In Harry's case, said Luigi, I wouldn't be too sure.

Wednesday

We became established members of the American tourist colony, which waxed and waned by turns. Some flew home to the States and others took their places. Only Sonia and I remained there like two fixed stars in an ever-changing firmament.

One Wednesday afternoon, when we were visiting the monastery of San Antimo with a party of four Americans, Luigi called us on the mobile he'd lent us. Something really stupid has happened, he said. Could you be at the café in La Pesta at five?

We were in two cars, so we told the Americans that one of our Italian friends had had a minor accident and needed collecting from the hospital.

*   *   *

It's really stupid. A really dumb business, Luigi said when he'd told us the whole story. We'll have to be very careful from now on.

The dumb business was connected with our blue Peugeot. No, said Luigi, the car itself is flat as a pancake – gone. I took care of that personally. They won't find it until after the next Ice Age. The problem is the licence plates.

Unknown to Luigi, someone had removed these before the Peugeot went into the crusher. The scrap merchants collected old licence plates simply because they were hoarders, and because people sometimes needed them for illicit purposes. Licence plates were really supposed to be handed in, but some of them ended up elsewhere.

That wouldn't have been so bad, said Luigi. It happens several times a month. But the guy that took your Luxembourg plates was involved in an accident, and he told the police where he'd got them from. Anyway, the Carabinieri turned up at the scrapyard today. The people there disclaimed all knowledge of the plates – and, of course, of the car to which they might have belonged.

Luigi was right, it was a bad business. There now existed a link between the Peugeot and him. And the house in the wood. And us.

Things are hotting up, he said, but only a little. So far, no one has discovered the connection. We all stick together round here, but we stick together even better if there's something in it for us. The first thing we have to do is slip the people at the scrapyard some money to make then stick to us even better.

Would ten thousand dollars do the trick? asked Sonia. Is that enough?

Far too much, said Luigi. Two thousand would be just right. Offer someone ten thousand dollars for a little silence and it may occur to them that, if ten thousand are so easy to come by, they ought to ask for a bit more. The two thousand must be in lire, of course. Then there's something else we have to do. The Carabinieri will come back. So far they only know about the plates, but it won't be long before they know what car they came from and who the registered owner is. And then things will really hot up. It probably won't be long before someone else appears on the scene.

Luigi proposed to spend the next few days working at the scrapyard. He wanted to make sure nothing happened. He knew the manager pretty well and had often worked there when he needed to earn a bit extra.

The Carabinieri turned up the following afternoon. They were looking for a blue Peugeot. They toured the scrapyard and took paint samples from the crushed remains of two blue cars. Then they came to the little office. Luigi was waiting for them with the entry ledger or log book, or whatever it was called. He showed it to the Carabinieri. They found no Peugeot among the entries.

Luigi stood beside them, looking bored. He told them he remembered a dark-coloured Mercedes with Berlin licence plates turning up some two weeks earlier. The driver had asked how much they charged for scrapping cars. A small blue saloon had followed the Mercedes into the yard, but he hadn't paid it much attention. He'd chatted with the driver of the Mercedes for quite a while. Was the blue car a Peugeot? He couldn't say for sure, but now he came to think about it – yes, it might well have been. He remembered that the people in the blue car had spent some time messing around with their bumpers while he was talking to the Mercedes driver. No, he didn't know what they were doing, but he remembered that the Mercedes and the small blue saloon had driven off together. So perhaps they'd been changing the plates.

I said to them, Luigi told us that evening, that it was possible the people in the blue car had helped themselves to some licence plates from our collection and left their own plates behind. Anyway, the yard hadn't scrapped any blue Peugeot.

Luigi even slept at the scrapyard. There was a small hut there for the use of staff. Also for moonlighters and illegal immigrants from Africa who wanted to earn some cash on the side.

Two days later a man turned up at the yard in a dark red Audi with Swiss plates. He got out slowly and stood beside the car, surveying the scene at his leisure. He was wearing a dark suit and a tie. Like someone in a thriller, said Luigi. I always thought mafiosi were better trained. I strolled over to him and said hello. He spoke Italian with a Slav accent but tried to give it a Swiss intonation. He held his ID under my nose. Interpol, Zurich, car thefts. What crap! The Mafia are getting worse and worse. There isn't any Interpol – I mean, no policeman would ever say he came "from Interpol". Interpol is just an information network, but they think Italians are dumb, and if we work at a scrapyard they think we're even dumber.

The man in the dark suit asked if the Carabinieri had taken any paint samples. Luigi proceeded to tell him the same story he'd told the Carabinieri. He added that the man in the Mercedes had told him scrapping cars was cheaper in Germany. There had been a total of four people in the two cars, and – if he remembered correctly – the small blue saloon that might have been a Peugeot was driven by a woman.

I then gave him a pretty good description of you, Sonia.

Thanks, said Sonia.

Anyway, we're rid of them for the moment, but they may come back. They know you're in Italy, after all. They may try again.

We're going to have to distract their attention before we fly to the States, I said, or they may watch all the airports.

So? said Luigi.

So I'll go to Germany and use my credit card there. We'll make a deliberate mistake. I'll go east and fill up somewhere using my credit card – leave a definite trail behind. This middle-aged man will go east, not west, and no one will realize he's going east so as to go west. I may make for Chemnitz or Leipzig. Or Erfurt or Dresden.

What car will you be driving?

I won't go by car. I'll take the train.

How are you going take on petrol if you go by train? asked Luigi. Or are you planning to drive the locomotive into a gas station and fill up with diesel?

Leave that to me, I said. I'll think of something. It's a long train journey, but I'll be back in three days at most.

Where will you spend the night? asked Sonia.

On the train, I told her.

Thursday

Next morning I went and had a really short haircut. Sonia waited for me at a bar, sitting at one of the tables outside.

My God, you look like something on a Wanted poster.

No, I said, like an ageing skinhead. I'm going to eastern Germany, after all.

Yes, she said, you needn't have imported any pit bulls from Russia, you've got enough of them already. But now you're going to get some decent headgear.

We went into a shop and she bought me a dark blue baseball cap with the Nike logo.

When we were outside in the street she eyed me from head to foot, then removed the cap and replaced it with the peak facing backwards. I took it off and put it on the right way round. Sonia turned it round again. We did that three or four times.

She smiled sadly. If only it were all for real, Harry. If only life were like this. I'd sit in a field and hold your head in my lap till your hair grew again. For weeks. Months. You must take good care of yourself from now on.

And you must take good care of our Americans, I said. We'll be needing them.

* * *

Luigi drove us to the station at Grosseto. He'd brought a box of ammunition for my gun. Just in case, he said.

Then he handed me a *Michelin* guide for Germany. Hotels and restaurants. Just in case, my friend. It gives street maps of the bigger places. Three-star restaurants too, of course.

Terrorist, I said.

Mafia lover, he said.

Skinhead, said Sonia.

What a team, I said. We hugged each other. Luigi took my cap and turned it back to front. No, not like that, said Sonia, and turned it the right way round. Then I boarded the train for La Spezia. It was just before three p.m.

* * *

I had decided to avoid Munich and travel to Frankfurt via Basel. I would have had to change in Munich, of course, and it was quite possible that I would be seen by someone who knew me. Some fellow cabby or neighbour, or one of my regular fares. I couldn't risk that.

This meant that my passport would be checked in Switzerland, but that was a risk I had to take. My Italian passport would surely be good enough for that – it had cost fifteen hundred dollars, after all. As far as the Swiss and Italian customs were concerned, I was Raimondo Vinciguerra. Luigi was sure the passport would withstand routine scrutiny on the train, even by Italian eyes.

At La Spezia I boarded the train for Milan, and by nine-fifteen I was in a couchette bound for Frankfurt. I wanted to be rested when I got to Germany. I shared the compartment with a young man from Livorno, a budding priest who was off to spend a semester studying at Heidelberg University. Excellent. I felt sure he didn't read any part of any newspaper in which my picture might appear.

The train pulled out of Milan station a little after half past nine. The came Como and Chiasso, Lugano and Bellinzona, but by that time we were asleep. We also slept through Basel and Karlsruhe. Then the young man woke up and got his things ready. It was around six a.m. when he left the train at Heidelberg. He gave me a bleary smile.

We got to Frankfurt's main-line station at seven. I breakfasted in the buffet and bought a ticket to Erfurt. A return ticket. No point in exposing myself twice to the gaze of ticket clerks who might have read some newspaper that carried a picture of me.

At eight I was on the Intercity to Erfurt. I left the train when it stopped at Bad Hersfeld at half past nine. Then I went to a florist's, bought a yellow rose which I put in my bag, and went in search of a petrol station. It didn't take me long to find one. The place was pretty busy, even for the time of day.

The weather wasn't particularly hot, but I put my bag in the shade, sat down beside it, and watched the cars that came and went. I was waiting for a well-laden car driven by a woman. After about ten minutes an anthracite-coloured Passat estate with Hamburg licence plates pulled into bay number three. There were two children on the back seat. The woman cleaned her windscreen while the petrol was flowing into the tank. I took the yellow rose from my bag and went over to her.

Excuse me, I said, holding out the rose, but I'd like to congratulate you. You're our three-thousandth customer this month, and we've got a PR scheme going. Until the end of the year, every thousandth customer

147

can fill up free of charge. You're number three thousand.

The woman took the rose, looking agreeably surprised. That's wonderful, she said. And my tank was nearly empty.

By now it was full. She replaced the nozzle in the holder, screwed up the petrol cap, smiled at me, and started to get back into the car. I couldn't let her drive off before the petrol was paid for or some pump attendant might have stopped her.

Hey, I said, kicking the near-side front tyre, maybe you'd better check the pressure in that one. It looks a bit low. Park over there. I'll be right back and I'll do it for you. I'd better tell them you're our three-thousandth customer or you could be done for bilking.

She laughed at that.

I went to the cashier, put my credit card on the counter, and said: Number three.

Her tyre pressure was okay. I gave the Passat a wave as it drove out on to the main road. The children looked out of the rear window and waved back.

You're a con artist, Sonia had told me. In the town I had lunch at a restaurant and paid by credit card. Then I went to an outfitter's and bought some slacks for myself and a dress and some lingerie in Sonia's size. Once again paying by credit card. They're for my daughter, I told the sales assistant. Could I change them if necessary?

After that I bought another travel bag and went and sat on a park bench, where I transferred everything from the old one to the new. Soon afterwards I spotted a big refuse bin in a courtyard and dumped the old bag in it. I'd left enough of a trail in Bad Hersfeld.

At half past twelve I boarded a train to Erfurt. It was

seventeen minutes late, but that gave me time to think things over. I had an idea. I wouldn't simply tour the area dishing out yellow roses every few hundred miles. That would be wasted effort.

At Erfurt station I called a hotel I'd chosen from Luigi's *Michelin* on the journey. To judge by the number of beds, it was quite a large hotel. Maybe that was a bad idea – in fact it might be unforgivably stupid and I would end up dead, even if death took a little while to catch up with me. I had reckoned that it might be some time – maybe not until the credit card accounts went out – before the police or the Mafia picked up our trail and concluded that we had probably gone east. Luigi and Sonia hadn't been sure how the police worked when they were reconstructing a route with the aid of credit cards. Sonia said she'd heard it could take only an hour or two if they were hot on the trail. But were they really hot on our trail? Under normal circumstances the hotel's registration system probably functioned much faster. There was a chance that it would function too fast – that someone would recognize me or my name – but I would have to risk that. It might even be the right course of action.

I walked to the big hotel where I'd booked a room. It must have had at least fifteen floors. The young woman at the reception desk in the spacious foyer double-checked my name – Harry Willemer? she repeated – and fed it into her computer, together with all my particulars. This took a while, and I thought I detected a look of consternation on her face. Then she gave me a friendly, neutral smile, handed me the plastic card that would open the door of my room on the ninth floor, and wished me a pleasant stay. I had booked a double room, telling her that my wife would be arriving tomorrow or the day after. I did that almost

149

automatically, but it might even be a help. If the receptionist had recognized my name and informed the police, they would wait before arresting me. I enquired about a place for my car in the underground garage. They didn't have an underground garage, just a car park behind the hotel. Typical East Germany. A hotel with fifteen or sixteen floors but no underground garage. Scared the foundations couldn't take it.

I still had to park my non-existent car, so I made my way back to the exit. After a few steps I turned to see the receptionist staring after me. Our eyes met. I returned to the desk and said: By the way, would you have the Telecom booklet that lists area codes? Could I borrow it for an hour?

She handed me the book. I went to the car park and had a good look round. It was a potential escape route, after all. Then I look the lift to the ninth floor.

The first thing I did when I reached my room was clean my teeth and wash my face. Then I sat down beside the phone and looked up the area codes for St Petersburg and Moscow. The Russian Federation had retained the country code 00 7, like the Soviet Union in the good old, safe old days of the Cold War. I dialled it, followed by the area code and any number that came into my head. I did this ten times or so. Six times the number actually existed, and I blathered something in English interspersed with the few scraps of Russian I knew, trying to spin out the call as long as I could. After ten minutes I was finished. If someone checked the telephone account for my room, he would find that I'd made six calls to Russia and two to Lithuania (00 370). Excellent.

Then I had another idea. I called Aliosha's mobile number. After the third ring a man's voice answered.

Yes?

Who's speaking? I asked.

Who wants to know? The man had a slight Russian accent. So the police hadn't confiscated the phone.

I'm a friend of Sonia's.

Well?

I want to make a deal with you.

The sort of deal you made with Aliosha?

Aliosha meant to kill us, I said.

You think he was the only one?

We're pretty well known these days, I said. If you kill us you could find yourselves in big trouble. We ought to talk.

When?

In a week or two, I said.

Where?

Maybe in St Petersburg. Maybe Leipzig or Dresden. I'll let you know nearer the time.

All right, said the man. We want that money – it's ours, after all. Then he added: Where are you now? Italy?

Italy? I said, trying to inject a note of condescension into my voice. It seemed to imply: Who on earth would want to go to Italy? I wouldn't have thought my voice capable of doing that. Then I said: I'll call you again in two weeks' time. And hung up.

After that I called reception. I would be out for a few hours, I said, so if anyone called me would they please make a note of the name. I had a shower, changed, stowed my gun and ammunition in the small, light rucksack I had in my bag, donned my baseball cap, rode the lift down, and left the hotel by way of the car park. I waited outside until a largish tour party arrived, then mingled with them and sat down in an armchair in the foyer as far as possible from the reception desk.

Roughly half an hour had elapsed when a man without any luggage came in. He walked straight up to the young woman who had checked me in and talked to her for a while. She fed some details into the computer. Soon afterwards she removed a sheet of paper from the printer. I felt myself smiling. If I was the person concerned, it was a printout of the phone numbers I'd called. Then she picked up the phone and dialled a short number. Having waited thirty or forty seconds, she shook her head and handed the man something. Probably a duplicate of my plastic room key. He walked off in the direction of the lifts.

As soon as the exit was obscured by a mass of people coming and going, I slipped outside and waited. Ten minutes later the man emerged. If he'd searched my room he wouldn't have found anything very helpful. I wondered what he'd thought when he found the lingerie for Sonia. I'd only bought the things as a way of using my credit card as often as possible, and to leave a trace of Sonia as well, but perhaps it had been an even better idea than I'd originally thought. The receptionist was bound to have told him I was waiting for my wife. If he was a policeman, they would wait until Sonia showed up – they would prefer to make a double arrest. If he was from the Mafia, on the other hand, they would act without delay. Harry Willemer could be tortured, after all. He would soon reveal Sonia's whereabouts.

I followed the man into the next street, where a dark green Ford was waiting for him. He got into the passenger seat. Five seconds later he had a mobile in his hand and was making notes on a pad. Shortly afterwards a patrol car drove slowly down the street, and the driver gave the Ford an almost imperceptible nod. This didn't look like a Mafia operation.

I returned to the hotel. My room looked untouched at first sight, but the bag containing the lingerie for Sonia had been replaced the other way round. I packed my things, left the hotel, again by way of the car park, walked to the station, and deposited my bag in a left-luggage locker. Then I went to a café, where I had a snack and a Pils with a cappuccino to follow.

Three hours later I was back at the hotel. I went in through the main entrance, just in case someone was waiting for me in the car park. I had been in my room about twenty minutes when the phone rang. It was the woman from reception. A gentleman in the foyer, one of the hotel guests, wanted a word with me. He had accidentally scraped my car while parking. Would I join him downstairs to go and inspect the damage?

That didn't sound like the police.

I said: The blue Audi 100 with the Frankfurt number plates?

The woman said something inaudible. Then, to me: That's right, the blue Audi 100.

No, it wasn't the police. Fast work! I wasn't prepared for this.

I was just having a shower, I said. Please ask the gentleman to come up.

The woman consulted someone again. Then she said: He'll be right up.

I had thirty seconds. A minute at most. I turned on the TV, took the gun from the rucksack, hurried out into the corridor, and hid round the next corner.

A tall, thickset man emerged from the lift. After a brief look round he went to the door of my room. He was much bigger and heavier than me – stronger too, without a doubt. He knocked and listened. When he put his ear to the door I stole out of my hiding place and tiptoed towards him. He knocked again. A TV

153

voice could be heard issuing from the room. The third time he knocked I was right behind him. I could see he was holding a gun.

Drop the gun and don't turn round, I told him in a quiet, affable tone.

He dropped the gun.

Shove it towards me with your left foot.

He shoved it towards me with his left foot.

Now lie down.

I picked up his gun and stuffed it in my waistband, took two steps forward, planted my foot on his neck. Then I unlocked the door and pushed it open.

Now crawl inside – slowly.

I didn't know what to do with him. He was lying face down on the floor of my room and I didn't know what to do. The best thing would have been to knock him out with my pistol butt. I couldn't do it, though. I just couldn't raise my hand. It was like a form of paralysis. What had Luigi said? *You simply aren't scared enough yet.* That was the probable reason, but I couldn't stand around there for hours, waiting for this guy on the floor to become scared enough himself to counterattack.

The guy on the floor must have sensed this. He suddenly rolled over, flexed both knees, and kicked me in the stomach with his heels. That was just what he should have done, but it was still a mistake, because it exempted me from having to think what to do. If you've ever done any boxing you know exactly where to hit someone. I did, at least, and when the man sprang to his feet I was quite calm. Oblivious of the pain in my stomach, I experienced a quite remarkable sensation of pleasure as I punched him in the solar plexus with all my might. He doubled up, gasping for air with his mouth wide open. The breath rattled in his throat as he tried to suck some air in, but it was like trying to pump up a tyre with a rent in it. He simply couldn't breathe. Where his lungs were concerned, air had become a foreign body. I caught him an uppercut with my knee and, when he straightened, gave him another punch in the solar plexus.

That was it. He was out for the count.

I manhandled him on to the bed, wrenched the flex of one of the bedside lights out of the wall and bound his wrists with it. I tied his feet together with the flex of the other bedside light and wound a towel round his head. Finally, I took the other twin bed and deposited it on top of him. First the bedclothes, then the mattress, then the wooden bedstead. That would keep him busy for a while – when he was in a fit enough state to busy himself with anything. I turned up the TV a bit and left the room.

I felt sure they would be waiting for me in the car park. The man had originally wanted to meet me downstairs, after all, so I made my way to the foyer. We've just been to the car park, I told the receptionist. Minor damage only. I'm going out for a bite.

She stared at me in surprise. The man had probably told her he was from the police. I bade her good evening, gave her a farewell wave, and walked out. Half an hour later I was on the train to Frankfurt.

But the fact that I was on the Frankfurt train didn't mean I was safe. I'd only been on board a few minutes when three skinheads started to harass people. They'd torn up a copy of *Playboy* and were sticking pictures of naked girls on the windows next to other passengers. No one made any attempt to stop them. I was fifth on their list. I debated whether to get up and move to another carriage, but that wouldn't have done much good. I resolved to keep a low profile.

What had Sonia said outside that Italian church? No punch-ups!

One of the trio stuck a page showing a naked girl on my window, then looked at me. I pulled it off and held it out. Here, I said, take it.

He grinned. Why?

Not my type.

By now the other two were standing beside my seat. I fished out my wallet and proffered a fifty-mark note. Take that, I told them, and go and sit somewhere else. And leave the other passengers alone.

That's not enough, one of them said. Nothing like enough.

Give us your mobile, said another.

I didn't have one with me, but I said: It's in my bag. I took my bag down from the rack, slowly unzipped it, very slowly took out my gun, and whispered so the other passengers couldn't hear: Go and sit down over there.

All four seats on the other side of the aisle were unoccupied. They duly sat down. You're getting out at Eisenach, I added.

But we need our things.

You, I told one of them in a low voice, go round the carriage and take those pictures down – and apologize to people at the same time. You can collect your things after that.

This is like a spaghetti Western, said one of the two who were still sitting down.

Sure, I said. We're taking a little trip down memory lane – and you're the bad guys.

I was starting to enjoy myself. Lucky Sonia wasn't there to see me. The other youth was taking down the pictures. He went round the carriage mumbling that it had all been a joke.

When he'd sat down next to the others he asked: Are you a cop?

No, I said, I'm a gangster. I always offer skinheads fifty marks. That's my contribution to German unity. If they won't accept it, I chuck them off the train. Now take off your boots, I added.

They started to protest, but I merely stared at their boots. They removed them.

At Eisenach I threw them off the train. That's to say, they jumped out on to the platform one after the other. Not much fun in bare feet.

Now stand outside my window till the train leaves, I said.

What about our boots? asked one of them.

No one'll steal them, they smell too bad.

When the train pulled out I watched them until they were out of sight.

Oh, Sonia Kovalevskaya, you really would have blown a fuse if you'd seen me. I had no choice, though. They would never have left me in peace.

*　*　*

In Frankfurt I failed to get a couchette on the train to Milan, so I had to try to sleep sitting up. When we reached Lugano at six a.m. a German woman sat down in the seat opposite me. Berlin publisher, East German background, bound for Milan. Very intellectual. I told her I was a tennis coach at a holiday hotel in Sicily, and she told me about her work. At some stage she began to tell me about an American author whose latest novel she had managed to acquire for an advance of one thousand dollars.

A mere pittance, I said.

She didn't agree. In her opinion, authors should

think themselves lucky that anyone took an interest in them and agreed to publish their books. They ought to be grateful for the appreciation. It took me some time to explain to her that, under the capitalist system, appreciation expressed itself in terms of hard cash, and that there was nothing outrageous or contemptible about this.

Given that many authors get advances of ten or fifty or a hundred thousand dollars or even more, I said, it's no mark of appreciation if you publish someone for an advance of a thousand dollars. That thousand dollars is a mark of supreme contempt. The absolute minimum. A slap in the face. You might at least have made it five thousand. Or even three.

She looked offended. I don't think she had the first idea what I was getting at. I'm really glad I'm not a writer any more.

We both got out at Milan. The publisher because she was probably going to pick up an Italian author on the cheap, and I because I had to change trains for Genoa. Before I boarded the train I called Sonia and Luigi. I told them I would be in Grosseto at 2.06 p.m., barring any delays. It was then eight a.m.

I was relieved to be on my own again. I looked out of the window and thought of Sonia and Luigi. For the first time in ages, two decades or more, I had the sensation of going home. Pavia, Tortona, Genoa, where I changed trains for the last time. Rapallo, Sestri Levante, La Spezia (one of my favourite places), Pisa, Livorno, Follonica. Finally, Grosseto. I felt exhilarated. My last homecoming had been a return to Ellen and Jessie, some time in 1975. And now, once again, someone was waiting for me – someone I looked forward to seeing. It was almost as if I had a future. I felt something akin to happiness.

Happiness at the thought of pulling into Grosseto station.

They were standing on the platform when the train arrived.

I've been looking back at the beginning of this file because my mental picture of Sonia and Luigi standing on the platform at Grosseto has just reminded me of something. Yes, that's what I wrote about the Mafia right at the start: that they wanted Sonia back. Sonia, the *girl*, the woman, who was with me. Sonia isn't a girl, she's thirty-eight years old, but that's what I wrote. It wasn't so wrong, either. When I got out of the train and she caught sight of me, she ran along the platform like a girl. Like a young girl, almost a child. She was wearing a dark blue summer dress with a black belt. I ran towards her and we exchanged a breathless hug. I was home. For a few moments I was home. And, when Luigi arrived on the scene and all three of us hugged each other simultaneously, I was home yet again.

Luigi said: I'm sure you did a lot of silly things in East Germany.

Yes, I said. More than you'll ever know.

* * *

We stopped in La Pesta on the way home. We sat outside the café and swapped accounts of what had happened in the last two days, playing corny pop songs on the jukebox while we talked. I didn't disclose all that had happened to me, because the other two were appalled enough to hear that I'd checked into a hotel in Erfurt.

Harry! said Sonia.

Did you kill someone else? asked Luigi.

159

I don't think so, I said. If I did, we'll read about it in the papers in the next few days. At least no one will think we're in Italy any more.

The German newspapers we bought in the next few days didn't mention the man I'd left with a towel wound round his head. The Mafia had doubtless done a discreet tidying-up job. He must have survived.

The American colony hadn't changed much in my absence. A new couple from Massachusetts had arrived, but they were too old for their passports to be of interest to us.

On the night of my return Sonia and I lay side by side for a long time, quite still, holding hands. We often lay in bed like that. I thought of those three skinheads in the train and what would have happened if I hadn't had a gun with me – what would have happened if they'd attacked me regardless. I would probably have opened fire on them. Yes, I felt quite sure of it. Not that they would have been any great loss. Sonia was right. They were pit bulls – repulsive warts on the face of the new Germany. Even so, it sickened me to think I would have shot them.

We're not going to die, I told Sonia in the darkness. We're going to get out of this somehow. But I don't want that gun any more.

If we fly to America, she said, we won't be able to take it with us in any case. But till then you must keep it. We *must* protect ourselves.

A *girl* . . . That's what I wrote right at the start. She was one, too. I pictured her again on the platform, recalling how she'd run towards me in her blue summer dress and how we both, for a few brief moments, felt at home when we embraced. At home with one another. But then, in my head, I once more heard those terrible words of consolation from Leningrad: *We all have to die in the end, don't be frightened.*

When I quit my flat and gave or threw away everything I owned, I went down to the river and burnt my mother's diaries as well as all my manuscripts and letters and photos. When they were alight I tried to save them, but it was too late. It was as if I had obliterated her. Tess had noted down so many things that mattered. For instance, her feeling of happiness just before an epileptic fit. *Life has nothing finer to offer,* she had written – I still remember it. *It's paradise. A boundless, entirely abstract feeling of happiness, devoid of object and motivation.* And then came the words she sometimes, laughingly, spoke aloud: *I'm an epileptic Buddhist.* No, that was no joke. Perhaps it's really true that happiness is merely an explosion in the brain – or, perhaps for Tess, the moments preceding the explosion.

But for me it was just an explosion – a terrifying explosion. Once, just once, I was alone with my mother when she had a seizure. I was eight or nine years old. There was usually someone in the house apart from my mother. One of my grandparents or our housekeeper, Marie, or Franz, who was a kind of business manager. But on this particular day my mother and I were alone together. It was around noon when she had the fit. We were sitting in the kitchen, talking, and suddenly it started. She collapsed on the kitchen's hard, flag-stoned floor and I screamed and screamed. I knew I mustn't restrain her, so I simply went on screaming. Then, still screaming, I raced upstairs and fetched the duvet and pillows from her bed and piled them up around her because I knew she needed something soft to lie on, and then I raced upstairs again and fetched the pillows and duvets from the two guest rooms and the bedroom where my grandparents slept when they

161

were spending the night with us. My mother lay in the middle of our vast kitchen in a big white cocoon – everything around her was soft and white – and I lay down beside her. I wasn't screaming any longer. I just looked at her and wept. I don't know how long for, but at some stage I must have fallen asleep.

It was dark when I awoke, and my grandmother, who had turned the light on, was standing in the doorway. Wide-eyed with horror, she stared at the two of us lying side by side on the kitchen floor, cocooned in pillows and duvets. She probably thought we'd both had a fit. *It's happened at last!* she was probably thinking. *He's started it too!* But then she must have realized how the bedclothes had got there, and she smiled at me. You look like a couple of skaters trapped in pack ice, she said, and she picked me up and hugged me very tight.

*   *   *

After I was born Tess regularly made notes about me and how I was developing. When I was six months old she wrote: *He looks at me with a thoroughly lucid expression and seems to understand all I say. Today I told him: It's time you started telling me things.*

That was pretty much what I thought when Jessie was roughly the same age. *It's time you started telling me things.* I remember only a few passages from my mother's diaries, but there's one story I still recall. Once, when I was four or five and had been admitted to hospital with a high temperature and everyone was afraid I wouldn't survive, she wrote down a Buddhist story in her diary. It was about a young woman whose little boy died when he had only just learnt to walk. In utter despair, she took her dead son on her back and went from house to house, begging for some medicine that would restore him to life. Everyone said: She's crazy – she's gone mad. But someone sent the girl to Buddha, the one person who might be able to help her. Buddha promised to bring her son back to life by means of a ritual. For that, he said, he would need a handful of mustard seed, but it had to come from a house in which no one had ever died. The girl hurried back to the village at once. She went from house to house, door to door, but soon discovered that there was no house, no family, in which no one had ever died. Realizing that death is inescapable, she burnt her son's body, went back to Buddha, and asked him to admit her to his order.

Ellen and I when Jessie was buried. When we walked the streets in silence all day long. When Ellen collapsed, sank into the ground. It was as if Tess had written that story down for us. But we're no Buddhists. We continue to go from door to door in search of those mustard seeds, looking for a family where no one has ever died and wishing we belonged to it.

What did you say, Harry?

I must have said something while lying in the darkness at Sonia's side, but I didn't know what it could have been, so I said: We're not going to die. We're going to get out of this somehow.

Yes, she said. Maybe you're right. Let's hope so.

Saturday

We occasionally played beach tennis with an American couple from Connecticut. Bessie and Michael Cameron. We'd brought the equipment from one of the black immigrants who peddle their wares on Italian beaches while their wives toil away picking up truck drivers.

We're off in three days, Luigi had told us the day before. To Los Angeles. The bad news is, no charter flight. Seems we Italians can't get cheapies to California. So it's three tickets on scheduled flights. I hope you can afford them – even four million dollars won't last for ever. I've already booked your seats in Bessie and Michael's names. Rome to Los Angeles, so get hold of those passports. I'll be flying from Rome to LA via London. We take off almost at the same time, ten and twenty minutes to eight. That's eight in the morning. We'll have to split the money between three bags. One each. If one of the planes crashes, at least there'll be a bit left over.

Luigi's smile can look positively evil sometimes. You must have those passports by tomorrow night, he said.

Bessie and Michael bore a reasonable resemblance to us. Once, down at the beach, I tried Michael's baseball cap on. Sonia looked at me and nodded approvingly. I watched Bessie and Michael playing. No, they certainly wouldn't be needing any passports in the next six days. They wanted to drink wine and eat well and go for strolls and sunbathe and play an occasional game of beach tennis. And Luigi would be bringing the passports back in a few days' time. By then we would be well established in Los Angeles.

The next morning we went to two wine tastings. Luigi came too – after all, he had to meet the couple. We planned to spend the afternoon at the beach. On the way back to town I complained so bitterly about the heat, saying I simply had to go home and take a shower, that Michael said: You don't have to go home, you can take a shower at our hotel.

Luigi said goodbye outside the hotel. Sonia and I asked for two towels from reception and we all went up to the Camerons' room and dumped our things.

You two take a shower, said Michael. We'll wait in the bar downstairs and have a cappuccino.

While Sonia was showering I searched the couple's rucksacks. I took the passports from their wallets and examined them. Excellent. They were classically poor passport photos. Only an absolute pedant would look at them twice. I put the passports in my own rucksack.

Hello, Mrs Cameron, I said when Sonia emerged from the shower.

Hello, Mr Cameron, she said. Don't you think you've been neglecting your wife a bit? American girls are very sensitive in that respect.

But I haven't had a shower yet. American girls are very sensitive in that respect as well.

We can soon fix that, she said, and pulled me under the shower.

* * *

Later on, down at the beach, we watched Bessie and Michael wade ashore hand in hand. Don't you think you're neglecting your wife a bit? Sonia whispered. She jumped up and ran down to the water's edge, and I ran after her.

We were far out, but we could still stand. I held her in my arms, and something inside me said: *If only it could all be for real.* And Sonia said: I really don't want to leave here.

There isn't any Europe for us, I said. Not any more. Not for a long time. Maybe never again.

That evening the five us went out for dinner. Luigi had reappeared. He was on excellent form. Oh, Europe! he said at one point. Europe is full of resentment and racism.

America too, said Bessie. The native Americans, the blacks, the Jews . . .

And the whites, Luigi said with a laugh. For a while it used to be fashionable to discredit dead white males. Plato, Aristotle, Einstein. Not so long ago – only the day before yesterday, so to speak. But the savages are no better.

Bessie and Michael stared at him in dismay.

No, no, don't let's be nasty to dead white males. While we're on the subject of racism, one of my favourite dead white males was Broca. Pierre Paul Broca, know who I mean? Died around 1880, co-founded the Anthropological Society of Paris. He was a serious scientist. Among other things, he located the part of the brain that controls the faculty of speech. He was also a believer in cranial content. He measured it by filling the empty skulls he was studying with shot. With lead pellets! It was really very ingenious. He tried to discover a relationship between intelligence, the size of the skull, and the weight of the brain. This wasn't too difficult, because he knew in advance that whites were superior to blacks and Asiatics, men to women, and Frenchmen to other Europeans – especially the Germans, of course.

Luigi looked at me and smiled. Swiss Germans excepted, naturally. But the Germans proved to be a problem. Broca discovered that they had bigger brains than the French. His explanation: Germans were physically stronger than Frenchmen, so they had bigger skulls. Where women were concerned, he didn't attribute their relative frailty to skull content, or there would have been no further excuse for denying them access to higher education. Man's age-old, atavistic fear of woman.

However, Broca really ran into difficulties when he found that the skulls of criminals and native Alaskans held more shot than those of genuine Parisians. He found himself in even deeper intellectual water when measurements taken at a morgue near the Seine revealed that the skulls of the corpses there were also pretty capacious. This he ascribed to the fact that the majority of the morgue's occupants had been drowned and most were suicides, many of them doubtless insane, and Broca had long known that many lunatics and criminals have brains of larger than average size. Apart from that, of course, the French were the race whose skulls held the largest quantity of shot. And besides, the rest were *French* lunatics and criminals.

Luigi surveyed us all with an earnest expression. Any criminals among us?

Everyone laughed.

But it's really fantastic, he said. Blacks and Asiatics, women and other Europeans. Racism, sexism and nationalism. When one of those three villains is hanging around, the other two won't be far away.

Bessie and Michael were entranced. Sonia and I were too. But Luigi had another little shocker in store for us.

The bad thing, he said, the really bad thing is that we're all racists. We're all a trifle racist, if not more. It's built into us, probably – built into the splendid human condition that's always invoked so solemnly. We're aware of it, that's the only difference between us and other less intelligent people.

Take me, for instance. A few weeks ago I watched a porn film about a Japanese woman. I'm pretty easily aroused in many respects, not because I'm an Italian, simply because I'm easily aroused – passionate by nature. Mind you, it's always hard to distinguish between passion and hysteria, especially in Italy. There are probably just as many easily aroused people in Holland as in Italy. Or in Switzerland – who knows?

But that's beside the point. Anyway, it was a long time before I felt anything. Why? Because the woman was Japanese. Her face didn't trigger anything inside me. No reaction. Things got better as the film went on. They probably made her face up differently – western-ized it. The film may have been one of those subtle, subcutaneous propaganda films that blind us to the fact that we're being converted. We're manipulated in such a way that we come to accept the unacceptable. Fundamentally, I'm no better than Broca with his buckshot.

Bessie was appalled. You call a Japanese woman *unacceptable*?

Yes, in that film. I was alone with her, after all.

And in real life?

In real life I'd probably fail to notice her. We fail to notice ninety-nine per cent of people. Of course, that's not so far removed from racism. Not long ago, one was always reading that Japanese on planes change places when they find themselves seated beside Europeans or

168

Americans because the Long Noses – the Caucasians, as you call them in the States – smell bad.

Bessie looked reassured. Reassured and thoughtful.

Luigi turned to her with a melting gaze. Bessie, he said, don't take me too seriously. I'm just a retired anarchist and bomber.

* * *

On the way home in the car Sonia said: Wasn't it a bit risky, provoking her like that?

No, Luigi replied from behind the wheel. Now she'll want to argue with me. We'll have a lot more to say to each other. But that wasn't why I said that bit about Broca. I said it because it had just occurred to me. You have to needle the righteous now and then.

We've got the passports, said Sonia.

I could tell from your faces. We're off the day after tomorrow. I've already booked your tickets. I paid for them with the credit card of a good friend of mine, by the way. A very good friend – so good that he'll disappear into thin air if anyone comes looking for him. But everything's paid for. Your hotel in LA is booked for four days. I wanted to rent a car for you as well, but that would be too dangerous. If you had an accident or got stopped at a roadblock, your Italian passports could land you in big trouble, Mr and Mrs Cameron. And you can't rent a car yourselves because you won't have any credit cards. You'll have to use cabs or shuttle buses.

I hadn't thought of that.

Credit cards are going to be a problem for you in any case, Luigi went on. You must never stay at any hotel longer than two days. People who pay substantial bills in cash are automatically suspect in the States, but you know that already. So you'll have to move on pretty often.

*   *   *

The flight to Los Angeles passed off without any major incident. We were an American couple and most of our fellow passengers were Italian. We spoke English with them, We were civil but not too sociable. Sonia said little in case her accent gave her away. We completed our US citizens' forms in the plane while the Italians filled in their own immigration forms. I helped our immediate neighbours with theirs.

Los Angeles International Airport presented no problems either. We went through the gate reserved for US citizens. We were both very tense, and I was glad we'd divided the money into three. It meant we had less to carry. The black woman customs officer at the counter smiled at me and said: How was Italy, Mr Cameron?

Great food, great wines, I said. But my wife was sick on the plane. I turned to Sonia, who had joined me at the counter. She really was looking pale. Poor baby, said the customs officer, giving her a sympathetic smile. It remained sympathetic even when she looked at Bessie Cameron's passport photo.

As we were walking down the long passage to reclaim our baggage Sonia came to a halt and hugged me. I was so scared, she whispered.

Me too, I said.

There were two customs officers with sniffer dogs in the baggage hall. The dogs were quite small. You always expect German shepherds in customs, but these were diminutive. They were probably searching for drugs. When our bags came into view on the conveyor belt like a pair of lifeboats, Sonia whispered: Do you think the dogs will smell the money?

Everything here smells of dollars, I told her. They're inured to it.

The dogs gave our suitcases a brief sniff and trotted on, tails wagging. They didn't even glance at us.

A shuttle bus took us to the hotel. We had a shower, ordered some beer from room service, stretched out on the bed and waited for Luigi. He turned up three hours later, smiling broadly, with a suitcaseful of cash.

You look like a million dollars in hundred-dollar bills, I said.

Right, he said. Allow me to introduce myself: Signore Fabri from Bologna. Carlo Fabri.

Sonia looked surprised. You travelled on a false passport?

Like all the best people, Signora Camerone. There was a time when I didn't possess a genuine passport, and I didn't want to run any needless risks.

Luigi, said Sonia, you're a hero of the Underground. She gave him a hug and kissed him on both cheeks.

There was a time, he said, when I wanted to be a hero of the working class. He went off to his room for a shower. Then we went and had a meal. After the meal we moved on to a bar and drank rather a lot of margaritas.

I won't be able to sleep otherwise, Luigi said, and I've got to fly back to Italy at midday tomorrow.

The next morning we had breakfast together. Luigi didn't want us to accompany him to the airport – he thought it too risky. You've been lucky up to now, he told us, but you mustn't tempt providence. Airports can be dangerous. Steer clear of them.

Sonia wanted to give him some money in return for all he'd done for us.

You've paid me back for all I've spent on your behalf. What else do you owe me? I've just spent a few weeks with my favourite enemy. I still love him. He's still the same, still sitting on a pile of unearned money.

We all laughed. Luigi looked at Sonia. And I've spent a few weeks with you as well. I'd watch all the Japanese porn films ever made if you were in them. I mean, you wouldn't have to play a leading role. It'd be enough if you walked across the street in some scene or other. I think blue movies attach too little importance to exterior shots in any case.

Sonia kissed him. Racist, she said.

Just before getting into the shuttle outside the hotel, he turned and said: I doubt if we'll see each other again, but if you ever pay another visit to Italy, the first thing we'll do is drink a cappuccino at the café in La Pesta.

After the next Ice Age, I said.

Sure, he said. And I'd so much have liked to found a commune with the two of you. I always detested the commune lifestyle, but with you, who knows?

After the next Ice Age, said Sonia, and Luigi set off on the return journey to Bessie and Michael Cameron, whom we would never see again either.

* * *

We stayed at our hotel for the prescribed four days. On the fifth day we called the Holiday Inn at Brentwood, booked a room, and took a cab there. The Holiday Inn is only a few hundred yards from the new Getty Museum. The hotel, which is a fairly tall high-rise of twenty-odd floors, looks ultramodern from a distance and utterly frightful at close range. There's an outdoor pool which isn't particularly beautiful either, but you can smoke there. They also have rooms for smokers, but I can't stand the smell in them.

When we checked into the hotel and were about to go up to our room, an oldish man of sixty or so was standing beside the elevator, desperately fiddling with his suitcase. I left my keys behind in Chicago, he said. It seemed he was an Italian businessman with a second home there. I need my suit, he said, almost hysterically. I've got a business dinner tonight.

I tried to open his suitcase with the keys of our own suitcase, but no luck.

The Italian businessman was still there when we came down half an hour later, but a hotel employee of Mexican appearance was working on the suitcase with a kind of jemmy. He wore a smart black mechanic's overall whose fifty or so pockets bristled with gleaming, impressive-looking tools. They hadn't been much use, obviously, hence his resort to the jemmy. I extracted one of the impressive-looking tools from a pocket, and two minutes later the suitcase was open. We specialize in burglary in Europe, I told the Mexican. The Italian thanked me, and Sonia and I took a cab to Santa Monica.

The next morning, when we went to have breakfast in the upstairs restaurant, the Italian and a business associate were breakfasting together. At least, they looked like business associates. Both were wearing smart suits and ties. The Italian, who was now the opposite of yesterday's bundle of nerves, came over to our table. He thanked me again and introduced himself.

My name is Fabri.

Fabri? I said. Not Carlo Fabri from Bologna?

No, he said, Giovanni Fabri from Milan. I divide my time between there and Chicago, but I have a cousin who's based in Bologna. His name is Carlo.

I shut my eyes for an instant and Luigi's face appeared. He winked at me.

I looked at Giovanni Fabri from Milan and Chicago and winked at him too. He winked back. Carlo Fabri from Bologna was evidently the kind of man that prompted one to wink at the mention of his name.

When we were alone again Sonia said: Did he wink at you too?

Who? I asked. Signore Fabri?

No, she said, Luigi.

It was the same with Ellen. Ellen often saw things she couldn't possibly have seen. Things that only went on in my head. It happened again and again. I still remember the train journey we took when I'd won my first and only prize for literature. We travelled to northern Germany together because Ellen wanted to take the opportunity to visit her parents. Ellen wasn't particularly interested in the literary scene, but if it could be combined with a visit to her parents, that was okay. We sat facing each other in the train, talking and reading by turns. At some stage I simply sat there, staring into space without focusing my gaze on anything in particular, and I pictured myself saying hello to a member of the jury whom I much admired but had never met. I suddenly became aware that Ellen was looking at me and smiling. Who did you just say hello to? she asked.

Ellen could look at the tips of my toes and guess what I was thinking.

And now Sonia had seen Luigi giving me a farewell wink.

This Kovalevskaya woman is growing on me, I said.

She smiled. We aren't Sonia Kovalevskaya and Harry Willemer any more. We've got serviceable Italian passports and our names are Raimondo Vinciguerra and Concetta Berlingeri.

Concetta, I said. I like that.

Vinciguerra isn't bad either. After all, we've been winning up to now.

Wednesday

We can't stay in this place, Sonia said over dinner in Santa Monica. It's no good, always having to take taxis, never being able to walk anywhere. We even had to take the shuttle to the museum when it was only a stone's throw away. We need some place with a decent public transport system.

She was quite right. Los Angeles can be a very exciting city when you know people and don't have to spend the whole time in public places. The trouble was, we couldn't afford to get to know anyone, and downtown LA is as dead at night as any one-horse town. You could introduce driving on the left and no one would notice.

So San Francisco is the name of the game, I said.

Yep, said Sonia. We had spent a lot of the time in LA watching television, and she was learning fast.

And that's the game we're going to play right now, she went on. San Francisco's public transport is as good as Munich's, so I've heard.

We took a cab to Union Station and caught a train to Oakland. Trains were safer than buses. On a train we could always get away somehow. At least a couple of carriages away.

This place looks like a church, Sonia said at Union Station. A tower, round arches, marble flooring. When you catch a train here you feel the entire world is holy and full of secrets. In Petersburg the subway stations are like churches too, like magnificent churches, but I never felt that they led to the outside world – that the world was holy. To me the world seemed bleak and dangerous and hostile.

When we got to Oakland we called a hotel in San Francisco and booked a room. Then we took a cab across Bay Bridge. I was apprehensive of what awaited us. We were entirely dependent on ourselves. There were just the two of us, and because we couldn't spend all day walking the streets, we would have to move from one hotel room to another until we found some place where we could live. A house or an apartment. But that might take ages. Meantime, the "game" meant taking a drab room in a different hotel every two or three days.

We would take our dirty washing to a Chinese laundry every week. My shirts would be ironed, we would have visited all the museums and seen all the movies, and still we wouldn't be truly alive. This had nothing to do with the Mafia. The Mafia was an additional factor. We would probably get on each other's nerves, that was the worst thing about this state of isolation. Yes, it wouldn't be long before we'd genuinely have visited all the museums and seen all the movies – and there weren't that many interesting movies in any case. As for concerts, it ruins the evening if you have to go back to a hotel room you loathe like a prison cell.

We had to do something, take the initiative, start to live again. We had all that money, and we couldn't do anything with it. Nothing much, anyway. We were like a couple of dogs standing guard over a pile of money. For no good reason.

* * *

On our third day in San Francisco I bought myself a laptop and a pack of diskettes, and Sonia found an interesting game in a gift shop in the Castro district, where the gays live in a clean, relaxed, pretty, not particularly exciting little community of their own. The shop sold Buddhist devotional articles, and Sonia found this drawing set there. Using a brush and special watercolours, you paint something on a sheet of paper – characters of some kind or a mountain, Fuji perhaps – and when the picture is finished it gradually disappears, until after a few minutes the paper is as blank as it was in the first place. The idea, I suppose, is to meditate on some picture you've painted in the knowledge that it will soon disappear for good.

Sonia was absolutely delighted with this, and now, as we have for the last four weeks or so, we often spend several hours a day painting and writing in our endless succession of hotel rooms. Sonia sits in front of the picture she has just painted, engrossed in its gradual reversion to a blank sheet, while I sit at the table or on the bed or window sill and write what I'm writing now. I don't possess a printer, of course, and if anything happens to the laptop it's possible that all I've written will vanish like the black characters and pictures on Sonia's drawing paper.

We write and paint and read and make long excursions into the city and go to movies or concerts. We talk a lot and smile at each other across the table during meals like two people who have just got to know each other and are gradually falling in love, and one day I told Sonia about Jessie, making it sound as if Jessie had been the daughter of some friends of mine. I told her about Jessie and the eighteen months the three of us spent in England. Jessie was four or five at the time, and I told Sonia how it was when she learnt English, how quick she was, and how at first, when she was lying alone in bed at night, she would make noises that sounded like English but weren't proper words. Already half asleep, she would quite instinctively alter the set of her mouth to accommodate sounds that might have been English. All those long, drawling vowels – way-wee-why-woe-woo – and all those short ones – bat-bet-bit-bot-but ... One evening, when we were back in Munich, we watched a Western on television together. She was sitting on my lap – she always sat on someone's lap when she watched television. Two of the characters in the Western had just fallen in love and exchanged a kiss, and Jessie looked up at me and asked, in English: Are they an item now?

Sonia chuckled at this anecdote as we sat there in the restaurant looking like two people who have just got to know each other and are slowly falling in love.

Are *we* an item now? she said with a laugh, knowing that we weren't.

Maybe, I said, knowing – sensing – that our relationship was steadily congealing.

We no longer made love. The last time we did, we had just become Bessie and Michael Cameron and Sonia had pulled me under the shower with her. No, I'm wrong, the last time was in the sea. Now, here in San Francisco, she put her hand on mine and said: What's to be done about Raimondo Vinciguerra and Concetta Berlingeri? What can we do to make them an item?

I don't know, Sonia. Let's go.

We're like a pair of ghosts, she said when we were outside in the street. Two ghosts that are slowly but steadily fading away. It hurts when you fade away. We've had such a good meal and you told me such nice stories about that little girl, yet I hurt all over. I feel as if I'm slowly dissolving in the pain.

Thursday

That was yesterday. Sonia has just gone to the cinema again. I didn't even ask her what film she was going to, I'm so benumbed. And that in the city where I was born a second time. Many years ago, when I was sixteen or seventeen. Yes, it was true what I told Sonia in Passau: that I'd gone to America for romance – that I made the perfect knight errant. They sent me to San Francisco, and there was black-eyed Susannah with her dark red hair, so dark that the red was just another form of black, and the Drifters sang *Save the Last Dance for Me* at a high school party, and we were just two teenagers in the middle of the sixties, and Susannah shook out her long hair, and a flock of blackbirds soared into the sky, and I wanted to see those blackbirds take wing again and again. Three months earlier, it seemed like the day before yesterday, I had been just another European youngster, a model-aeroplane-building youngster with two zits on his face, and now I wanted nothing better than to see those blackbirds take wing again and again. I wanted to die in that hair. That was how it was when I was born a second time: wanting to die in Susannah's hair. The Drifters sang *Saturday Night at the Movies* and *Under the Boardwalk* and *Some Kind of Wonderful* and *Please Stay* and *There Goes My Baby*, and whenever I visited San Francisco later on I looked up the Timmermans in the phone book but never called, and a few years later Susannah's surname was Mitchell, and a few years later still I sent her my first book, just to let her see what I was doing with my life, and many years later Susannah's surname was Timmerman again, but we never saw or phoned each other throughout that time. We were both created for different lives, even though I sense those blackbirds taking wing whenever the thought of Susannah crosses my mind. A fluttering, rustling, infinitely gentle sound that goes right through me. But for Susannah, I would never have had a life with Ellen. Ellen would never have noticed me but for Susannah and what she made of me.

But now my life with Ellen no longer exists. It hasn't existed for a long time. It's all gone. I abandoned everything, destroyed everything, obliterated nearly every trace of myself. I burnt my boats. I never wanted to write again – I *couldn't* write any more, and I was utterly uninterested in doing so. I took off into limbo with someone I didn't know at all when my one desire was to roam the world with a begging bowl, and now I'm sitting here *writing*.

It's very strange, almost as if you *have* to leave traces behind. Or as if you can't stop being a writer even when it's the last thing you want to be. I shall finish this however it turns out, and in the end some faulty circuit, some faulty contact may wipe it from the laptop's memory as if the whole thing had never existed. If that happens, so be it.

What I enjoyed most about writing was the writing itself. The way you cast a spell over the world while writing. The initial uncertainty, and then the stage at which you know that nothing can stop you – that the book will almost write itself from now on. I never changed my way of life when working on a book. I did all the things I used to do in normal times, never shutting myself off from anything or anyone. But the spell persisted. I wrote my first novel when I was twenty-one. Ellen was pregnant, and Tess died that December. I couldn't shut myself off from anything. I was demented with happiness and grief, and I wrote and cooked and argued with people and read and did the washing-up and worked as a waiter four days a week and played basketball, and later on, when Jessie arrived, I was always her father first and someone writing a book second. When Ellen was awarded a grant to study in London, we took some of the money I'd inherited from my mother because I couldn't get a job in London for those eighteen months. Jobs were reserved for Brits, so I wrote my second novel in London on the grant from my mother. I wrote whenever I could find the time, but Ellen and Jessie always came first. And all that happened pervaded the book like a warm glow, and the book, the act of writing, pervaded all that happened.

You only love me because you love your book, Ellen often said.

And I said: I love my book because I love you. Without you I'd never write it.

Ellen said: I always thought writers were reclusive oddballs who cut themselves off from the world like St Jerome in his cell, but it seems I was wrong. It's quite different. Everything becomes transparent somehow, and it's infectious. When you write you make everyone around you happy.

Yes, that was it: I was a happy author. Was I successful as well? No. Harry Willemer the cabby was a great deal more successful than Harry Willemer the author. Strictly speaking, I've always had jobs that earn you tips – waiter, author, taxi driver. The only difference between them is, most authors get nothing *but* tips. They accept fees for which no waiters or cabbies would work – unless, of course, they come from the East or the Third World. Most authors can be bought pretty cheaply. They're game for almost anything, any form of prostitution, as long as it jacks up the price a little. That's why they harp on morality so much. I've driven all kinds in my taxi – rock stars, television people, parliamentarians, even the occasional writer. One night around a year ago I drove two of our younger authors to a bar after some literary shindig or other. I can't read their stuff. I usually give up after a few pages, but they were very amusing in the back of my cab.

They were talking about a fellow author who had apparently intimated to a literary editor that the review of his latest novel ought to proclaim him Germany's answer to Philip Roth. Oh well, said one of the two young writers, at least he's got the hairstyle.

Really? said the other. Is Philip Roth's chest *that* hairy?

We all laughed. Why can't these guys be the same in their books as they are in the back of a cab?

* * *

What else did I enjoy about being a writer? The moment when I held my first book in my hand, of course. But that sensation doesn't last long. Less than a week, and it only applies to your first book. I soon realized that you don't write for yourself. Nor to please your friends. Nor for the ones you love. It was like that with me, at least. You always write for the public. You write to conquer strangers, people you've never heard of. It's the old erotic syndrome: not the girl next door but someone far away, some total stranger. I don't know how it is with women, but that's how it is with me:

someone from somewhere quite different, someone entirely unfamiliar, someone we've always been seeking, always knowing that they must exist. Or always fearing that they can't possibly exist.

It's like anonymous sex. The fact is, of course, that readers whom you may have conquered are by way of being friends (although you never meet them). So you stop writing for them. You even have to disappoint them, perhaps, and go on writing, on and on, for a succession of other total strangers. Yes indeed, writing really is quite like anonymous sex.

That's all I liked about writing. Nothing more.

No, wrong! There were two more things I miss these days. I never wrote direct descriptions or pen portraits of people. I always thought it important to describe them in such a way that they wouldn't recognize themselves. And then this remarkable process sets in: you invent people, really invent people who are nothing but fictional characters, and in the end, when the book is finished, they're just as real as people in real life. You think of them and remember them like people you really know – people you've spent a lot of time with.

* * *

Yes, that's all that mattered to me about writing. Nothing else. And literary criticism? Barring a few exceptions, I've never thought much of critics and reviewers, even when I've sometimes rejoiced at what they've written. When my first novel came out, someone called me the Easy Rider of modern German literature. That gratified me even though I didn't particularly like the film or Dennis Hopper – or motorbikes either, to be honest. But the reviewer had a point: I belonged to the light cavalry brigade, though you probably couldn't have raised a brigade of us. Our kind aren't that numerous, or weren't.

But all that has ceased to interest me. It's not even an academic problem any more. It's nothing at all.

Saturday

For some weeks now, Sonia and I have been going every few days to a Chinese massage parlour on Sutter Street. Our backs are giving us a bit of trouble, but I think it's partly because of the strain we're under.

We take the elevator to the top floor and come out in the massage parlour itself. The sign on the reception desk says they don't accept American Express, but we can only pay cash in any case. I'm afraid we've only got American Express, I told them. It wasn't necessary, but that's how tensed-up we are – how careful to cover ourselves the whole time. We avoid attracting attention. Everything has to be explained away and ironed out.

In the cubicles we're pummelled for half an hour or an hour by diminutive Chinese masseuses. They actually climb on top of us and trample around for a considerable time, probably because they're so small. It's quite sexy. No doubt that accounts for the notices on the cubicle doors, which state that "indecent behavior" will not be tolerated. We had a good laugh about that after our first visit, because the temptation was considerable. Sonia found it so too.

I didn't feel like a massage yesterday, so Sonia went on her own. I picked her up at five. A young Chinese got into the elevator with me. I made some remark about the weather and he gave me a supercilious smile. The elegant Chinese woman at reception told me that

Mrs Berlingeri would be a bit longer today, and I thought no more about it.

Then she said something in Chinese, rather sharply, to the man who had come up in the elevator with me. She produced a white bath towel, tossed it to him, and indicated the door to the shower. That presumably meant: Have a shower first.

Two minutes later the elevator door opened and a couple of sinister-looking Chinese emerged. I said Hi, but they ignored me, perhaps because they knew no English. They engaged the good-looking receptionist in a brief but heated conversation and kept edging towards the door that led to the massage cubicles, but the receptionist barred their way. That was when I first became scared.

Had they come for Sonia? Had the Mafia caught up with us already? We were trapped in here. There was no staircase – or rather, there had to be one but I'd never seen it. There was only the elevator. I waited, never taking my eyes off the two men. At last, having apparently overcome the receptionist's objections, they strode through the door leading to the cubicles. Moments later the third Chinese emerged from the shower cubicle. He had knotted the white towel round his waist and draped his clothes over his right arm. Perhaps the clothes concealed a gun. Yes, I was sure of it! I jumped up and thrust him back into the shower cubicle. He shouted something in Chinese and the receptionist stared at me in horror. I yelled at her to press the elevator button, then wrenched the shower door open and hauled the Chinese out again. His towel slipped to the floor. At that moment Sonia came out into reception followed by a masseuse.

Harry! she cried. What's the matter?

Are you all right? Why were you so long? Did anyone do anything to you?

No, we started late, that's all.

I apologized to the Chinese, wound the towel round his waist and held it there until he took hold of it himself. I could almost have hugged him – in fact I felt tempted to give him a tip. I muttered something about having had a nervous breakdown and not being entirely over it yet. I wasn't sure if he understood, but he looked relieved.

Then I apologized to the receptionist. Sonia tipped her masseuse twenty dollars.

Boy oh boy, she said when we were out in the street, are we getting jumpy! I thought you were going to kill the poor man. You should have seen the look in your eyes.

Hang on a minute, I told her.

We went into a shop across the street and watched the door of the building that housed the massage parlour. After a few minutes the two sinister-looking Chinese emerged from the narrow doorway, one after the other. They looked in both directions, then nodded and walked off. One going left, the other right.

We're getting really hysterical, I said.

Yes, said Sonia. It really would be hysterical to tangle with the Chinese Mafia as well. We've got enough on our plates with the Russian variety. Then she said: Harry?

I looked at her.

Your reaction was absolutely correct, she said. Thanks. We *must* react hysterically, we've no choice.

There was a time when I didn't react hysterically. In another life. I still recall being mugged, so to speak, in New Orleans. It was Saturday night and the streets were teeming with people, and at some stage I was accosted by a black man. Very amiably, he pointed to my shoes and enquired, with an admiring smile, where I'd bought them. I had proudly worn Clarks for years, and I told him so. Great shoes, he said. I'll shine them for you right now. It'll cost you twenty dollars. Payable in advance.

He looked round, still smiling, and I saw that another three black men were watching me expectantly. I hadn't much time for reflection. I said: Twenty dollars is over the top. You can have five, and you needn't shine my shoes. I gave him five dollars and disappeared into the crowd.

I told Sonia that story.

Cool customer, she said in English. She really was learning fast.

We were all cool once upon a time, I said, but now we've got to turn over a new leaf.

How do you propose to do that? she asked.

We must do something with your money or we'll be completely stymied. As things stand, all we can do is bolt from one hotel to the next.

With *our* money, she said. We're in this together, Harry – Raimondo, I mean.

We need a bank account and some credit cards, I said. The money's no good to us without them. But we're foreigners. We don't have a fixed abode – far from it – and I've no idea what one needs to open a bank account in the States.

So? said Sonia.

I know someone in San Francisco who may be able to help us. I don't know what she's like these days, but it's a possibility.

She?

Yes, an old girlfriend.

An old *girlfriend?*

A very old girlfriend. We haven't seen each other for thirty-five years, but she'll help us if she's anything like the person she used to be.

For old times' sake?

For old times' sake.

I see, said Sonia.

I could call her, I said. She may be away, but I'll call her.

And then?

Then I'll try, very cautiously, to find out what we can expect of her. How much we can afford to tell her. There was a time when I could tell her anything.

In that case, said Sonia, let's hope she hasn't changed. How old were you then? Sixteen, seventeen? A child.

I was an infant prodigy, Sonia. Bear that in mind.

You don't sound hysterical any more, she said. Not in the least.

Tuesday

Fritz! Susannah's voice on the phone. Is it really you? And you're actually here in San Francisco? Jump into a cab and come over right away. Or shall I pick you up? We must meet up at once. I haven't painted my face yet, but I'll be relatively presentable by the time you get here.

Susannah called me Fritz from the start. It was the nickname they gave me in school because they called all Germans that. I didn't resent it. My grandfather's name was Fritz, so in a way I felt proud to be called Fritz. Very proud, in fact.

It completely disarmed them, Susannah told me at the time. They thought it would bug you, but you accepted the name as if it had been made for you.

The others have probably forgotten me long ago, so Susannah is most likely the only person in the world who still calls me Fritz.

She lives in one of those handsome houses on El Camino del Mar, out by South Bay. I told her it would be better to meet on neutral territory.

Oh, she said. Are we at war?

We aren't, Susannah, but I have to be careful. I'll explain later.

Okay. Let's meet at Enrico's, then. Two hours from now. I'll book us a table on the terrace.

I walked to Enrico's by way of Chinatown. Susannah was already there, sitting on the terrace. She got up when she saw me and came to meet me. Red lips and big, dark eyes. She came right out on to the sidewalk, and a flock of blackbirds soared into the sky. Fritz, this is lovely. This is wonderful. I never thought it would happen. You're looking tired, though.

She led the way back to her table. Enrico's is my favourite place, she said. I'm a smoker, and one can smoke out here on the terrace. It's probably the only public place in the States where you can smoke sitting down – unless you're prepared to sit on the steps of some church like a wino.

She was very much the old Susannah. We ordered champagne. And some scallops as a starter. Now tell me your life story, she said. Tell me all that's happened in the past thirty-five years. She laughed. No, first you must tell me why we had to meet on neutral territory.

I told her. I told her the whole story, from the moment when Sonia got into my cab. She listened quite calmly, sipping champagne and smoking. No, I didn't try, very cautiously, to find out how much we could afford to tell her. I told her *everything*.

When I was through she said: The Russian Mafia? This is a bad business. Why do we let these people into the West at all? Anyone would think we didn't have enough crooks of our own. But . . . if you've been away from Munich for so long, won't anyone be missing you?

No, Susannah, but that's another long story. Another bad business. Nothing I can tell you right now.

I understand, she said. Well, if I've got this straight, what you need right now is a bank account or some-where to stash the four million safely. You also need some credit cards. Opening a bank account would probably be too risky at the moment, but you could give the money to me. I could tuck it away for you.

Wouldn't it raise too many eyebrows if your bank balance suddenly jumped by four million?

I'm a wealthy woman, Fritz. A very wealthy woman, and our local brand of capitalism is pretty permissive. I'll tell you a story. A few months ago a friend of mine wanted to buy a house in Berkeley. A pretty little house, guide price one million dollars. The realtor was expecting another bid at the weekend, so my friend said, if the other bid was higher he was prepared to pay more than the million they'd provisionally agreed on. On the Monday he called the realtor to clinch the deal, only to be told that the house was already sold. My friend was pretty annoyed, having wanted a chance to increase his offer, but the realtor told him that the other party, a guy from Silicon Valley, hadn't just offered a tad more, he'd offered two million cash. It turned out that he hadn't wanted the pretty little house at all, just the site. He wanted to buy the *view*, that's all. He's had the house demolished and is currently building himself a new one on the site. All I meant to say was, I won't have any great difficulty in shoving your four million into an account.

That sounded very reassuring.

You'll need credit cards as well, of course. And two cell phones, so you can keep in touch. And you shouldn't go on staying at hotels, it's too risky. You could stay at my place. I've got plenty of room.

No, Susannah, that's out – far too dangerous for you. There mustn't be any obvious connection between you and us. I don't want to involve you in our troubles. We'll go on staying at hotels for another few weeks, moving on every four or five days. Then we'll see. We can't take much more of the way we're living now.

* * *

When I got back to the hotel Sonia was lying on the bed reading a book. *As I Lay Dying* by William Faulkner. Couldn't you find anything more cheerful? I asked.

It's very funny as well, she said, but we can't shut our eyes to things. We mustn't avoid life.

You mean death, I said.

Or death. Well, how did it go, this reunion with your old girlfriend?

I told her. In two days' time, I said, we'll meet up and transfer the money to Susannah's car. She's going to get us some credit cards and mobiles.

You're crazy, Harry, said Sonia. You want to trust some woman with four million dollars, just because you slept with her when you were sixteen? You really are an incurable romantic.

We don't have any choice, Sonia. Susannah's a wealthy woman, she doesn't need our money. Many years ago she made some interesting discoveries in Silicon Valley. Software. She knows Robert Noyce and all that bunch. Anyway, she was wealthy already. She comes from a very well-to-do family. She has everything a person could want. Being born into California's upper-middle class was the best thing that could happen to anyone in the second half of the twentieth century.

Then she probably hates all Russians, said Sonia. Or all communists. That was another American speciality in the second half of the twentieth century. They even used their art as an argument against us.

Susannah is far too intelligent for that, I said.

Let's hand over the money in two instalments, all right? *I'm* an intelligent woman too.

Have it your way.

Saturday

It wasn't such a bad idea, handing over the money in two batches. It was much less conspicuous, so two days ago I took a taxi to the Fairmont Hotel. A page relieved me of the suitcase and escorted me up to the room, which had been booked in Susannah's name. They all know me at the Fairmont, she'd told me. It would have been pointless to check in under a different name. Besides, some IT executives are holding an informal meeting here. I'm still a kind of consultant. A very well-paid consultant.

The money she earns as a consultant goes to an old folks' home in San Francisco. Not a home for the rich, Fritz, if that's what you're thinking. I work there two days a week. I feed the old people, change their diapers, turn them over so they don't get bed sores, deal with their financial problems, talk with them, go to their funerals. That's my life in broad outline: a big house on El Camino del Mar, my job as a consultant, the Fairmont Hotel, and the old folks' home. I'm a woman in her prime, a woman of the world, but the boundaries of that world are already in sight.

We had a coffee in her room and she handed me the cell phones and two credit cards. The cell phones, she said, are registered in the name of someone who died last month in Mexico but still has an apartment here. You see? I'm beginning to think like a criminal. The credit cards were more of a problem. This is one of mine. Your girlfriend will have to practise my signature a bit, but that should come easy to someone from the Mafia. Your card belongs to Carey, my son. He's a wonderful boy. He's spending three months in Asia, and the bills are sent to me. He left this card behind by mistake. It's the best idea I could come up with. So go easy on the credit cards and pay cash whenever you can.

We stowed the money in a suitcase Susannah had brought with her, put the suitcase in her car, and drove down into town. Susannah dropped me off somewhere. Same procedure tomorrow, Fritz, she said. She smiled at me when we said goodbye. Don't look so depressed, everything will turn out all right. I'm already working on it.

I sat down on a bench in Jefferson Square with the empty suitcase beside me. It was two o'clock in the afternoon. Eleven p.m. in Europe. I dialled Ellen's number. Then it occurred to me that this was a mistake. I hung up before she could answer. Ellen's number might crop up in connection with that dead man in Mexico.

I went to a Walgren supermarket and bought myself a phone card. Then I looked for a phone booth and dialled Ellen's number again.

Where are you, Harry? What are you doing?

I'm still alive. I only called because I want you to have my mobile number.

But *where* are you still alive?

In the States.

Good, she said. There was a brief report in the paper a few days ago. Just a few lines. They've extended the manhunt to Eastern Europe.

I gave her my number.

What are you going to do now?

We may buy a house. Look for work of some kind. But both will be difficult.

A new life?

A *kind* of life, Ellen. I don't have a real life any more. I haven't had for years.

Harry?

I didn't speak, just listened to her voice saying my name. Harry?

Then I said something I never meant to say again. I said: What did you say, Jessie?

I sensed that she was smiling, saw her face in my mind's eye.

Harry, I'm with you. I'm with you all the time. Day and night.

The airbags inflated. They slowly, softly inflated.

That's good, I said. Very good. Now hang up. I don't want to.

* * *

Yesterday afternoon I took the second batch of money to the Fairmont. Everything went the way it had the first time. Without a hitch. As I was leaving Susannah said: We ought to have dinner together tonight. There are a few restaurants in the Bay area where nobody knows me. We definitely ought to celebrate the homecoming of four million genuine American dollars. Besides, I'd like to meet your Russian girlfriend.

That evening Susannah drove us across Bay Bridge to a Thai restaurant in Berkeley. Sonia was very subdued, almost hostile, not only in the car but during the meal as well. She stiffened slightly whenever Susannah called me Fritz, as if the name symbolized a world from which she was excluded. Which was true. Even before we'd reached dessert she said she wanted to call a cab and go back to the hotel.

No, Susannah told her, we'll all go together. I'll drive you back to the hotel. Then, if Fritz feels like it, the two of us can go and have a drink somewhere.

For the past three days we've been staying at a small, old-fashioned hotel on Bush Street. They've got one of those ancient, openwork elevators. You have to close two latticework gates before it consents to embark on its juddering ascent in a slow, noisy, uncertain, experimental manner, like the first lift in the history of the world. Susannah and I stood outside the hotel, looking through the glass door, until I saw Sonia get into the elevator, close the gates, and start to ascend. It was a mistake. I would have felt easier in my mind if I'd gone up with her.

Susannah and I drove to the new Marriott and sat in the bar on the top floor. It was surrounded by glass and had a panoramic view of San Francisco. We drank margaritas.

I'm glad you're back in San Francisco, said Susannah. I should never have let you return to Europe.

I laughed, and she laughed too. But you were a minor, she went on. You had to go back to your mummy and daddy – or rather, to your mummy. I seem to recall there wasn't a daddy, was there?

No, no daddy.

My God, Fritz, thirty-five years and I'm still fond of you. That's pretty unusual, if you know what I mean. Women have this genetic quirk that compels them to build a nest, and old love affairs can be very obstructive from that point of view. When a woman's through with a man she's really through, because these things get in the way of nest-building. I'm not exempt from the quirk myself, but I also possess a memory. Besides, my nest-building days ended long ago.

Jeff and I had some good times together at first. Tempestuous times. And we had Carey, who needed a nest. Jeff slept with a lot of women because he thought a psychologist should have plenty of experience. But he'd have slept with a lot of women if he'd been a motor mechanic. He was a pretty good mechanic too, incidentally. In every respect. I didn't like it, but we stayed together until Carey didn't need a nest any more. Jeff has been working as an adviser in Washington for the past few years. I reckon they can use some of his experience there.

We did the right thing, I think. In our lifetime there have been all kinds of stupid theories about love, and one of the silliest is the theory that another person – *one* other person – can never satisfy all one's requirements. That's what everyone thought in the sixties and seventies. In Europe too, probably. As if we needed a different lover for each of our personal requirements. The problem lies elsewhere, in fact. Most couples aren't all that fond of each other, so they soon get bored and start looking for someone else. By soon I mean after the first really violent row. And now, for the past few years, people have been citing life expectancy: now that we're living so long, they say, you can't expect us to spend a whole lifetime together. It's not as if they divorce and embark on a new life at seventy-five. They get divorced far earlier, usually several times from several people. Half of all American children born in the sixties saw their parents get divorced before they were sixteen. Greater life expectancy doesn't come into it.

Susannah paused. Then she said: The truth is quite simple and quite brutal. Most people aren't made for love. They have a few violent attacks of infatuation in

199

their salad days, and then it's over. No, most people don't have the stamina. They're much better at doing other things: building homes, paying off mortgages, saving money, planning vacations, bringing up children. They can even pull off really great divorce settlements, absolutely fair and equitable separations. And so they should. Most people are extremely competent in these matters, if you discount the way they bring up their children. It didn't take Jeff and me long to see we were going down the same road, but we didn't divorce until our son had started his second year in college. We earned a lot of money during those years. We dabbled a bit in politics and refrained from making any excessive contribution to the over-population of the Western World. And we didn't divorce until our son was eighteen, not sixteen. Carey really is a wonderful boy. He had a good ... well ... nest.

She surveyed the panoramic view of San Francisco with a smile. We often said that Carey learned more about the world during meals at home than in school or elsewhere. And he ate much better, too.

A few centuries ago, she went on, someone in Europe invented the concept of romantic love, which is beyond most people's powers of endurance. Then along came all these novels and movies, and now everyone hankers after a wonderful, exciting, crazy romance for which they're completely ill-equipped. And they come to grief.

Still looking down at San Francisco, she said: My God, now I'm talking like an American courtesan! But then, I *am* an American courtesan.

We both laughed. I didn't want her to stop laughing – ever. I felt as if her laughter could save me. Her mouth shimmered in the gloom of the bar. She threw back her head, and a flock of blackbirds flew out into the night.

What are you thinking of? she asked.

I'm thinking of a Californian girl I used to know. She was very beautiful and very . . . well, on the temperamental side. She made me feel that she was the whole world – that no one could ever wield the same fascination over me.

And?

That was long ago. Looking at you here and now, I'd find it very hard to decide between that girl and the woman sitting across the table from me, who's over fifty.

Which would you choose?

I've run out of choices, Susannah. I'm finished, and not just since this business with the Mafia. I've been finished for a long time.

Is that why no one will miss you back home?

Yes.

Tell me why no one will miss you.

I told her. I told her everything, the whole terrible story that was my life.

We didn't speak for a long time after that, just gazed out into the darkness and across San Francisco.

You did a terrible thing, Fritz. I would have left you in Ellen's place. I couldn't have gone on living with you either. You must have known it would end your life together. Some things ought never to happen, but if they do, they must only happen once. There isn't a second chance. There *mustn't* be a second chance. It may sound strange, but I've a feeling that all this has something to do with me.

It probably has, Susannah. What happened between us, between you and me, was a promise. Something absolute. Everything that came after it had to mean as

201

much. And I broke that promise, destroyed it. It didn't affect Ellen alone. Or Jessie. It affects you too. It affects all women.

Susannah looked at me sadly. I'd like to turn the clock back, she said. I'm not talking about a romantic time warp. I don't mean a romantic foray into the past, nice as that might be. I mean I'd like to restore your innocence. I'd like to turn the clock back to the moment before that thing happened between you and Ellen. And I'd like you to be as innocent as you were when you first arrived here. I remember it well. You had a slight German accent. No, it wasn't bad, not guttural or anything, just *slight*. Do you remember?

No, I don't.

At school they called you Fritz the very first week, but they'd have done that even if you hadn't had an accent. And I soon fell in love with you, very soon, and we became inseparable. We were together as often as possible, which was very often. So often that nothing else mattered. Your basketball steadily deteriorated. You were soon relegated to the reserves, I seem to remember. And you soon spoke my language more and more. No, I don't mean English, I mean *my* English. My intonation and certain phrases I still use today. You can say "hell and damnation" like no one in the States but me. And "holy cow". And my address, "El Camino del Mar". It's quite wonderful. You speak like me. You've adopted my rhythms. I'm your mother tongue. I've been with you all these years. Whenever you spoke English I was there.

Not only then, I said. And Jessie was there – suddenly Jessie was there speaking English in London. She used to say "fiddlesticks" and "holy cow" and "hell and damnation" and "I bet you a dollar to a doughnut", just the way Susannah said them. And in England she'd say "I bet you a pound to a doughnut". She always giggled after that. In some funny way, there was something of Susannah in Jessie.

It was very strange. I'd said that there was something absolute between me and Susannah. I'd said it because it was true. It had started with the Drifters and *Save the Last Dance for Me* and *Saturday Night at the Movies* and *Under the Boardwalk,* and all at once it was something absolute. As it was with Ellen.

A promise for all time. Without end. Even when you break that promise, it still exists. And Jessie was a part of it. There's an old saying that men always want sons. It's only dinned into them by the mother-animals, perhaps because they need someone who can defend their nest in the future. I think men want daughters. It was so with me, at least. Men like me want daughters. Why? To prevent the image of love from disappearing. The image that love holds for them. Ellen's image. Susannah's image.

*　*　*

Susannah drove me back to the hotel. I got out two blocks away, and I didn't know what I was doing there. It surprised me that she'd driven me back because I couldn't think why I should ever go back to the hotel at all. It was as though I had no business there.

I wanted to smoke a cigarette before returning to the hotel, but the wind was so strong my matches kept going out. I went round the nearest corner and managed to light up there. A moment later a young man came up to me and asked for a light. We went back round the corner. He was a Mexican who had moved from LA to San Francisco a few years ago after some trouble with a street gang. He complained of having to smoke outdoors so often in the States, but he knew of a bar nearby where everyone smoked. He asked if I wanted to go there with him. His name, he said, was Pancho.

Come and have a drink, he said.

No thanks, I said.

Come on, he repeated.

No, I've got to get home.

Oh, come on, he said again, gripping my shoulder.

Sonia! My whole body exploded. Something seemed to detonate in my brain. They've got Sonia! They've got Sonia, and they want to lure me away from the hotel!

Come on, he said, tightening his grip. I drove my knee into his gut, and he doubled up. I hauled him upright and repeated the process. Then I ran off down the street to the hotel. We each had keys of our own. I unlocked the glass entrance door and raced up the narrow stairs to the third floor.

As soon as I'd unlocked the door to our room I dashed inside with my fists raised.

Sonia was sitting up in bed, painting one of those pictures that disappear so quickly.

Harry! What's the matter? Are they after you?

No, I said, taking her in my arms. I blew a fuse again, that's all.

And I thought you'd forgotten all about me.

We lay awake for a long time, I don't know how long. Two or three hours, maybe. When I thought Sonia was already asleep, she said: I'm not jealous. We aren't in love, you and I – we don't even think we're in love. No, it isn't that. It's just that I've lost the little bit of future I had left. I suddenly felt so awfully alone in that restaurant. I just couldn't bear it any more.

I'm sorry. I'm so sorry.

204

You needn't be, Harry. It's just that, if we do have a little bit of a future left, all we've got is ourselves. I've got you and you've got me, even if you can't stand Russians. And there you were with Susannah – with a past that has no future but is destroying *my* little bit of a future. And it hurt a lot. It was like dying before one's death. Can you understand that?

Yes, I said, holding her tight with Susannah's face in my mind's eye.

Are you sleepy?

No, I said. Why?

I want to tell you something. It's just a corny novel I read as a child. An English historical romance of the nineteenth century. We had a lot of those books at home, and at fourteen or fifteen I devoured them all, just as all the children in our family had probably done for a couple of generations before me. But this book was different. It was dark, very dark – extravagantly so. It was the story of King Harold. I've been thinking about it the whole time tonight. Do you know it?

No, I said, so she told me the story of King Harold, who fell at the battle of Hastings. Edith Swan-Neck, who was his mistress, found him lying among the dead on the battlefield. Before the battle began Harold had sworn a false oath, and he died without being able to expiate that mortal sin. Edith disappeared from that day forward. No member of her family ever heard of her again. Years went by, and everyone forgot her. She had simply vanished from the memory of man.

On the other side of the English Channel, in a rocky, wooded wilderness, stood a convent noted for its strict observance of monastic rules. One of its long-standing inmates was a nun who had taken a vow of eternal silence. Her fellow nuns admired her greatly. She knew no rest by day or night. Whether early in the morning or in the stillness at noon, her figure could be seen kneeling in front of the crucifix in the convent chapel. Whenever anyone stood in need of help or consolation, she was always the first to appear. Not a soul in the neighbourhood died but the tall, pale-faced nun would first bend over the deathbed and brush the dying man or woman's forehead with her bloodless lips, which her vow of silence had sealed for ever . . . Are you still listening, Harry?

No one knew who this nun was or where she came from. Twenty years earlier she had appeared outside the convent gate, wrapped in a black cloak. After a long conversation with the abbess, she had remained in the convent ever since. The abbess of those days was long dead, but the pale-faced nun still walked the cloisters like a ghost. No one now living in the convent had ever heard her voice. The younger nuns and the poor of the entire district bowed to her as if she were a saint, and mothers brought their sick children to her in the hope that her touch would cure them. Many people believed that she had been a great sinner in her youth, and was atoning for her past.

Then, after many years, the hour of her own death drew near. All the nuns in the convent, young and old, gathered around her deathbed.

A priest entered the dying woman's cell. Having released her from her vow of eternal silence, he urged her to reveal who she was and what sin or crime was weighing on her conscience.

She sat up with an effort. It was as if her bloodless lips had been paralysed by her long silence. They twitched for some minutes, soundlessly and spasmodically. Then, at long last, she managed to speak. The voice she had not used for twenty years sounded muffled and unnatural . . . Are you still listening, Harry? Are you still listening?

I am Edith, she said with difficulty. I was mistress to the ill-fated King Harold.

The other nuns crossed themselves on hearing the king's name, but the priest said: My daughter, in your lifetime you loved a great sinner. King Harold was anathematized by our Holy Mother, the Catholic Church, and can never be forgiven. He will burn in hellfire for ever. But God sees your humility and accepts your penance and your tears. Depart in peace. Another, immortal bridegroom awaits you in paradise.

A sudden flush suffused the dying woman's hollow cheeks, and her sunken eyes flashed fire.

I want no paradise without Harold! she cried. The nuns looked appalled. If Harold is denied forgiveness, God need not summon me to him!

Rigid with consternation, the nuns heard Edith call upon the Almighty: Your son's sufferings endured for a few hours only, yet for their sake you relieved mankind of its burden of sin. I have been dying a slow, agonizing death every hour of every day for twenty long years. You have seen my sufferings. If they count for anything, have mercy on Harold. Give me a sign before I die: when we say the Lord's Prayer, cause the candle before the image of Jesus to ignite itself. Then I shall know that Harold is forgiven.

The priest intoned the Paternoster, solemnly and clearly enunciating each word. The nuns recited the prayer in a whisper. Every one of them was filled with compassion for Edith.

Edith lay there, her body already writhing in its death throes. Only her eyes, which were fixed on the cross, retained a spark of life.

Still the candle remained unlit.

The priest came to the end of the prayer. Amen, he said sadly.

The miracle had not occurred. Harold had found no forgiveness. A plaintive curse issued from Edith's lips. Then she died.

*　　*　　*

I felt quite numb with horror for several days, said Sonia. I was fifteen, Harry, and overwhelmed with despair.

Yet another indication of what a merciless, implacable religion it is, I told myself. Obsessed with power – abominable! But it has already lost the battle. It won't survive for much longer.

I don't want to start a political argument, Harry, I'm simply telling you how desperate I felt, just the way I did tonight. There was no future any more, only despair at the absence of compassion, at the fact that the world is a cold and pitiless place. There's a feeling many Russians have: People hate me, so I'm a Russian. And then, when I was fifteen, it was: God hates us, so we're human beings.

And all that in the home of a general, I said. I mean, fancy a book like that in the home of a Soviet general.

Yes, it was subversive literature. Our system wasn't much better than this God. It was just as merciless and implacable. And now it's as if there's a curse on my country, not only on me. Look at our history. Glorious Petersburg, and what came of that? The October Revolution, and what came of that? The Great Patriotic War, and what came of that? Our hopes have always been dashed. We defeated the Germans who wanted to enslave us. We and the Americans won that war together. And what are we now? First the Evil Empire and now the land of eternal inefficiency. Your country – not you, Harry, not you – committed the worst crime in human history, and how are you faring today? You with your big cars and long holidays and fat incomes and weight problems! Even your pigeons are fat because you feed them all the time. As for the swans on the Isar, they can't even take off, they're so well-fed. You've got *everything*. All we've got is swans that can still fly. Is that fair? Not you, Harry. I'm not talking about you. I'm talking about my country, which is once more choking on its own incompetence and self-pity and despair. We're choking on failure, even though we're such experts at it.

I held her tight.

I know it sounds as corny as that novel, she said, but I want no paradise without Harold. I can't put it any other way. Even though we aren't in love, I want no paradise without you, Harry.

Paradise doesn't exist, I said. That's a bad thing, I suppose, but neither does that merciless God of yours exist. Don't be scared.

So where is paradise, Harry? Tell me – tell me where it is.

It's here. It could be here. It's just that we won't get there together.

*   *   *

We must have fallen asleep at some stage. I thought of Tess as I was drifting off. Or did I dream of her? It was the day she died. We were in her bedroom, Ellen and I. Darkness had already fallen. December. December 1968. Jessie was born four months later.

Bring me a glass of wine. Please.

You aren't supposed to drink any wine.

Epileptics aren't supposed to, I know. But I always have.

I brought her a glass of water.

She pushed it away. I said *wine*, Harry.

I brought her some from the kitchen. She was too weak to drink it, but she sniffed the glass.

Thanks.

Ellen wiped her face with a damp flannel.

Tess looked at me. There was laughter in the distant depths of her eyes. Once could scarcely see it. It was only a tiny laugh.

A grand baby you're going to have, the two of you.

All at once she gripped my hand. Hold me tight, Harry.

She looked at Ellen, and Ellen held her tight too.

I've got to go. And I want to. But hold me tight.

I rested my cheek against hers. Her fingers were enlaced in my hair. You always had such lovely smooth skin as a child, she whispered, and now you're all stubbly. You might at least have shaved beforehand.

We laughed, all three of us. Some time later I glanced at the ceiling, then back at Ellen and Tess, and something left the room. Just a brief glance at the ceiling, and then we both looked at Tess, Ellen and I, and something left the room.

* * *

Jessie was born four months later. While she was sleeping peacefully in bed beside Ellen and I was sitting on a chair beside them, there it was again. A brief moment, and something came into the room – something I already knew.

Ellen said later: One goes and another comes. What a strange family.

* * *

Sonia and I didn't wake the next morning until two Mexican chambermaids opened the door to do our room. For an instant I thought they'd come to avenge the young Mexican I'd beaten up the night before. I thought they might be planning to suffocate us in our sleep, but they gave us an understanding, apologetic smile. It was just after eleven. When we moved out of the hotel half an hour later we left a hundred-dollar tip on the bed. Far too much, really. Too likely to attract attention, but I felt a hundred was right. It was a glorious, cloudless day in San Francisco.

Wednesday

Sonia wanted to take the ferry to Sausalito and look at some houses. I'm thinking of the future, Harry. I'm dreaming of a future of some kind. It's only a game, something to pass the time. Maybe we'll find a little house over there that isn't too expensive.

We went to the ferry port by streetcar. Sonia planned to go to Sausalito on her own, and I had already arranged to meet Susannah at Enrico's.

Susannah came there straight from the old folks' home, where she always starts work at six in the morning. She was looking exhausted, but she smiled when she saw me.

Ah, Fritz, she said when the waiter had brought the wine. It isn't easy to watch old people deteriorate and lose their wits, but sometimes it's like a miracle. When a life is ending and the truth becomes visible once more – visible for the first time, maybe – it's like a miracle sometimes. One of our old men has five pianos in his room. Five pianos and a bed, that's all. There's nothing else in the room. And I always have to play two-handed with him when I'm there. Bach and Mozart. I don't know what that means, not yet, but I'm definitely going to find out. We sometimes have wild Bach and Mozart parties. Above his bed is a little old hippy poster with a poem on it. I know the poem by heart. It goes like this:

In a room that knows your death

A closet freezes like a postage stamp.
A coat, a dress is hanging there.

Susannah looked at me. It's horrible, Fritz. Some demented hippy poet probably nailed it to a tree sometime in the sixties. How would it go in German?

I said: *In einem Zimmer, das deinen Tod kennt*
Friert ein Schrank fast wie eine Briefmarke.
Ein Mantel, ein Kleid hängt in dem Schrank.

That sounds just as horrible, she said. Until three months ago we had another old man at the home. I used to think of you when I was with him, because he came from Germany. From Hamburg. He had around two hundred dolls in his room. He was always making dresses for them, forever undressing the ones that could withstand immersion in water and bathing them in a particular way. Naturally, everyone thought they knew what was going on. They thought the old boy was a paedophile who had flipped and was now doing what he used to do, over and over, but quite openly. He was confessing the sins of a lifetime, washing the children he'd abused and making them new dresses.

In fact the truth was altogether different. There was quite another background to the story of the old man with the two hundred dolls. Both his daughters were killed in an air raid during the war – that terrible raid on Hamburg in 1943. He went mad after that – well, maybe not immediately after that, but anyway, he emigrated to the States and learned English and scraped a living somehow, and eventually he went insane. After that he was just a man who bathed his dolls and made dresses for them, like someone destined to do so for evermore.

213

Susannah didn't speak for a long time. Then she said: I stole one of his dolls when he died. After all, he had two hundred of them. No one's going to miss it. It sits on a chair beside the desk in my study, watching me while I work.

Jessie! For a moment it was as if Susannah had saved Jessie. For one brief, luminous moment. One day, perhaps, I shall be an old man in a home, bathing and dressing my dolls. A crazy old man kept alive by that ritual alone. But it isn't so crazy, retrieving what you've broken. Retrieving it over and over again. Perhaps it's like that when you're an old man. You become diminished. Some relive the process that ruined their lives, others do their exercises in front of the TV under instruction from attractive young women in chic leotards. Then they switch channels to the latest market prices. A touch of sexual titillation in the morning, then off to Wall Street. Capital appreciation for their grandchildren's benefit.

I made a call, said Susannah. To Washington. To see what can be done about you, you and Sonia. How you can be protected. I'm an American courtesan, my dear Fritz, and I've got some good connections with the royal court in Washington. We'll know more in a few days' time. Maybe we'll house you in the Pentagon, and when you're dead they'll make a Hollywood biopic about you – *The Spy Who Loved Me, Part Two*. Or I'll marry you and we'll adopt Sonia. That's an idea, isn't it?

She threw back her head. Her laugh was like a door opening. A flock of blackbirds soared into the sky.

What are you looking at? she asked.

There's a flock of blackbirds in the sky.

San Francisco isn't noted for its flocks of blackbirds, she said, but I know what you're getting at. The laugh

214

was only in her eyes now, there and in the fine lines round her mouth. It was a classically ironical smile. I read the book you sent me, she said. Your debut novel. I heard no more from you after that. I know those blackbirds. I recognized one or two things in your book.

Did it surprise me you'd become a writer? Actually, it didn't. Although you're too impetuous to be one. You aren't the kind that sits on literary eggs and hatches them out. Mind you, there was always going to be something in your life that would prevent you from playing really good basketball, I realized that quite early on. That being so, what else could you have become but a writer? You were made for it. Made for women, I mean. Just as I'm a courtesan, so you're my, well . . . my troubadour. But you troubadours don't perform for us courtesans, only for queens and princesses. Or do you?

Oh, Susannah!

You haven't asked how I managed to read your book. I didn't know German, or had you forgotten?

I hadn't forgotten. Susannah was interested in everything. All things and all languages. She wanted to know and be able to do everything. I had taught her a bit of German, but we hadn't progressed beyond a few phrases and numerals.

I could still hear her reciting: *Eins, zwei, drei . . . vierundsechzig, fünfundsechzig . . . neunundneunzig . . . hundert! hundert Jahre reichen nicht für uns* – a hundred years won't be long enough for us!

My parents mustn't know I'm learning German, she had told me then.

Now she said: My mother hated the Germans. All Germans without exception. But my mother was just a stupid Jewish momma who was keen to have children.

215

Sons above all. When she got to hear about you, she seethed with hatred and disgust. But my father was a shrewd man. It wasn't that he didn't hate the Germans too; he didn't give his hatred houseroom. His argument was that everything between us – every row we had – would turn into a German–Jewish conflict. That it would destroy us. There would come a stage when that conflict was all we had left.

You had absolutely no idea that I was Jewish. I had to tell you. You were a total innocent. You found the information interesting but unexciting. Your reaction would have been just as neutral if I'd told you I was Norwegian.

I've always been a clever girl, Harry, and I fully understood what my father was getting at. But I didn't accept it, even if he was right. He was probably right when he said that the best thing that could happen to me in Germany would be inverted philosemitism – that people would drown me in it. Not you, Fritz. You're probably not entirely free from it yourself – it would be unnatural if you weren't – but you would even have fallen in love with a Norwegian if she'd been like me.

My father was afraid I might become a kind of Jewish trophy wife. I doubt if it would have happened, but now, after years of experience, I think it's possible.

The ironical smile had left her eyes and given way to a kind of disquiet. A disquiet that went back a long way. When Ellen was pregnant and it had become clear that our daughter would be called Jessie, I said that, if the baby turned out to be a boy after all, David or Daniel might be nice names. Ellen simply laughed at me. No child of mine is going to have a bogus, philosemitic name like that, she said. I'm not playing that little game.

I was really thinking of Davy Crockett.

216

Forget Davy Crockett, Ellen told me. As for Daniel, I suppose you were thinking of Daniel Boone? Anyway, it's going to be a girl.

Clever girl, said Susannah. A woman after my own heart. And she was twenty or twenty-one when she said that? Still, Jessie – or Jesse – is also –

Jessie is Jessie, I said. It's neither more nor less philosemitic than Anna or Maria.

True. The ironical smile had reappeared in Susannah's eyes. I sometimes think it will never release its hold over me, but I thought that once before.

We're the Germans' bad dream, she said. Maybe even *your* bad dream, but I doubt it. They're putting up one Holocaust memorial after another in Germany. Like guilt-ridden squirrels. Remember that unnecessary Gulf War? It very soon became an attack on the state of Israel by Federal Germany through the medium of Iraq. "Auschwitz in the desert" – I remember it well. That really infuriated me, but the propaganda worked. They made you cough up eighteen billion worth of war reparations and three submarines for Israel. Am I right?

And last year, when it came to that crusade against Serbia, you couldn't bear to stay out of it. "No more Auschwitzes" – that's what your fusty foreign minister blithely crowed to the world at large, although he knew perfectly well you wouldn't have been able to stay out of it in any case.

Susannah, I said, the German–Jewish dialogue doesn't interest me. There are too many lies lurking on both sides. Too many cries of triumph whenever someone blunders.

It doesn't interest me either. I only wanted to tell you why I managed to read your book. My father wanted me to break with you, but I refused. Even if he was right. There was a scene one night. Anyway, I shouted at him: You can't prevent me from committing *Rassenschande*! I used the German expression – racial dishonour. We don't have a word for it in English, but that doesn't mean we don't have the concept.

He went for me when I said that. He *hit* me. My dear, sweet daddy actually struck me! Don't look so shocked. It didn't hurt. He wasn't very strong, physically. It was more of a gesture than anything else, but I never forgave him. For hitting me that one and only time in my life. And for hitting me because of you.

You know the rest. The clever girl eventually gave way. But I'd have run away with you if you'd said a word – just one word. It's the age-old conflict. It often happens: the past, the family, one's nearest and dearest versus the new, which is equally near and dear to one. Next of kin versus next of skin. Yes, I'd have run away with you, even if it wouldn't have done us any good.

But there's something else you don't know. I'm old enough now to see it – and say it. Say it to *you*. The first time I saw you and learned where you came from, I wanted to *have* you because we were the most unlikely combination in the school, and because I knew how my family would react. I wanted you as a demonstration of power. You yourself were secondary. That's how it was at first, Fritz, but not later on. I wanted to win. In school and at home. I'm just like the Kennedys in that respect: I always want to win. No, you weren't important at first. You were already in love with me when I was using you merely to stir things up a bit. That's the truth. And afterwards you meant *everything* to me.

When you'd left here and gone back to Europe, I learned German. Frantically, because I wanted to hang on to you. That was one reason. The other was my family. Learning German was my love song and my revolution.

She gave me a radiant smile, and her words resounded in my head: *You were already in love with me when I was using you merely to stir things up a bit. That's the truth. And afterwards you meant* everything *to me.* And Susannah was sitting opposite me and was beautiful. Quite simply beautiful.

You're so beautiful, Susannah, I feel like throwing my glass of wine in your face.

Don't you dare!

I didn't dare. I kicked her shin under the table instead. It was so good when we laughed, and a dynamo started spinning in my head: *You weren't important at first . . . You were already in love with me when I was using you merely to stir things up a bit.* I laughed with Susannah, and the dynamo kept spinning and spinning, and I felt the pain of that sixteen-year-old youth, the pain he didn't feel because he knew nothing, but it hurt just the same – hurt terribly. All at once I felt incredibly alone in Susannah's company. All at once I had *two* reasons for throwing my glass of wine in her face, but the glass was already empty. And I couldn't free myself from her even if I'd wanted to – even though I knew that now, today and tomorrow and the day after, I would be unimportant to her once more. I looked at her and wanted to look at her for ever, wanted to write down all she said, she alone. What *I* say is unimportant. And, in spite of everything, that dynamo exists and goes on spinning.

Wednesday

For the past two weeks I've been going jogging with Susannah every few days. I'd sensed that I was getting a bit out of condition; it was so long since I'd taken any exercise. I feel the hills here in San Francisco. Sonia doesn't want to come with us, so Susannah and I go jogging in Lincoln Park or Golden Gate Park. Mostly in Lincoln Park or down at Baker Beach. We arrange to meet somewhere in town, and Susannah picks me up in her dark red Volvo estate.

It always feels strange when I'm jogging with her. We're suddenly young again. We run side by side and talk and survey our surroundings, and I sense her skin although we're nearly a yard apart. I sense her skin the way you sense a light, pleasant breeze. I sense the fine hairs on my arms, or is it the hairs on her arms? And I sense her voice all over my body. Her presence and her voice are like the air that pervades my body. We're young again – fresh and innocent. I haven't killed anyone and no one's after me. We're young again, that's all. We don't even know we'll fall in love. We don't know anything yet. There's just the wind and the air and our skin, and I never want to stop running beside her and talking with her, talking about no matter what. What we talk about is quite unimportant because our voices are music, and I look at Susannah's face and say: *Gee, you're so beautiful it's starting to rain.*

Where does that come from? she asked.

Some hippy poem, I told her. Death isn't everything.

The first time we drove to her house after jogging, I said: I shouldn't come in. It's risky for us to be seen together too often.

But you're bathed in sweat, she said. I can't deliver you to Sonia in that state.

After showering we sat in her living room, and she said: Okay, now we'll do something *bad* for our health. Scotch or a martini? Or a margarita?

Wednesday, Later

Susannah handed me a letter today, after jogging.

I wrote it, she said, because I don't want to talk about it. And because I wanted to talk to you last night and couldn't. After all, you weren't there.

I've only just read the letter:

* * *

Fritz, it's after midnight already, and I'm sitting here at my desk. The doll I stole from the old folks' home is sitting here, looking at me. I'm writing this because I want to talk with you, and because you aren't here. I'm always wanting to talk with you, and wanting you always to be there. That's one of the two reasons why I'm writing to you now.

The second has to do with the guilt-ridden squirrels who pile one Holocaust memorial on top of another.

I think it was unfair of me to say that. Unfair because I didn't say all there is to be said on the subject. I'm not a professional Jewess, you know that. I'm a citizen of San Francisco first, then a Californian, and after that an American. And only then – a long way after that – am I Jewish. For my mother it was precisely the other way around, even though she was a second-generation American.

All the same, ten or eleven years ago a woman from Cologne told me there would always be problems with the Jews and memorials. If the Germans didn't erect any memorials, they would be accused of suppressing their crimes against the Jews. If they did erect memorials, they were bound to be told they were doing so only as a form of self-redemption.

I think the woman was right. The sufferings and hatred of the Jews are irreconcilable. Permanently so. There would have been an end to the hatred – not to the sufferings and the horror – only if Germany had undergone what happened to Japan, but on a far larger scale . . . Two, three, many Hiroshimas. It very nearly happened, too. That, I think, is the truth no one utters because no one could live with it. There's no end to the hatred, I know that. I looked deep into my mother's soul a few times in my life. Very deep.

And there's something else that has nothing to do with hatred. Whenever the word "German" or "Germany" crops up, the first association that springs to mind is the word "Hitler". Throughout the world. Invariably. Over fifty years after the crime. A mark of Cain is also a memorial.

Those who did what the Germans did are bound to suppress it. They have to do good and suppress it. It's perfectly natural – essential, too. No one can live without suppressing something. That's one point. Moreover, total suppression is impossible. The thing suppressed is always there. But this memorial mania – this ostentatious accumulation of memorials – is sick. As sick as the crime at the root of the mania.

But you Germans do something else as well. Something quite wonderful. I occasionally read German newspapers – not often, but often enough – and there's hardly a supplement, hardly a weekend edition or books section, that doesn't refer to those days, to those crimes and the war. Thinking about them is far more important than any memorial. Of course, it's often mendacious and hypocritical. False and mealy-mouthed, like the following extract from a newspaper article: "The fact that so many citizens of the Jewish faith, to quote the words of Ignaz Bubis, are seeking to bring about a new efflorescence of Jewish life in

223

post-war Germany is a boon we have far from deserved, an obligation laid on all non-Jews."

That's political kitsch, and unctuous enough to slip on. "Citizens of the Jewish faith!" Holy Cow! I, for example, am not a citizen of the Jewish faith. That faith is as remote from me and close to me as Christianity. Or Islam. I'm simply a Jewess of no particular faith. An American Jewess. I simply had Jewish parents and grandparents and so on. Didn't your Ignaz Bubis give any thought to people like me? To the poor, innocent, godless, well-heeled girls from San Francisco or Braunschweig? Don't they have a right to live and flourish in post-war Germany?

Yes, many of those articles are mendacious and unctuous and hypocritical. And many Germans flaunt the name of some chance Jewish forebear like a title of nobility. The same forebear whom, sixty years ago, they . . . no, forget it. All public life is inseparable from hypocrisy. All political life. The moment of truth is a very rare occurrence. What goes on in the minds of those who kneel and lay wreaths and do penance in public? Are they thinking what we'd like them to think? Or are they thinking of their lovers, their slipped disks, or the fact that they've just performed a great historic act? We don't know. Only they do.

In private life, too, the celebrated moment of truth is usually delegated to art, and art is often just a sham. Still, it's great that such articles get written. The fact that people keep writing and thinking and shamming – that's the memorial. It's a shaky memorial and always will be, but it will – I hope – always be there. At least for the next fifty years.

This has nothing to do with us – with you and me. I've written this only to prevent you from thinking me the kind of person who's impossible to satisfy, with or without a memorial. That's all.

The doll is sitting here, watching me. A doll from Germany, that's what I always tell myself. She's related to you.

224

I like her. And I'm so close to you now, I'd like to go on writing for ever.

Your
Norwegian Susannah

Thursday

The night before last I called Susannah because Sonia wanted to invite us to dinner. At the Thai restaurant in Berkeley where she'd felt so alone.

That's fine, said Susannah. I've got some news to discuss with you both. News from Washington. And another thing: it's very brave of your Sonia to want to pay that restaurant another visit.

* * *

Well, said Susannah after the first course, you've got several possibilities. I have some good connections in Canada and Australia as well as the States. We could tuck you away someplace without the aid of any kind of government authority. Even in Australia, if you like. Australia is a proven convict island, after all. But I'd sooner keep you here in the States.

The safest thing would be the witness protection programme. You're witnesses against the Mafia, so to speak. I could fix that. You'd be provided with an entirely new life – a legend, as they call it. However, it would mean we could never see each other again. Worse still, you couldn't stay together. You'd have to live in entirely different parts of the States.

No! Sonia sprang to her feet. A few people at the neighbouring tables looked over at us. I can't live here without Harry!

I felt the blood shoot to my head. *I want no paradise without Harry,* she'd said when she told me the story of King Harold.

The situation looks like this, Susannah said when Sonia had recovered her composure. In Washington they think it would be dangerous to provide you with a new life together, because a couple is just the combination they're looking for. Mind you, the true reason may be political bigotry. There are people in this country who almost go mad when the Germans and the Russians get together. President Putin went to Berlin in June or July. The Germans regarded it as a perfectly normal state visit, but the *New York Times* devoted a long article to the event. Europe usually merits a mention only when a world war breaks out – if our newspapers can find room for it.

So no witness protection programme for us, I said. It would wipe us out completely.

Sonia smiled at me.

Give me a little more time, then, said Susannah. I can try again.

* * *

In bed that night Sonia said: What is it with you and Susannah?

It's a long story, I told her.

I know that. But what are you planning, the two of you?

We aren't planning anything at all, Sonia. But something has happened to us – something that happened once before. I can't pretend I didn't want it to happen, and I can't pretend I'm unhappy about it. But there's something more important: love is so often used as a pretext for the stupidest, simplest, meanest actions. I

227

don't play that game. The name of my game is Susannah. And Ellen, of whom you know nothing. And Jessie, of whom you also know nothing.

What about me, Harry? Where do I fit in? Don't I belong in your game?

You're fourteen years younger than me. A different generation.

Well? What difference does that make?

Just think: when I was twenty you were six. A child. Really a child. A *little* child. It's quite impossible. But you're very close to me, Sonia Kovalevskaya.

Closer than one would expect of a Russian, eh?

Stop that. I don't know where you fit into my game, but you exist, and I like you, and you're very close to me, and – if it's of any interest to you – every time we made love it was like a miracle. It was like something absolute – something that swept away all resistance, and wherever we have to go I'll go there with you. I won't leave you on your own. I'll stay with you for as long as you can endure my company. We're in this together. That's what you said once, wasn't it? And there something else, dramatic though it may sound: we're together on the brink of eternity because they'll hunt us for all eternity. We may die together – you could be right – but we may also live together. For a while. For a little while.

Friday

A bright, luminous day. Susannah had to go to Sacramento. Sonia and I spent the whole day roaming the city hand in hand like two tourists in love. Sonia had brought a street map. After all, she said as we set out, we may live here. We bought some fruit in Chinatown and ate it sitting on a bench. Sonia tried on a lot of smart clothes in three different boutiques. In the end she bought a pair of shoes.

We went into a church and sat down in a pew at the back. Mass was just ending. The priest was Chinese. His congregation comprised a few disabled people in wheelchairs, six or seven old folk, and a handful of those inordinately fat Americans for whom Sonia, saddened but sarcastic, had recently coined the term "jumbo citizens". They nearly all took Communion.

When the priest finally turned to bless those present he glanced at his watch as he spread his arms. Sonia nudged me and whispered: The representatives of eternity are in a hell of a hurry round here.

Who knows, I whispered, perhaps he's due at a funeral.

When we were outside again I sat down on the church steps and smoked a cigarette.

Some time early in the afternoon we watched a couple playing tennis in Alamo Square. They weren't particularly good.

A little while later we walked to the nearest bus stop because Sonia wanted to go down to the sea. She studied the timetable and compared it with the street map to try to find the most interesting route. Maps and street maps always faze me. Sonia could see that I was entirely dependent on her.

You're a pretty poor map-reader for a taxi driver, she said while we were waiting for the bus. I sometimes wonder how you found the way to Luxembourg.

We laughed and went on waiting for the bus, which ought to have turned up long before. Two buses had already passed us going in the opposite direction. Having waited for nearly half an hour, we were about to walk on when our bus appeared at the end of the street. We got in at the same time as an old Chinese woman who was loaded down with shopping bags but refused our help.

We showed the Chinese driver our Muni Passes. Sonia and I have made it our habit always to stand in the middle of the bus, near the centre door, where we have a good view of the whole of the interior. There have been a few incidents, for instance when people spoke to Sonia and I had to watch what was going on quite closely. Usually I signal to her that we're getting off at the next stop. I always stand there like a protective wall. It was the same with me and Jessie when we went cycling together. I always rode on her left and slightly to the rear, so that I could intervene at a moment's notice. And when we were crossing an intersection I always rode alongside so as to shield her body with mine. I had a sensation of infinite strength when I rode beside her like that – the feeling that I was proof against any car or truck.

Our stop was only fifteen or twenty yards beyond an intersection, and the bus still had several intersections to cross, but the driver put his foot down and turned off so sharply that we were all thrown sideways. Several of our fellow passengers were hurled against the seats on the left-hand side. Hey, what are you playing at? they shouted, and one young man yelled: Stop! Stop, you fucking asshole! The driver yelled something back – I didn't catch it – and laughed. I threw myself at Sonia and held her tight. I felt preternaturally strong and huge like the colossal barrier that had once shielded Jessie. Now they've got us! I told myself. They've got rid of the real driver and hijacked the bus, that's why it's all taken so long. I had a sudden vision of the Chinese in the massage parlour.

The people on the bus continued to shout and protest until they forced the driver to pull up. We opened the door and jumped off. Nearly all the other passengers got off at the same time. I took Sonia's hand and we ran and ran until we were out of breath.

My God! Sonia panted. What was all that?

Maybe just a change of route, I said. On the other hand, maybe they planned to hijack the entire busload and pick us out later.

Wouldn't that have been a bit overcomplicated?

Yes. Perhaps it was just a change of route after all. Or the driver simply flipped. But perhaps they don't want to grab us yet. Perhaps they're using these Chinese to unnerve us. Perhaps they only want to keep us dangling, blind us to what's really going on. I don't know. All I know is, we'd better be more careful. We should steer clear of anyone who looks Chinese.

Sonia looked round. In this city? she said. That's a tall order.

Yes, I said. Maybe that's just it. Maybe the Chinese are simply meant to hem us in until we go mad.

When we were sitting in a restaurant an hour later, Sonia said: Harry, I think that business with the bus was just a coincidence. The driver flipped, that's all. We mustn't drive ourselves insane.

231

Saturday

With Susannah in her garden after jogging. More precisely, in the doorway leading to her garden. It was cool there. We were drinking Scotch. Susannah had showered and put on a dark brown dress with an abstract floral pattern in grey. If only this could be my life, I thought. If only I didn't have to be scared of Chinese bus drivers, I thought. If only a volcano would suddenly erupt *à la* Pompeii, and nothing would ever part us again. Susannah and I would sit gazing at each other for all time, an eternal memento of love in the twentieth century for all who came after us. Susannah Timmerman and Harry Willemer. Fritz. We would still be sitting there even if love became extinct, and people would wonder what we'd been doing a few hundred years earlier – wonder why we were holding glasses in our hands, and why our faces wore a smile. They would debate all these matters in sage dissertations.

The smiles of love, Susannah said once.

She looked at me thoughtfully. Your eyes are filled with death, Fritz. You must start to live again. I sometimes think you're back in the land of the living, but then I see death in your eyes once more. I'll bring you back, though. You've simply got to mingle with people again, you and Sonia. I almost said you and your little Russian, but that would be unfair. You must mingle with people, that's all. I'm throwing a party next Saturday night. A house and garden party for forty or fifty guests, complete with Chinese lanterns and all the trimmings. I'll rent some of those gas heaters restaurants install on their terraces so diners can sit outside when it's chilly.

Too risky, I said. I don't mean the gas heaters, I mean the party. In my head I could already see the lanterns. Green, red, blue, yellow. Will anyone from Europe be there? I asked. Anyone who reads European papers and might recognize us?

No, said Susannah. They only read the financial section and the stock market reports. The only person who might be dangerous from your point of view is a professor of German language and literature from the East Coast, but I doubt if he reads newspaper reports of Mafia crimes. He comes from Ohio and is married to a German. A very nice girl. Guys like him always marry their personal language laboratories.

At that moment Susannah was both seventeen and fifty-two and everything between and before. *Guys like him always marry their personal language laboratories!* She sat there in her incredibly elegant gown, with her black eyes and her dark red hair, which is so dark that the red is just another form of black, and in that dark red hair are a few fine, almost invisible strands of grey that prove what I've no need to be told – that the red is genuine – and her face once more wore that ironical smile, and the whole world and the whole of life were just a wonderful game.

Susannah Timmerman, I said, you're the greatest.

She laughed. I know. That's precisely why I'm here on earth.

Who am I supposed to be at your party? I mean, how will you introduce me?

Oh, she said, I'll simply tell everyone you're Fritz from Munich. He's lent me four million dollars, and in return he's being allowed to use my son's credit card. As for your Russian girlfriend, we'll tell them she's little Sonietska from the Mafia – or shall we say the KGB? – and she gave you the four million you lent me, and in return I'm letting her use one of my own credit cards. OK? They won't believe a word of it.

So what *will* they believe?

They'll believe you're my new lover. Besides, I'll dance with you all night long. That's my plan, anyway. As for your little Sonietska, she'll simply be your little Sonietska.

Monday

At the party on Saturday, Susannah introduced me to some of the guests as they arrived in dribs and drabs. Later on, with a discreet little jerk of the chin, she steered me in the direction of this or that person standing somewhere in the garden or the house.

That's Ahmed over there, she told me, indicating a short, rather tubby man with a swarthy complexion. He's a Palestinian married to a fat Texan housewife. He speaks with a strong Texan accent. Ahmed is in clocks and watches – fuses for time bombs, probably. Wherever there's dancing, he's there. He loves dancing with great big Western women. It's nothing to do with sex or eroticism. He gets a kick out of *leading* them, that's all. I always dance with him a couple of times. He's a very nice person – time bombs aside. My God, Fritz, when I think of it: a German, a Russian and a Palestinian – what a mixture! Our arch-enemies.

Susannah delivered a little speech when all the guests were there. Then she took me by the arm and introduced me. This is my friend Fritz Brisante from the South Tyrol. He produces an excellent Chardonnay. She gave me a long, ironical look that said: Now make something of your new identity!

Before I could say anything she made the following announcement: Fritz is going into a Buddhist monastery for a few years. That's why I shall only dance with him tonight.

No! Ahmed protested. You must save *one* dance for me!

Everyone laughed, and Susannah danced with Ahmed.

Watching them, I wondered how it would have been if I'd lived with Susannah. Would everything have turned out exactly as it had? Would we have been as happy and unhappy as Ellen and I were? I don't know.

When we were dancing together she said: It's true what I told you recently. I should never have let you go back to Europe. I pretty soon grasped what sort of person you are. I mean, we were only sixteen and seventeen – only children, but we very soon stopped being children. Suddenly it was all so different. It was as easy as it had been at first, and as difficult, and I pretty soon grasped what sort of person you are. One could already tell. She looked at me with her eyes wide. I should never have let you go back to Europe.

I laughed, and she laughed too. But you were a minor, she said.

Then she said: I didn't have to wait for some prince or Mr Right, I realized that very early on. My family was much too rich for that. Besides, I had a few assets of my own. I could have had any man I wanted. That's the way American women look at things, and it's not so bad. But I wanted *you* because you're different. With most men it's wham bam, thank you ma'am. The same goes for most husbands. They aren't all that interested in women and prefer to hang out with the other guys. But you're different, you're genuinely interested in women. It isn't wham bam, thank you ma'am with you, even though it was always very, well . . . very stimulating.

Or exciting? I said.

Yes, she said, if you like. It was always very exciting.

Mostly, I said.

236

Yes, mostly, she said. If you like.

No, always, I said. For me, always.

Mostly, she said. Mostly is pretty damned often.

She became serious again. A few of the people dancing nearby were listening to us. Susannah had never been the subdued type.

Let them listen, she said. They may learn something. Still dancing, she took hold of my left earlobe and drew me closer. I think I know why you're the man you are: you're half woman yourself. I mean, there's something inside you that responds to what women are. It's the same with all men who get on well with women. Ultra-masculine men and gays are only interested in their own sex. There's nothing in them capable of responding to women.

Oh Susannah! I said.

I know, she said. You're a very good boxer. I saw you once in the school yard. You only had to show what you were capable of and that was enough – you didn't have to throw a single punch – and you're probably an excellent shot, and you feel at your best when you can fight, and you probably kill three mafiosi every few years, but you're still half woman.

And you? I said. What are you then?

She looked at me and laughed. Hadn't you noticed? I'm just the same as you – roughly half man. And if I were a man and you were a woman, everything would probably have gone exactly the same way. There would have been no difference. Nothing would be different *now*. Isn't that great? Maybe our ethnic chemistry is wrong. No, not ethnic, that's nonsense. It's our historical chemistry that's wrong, but our molecular balance is right – if there *is* such a thing as molecular balance.

She beamed at me like someone who has just registered an extremely interesting patent, then leant forward and sang, slowly and softly, in my ear: *If you were the woman/and I were the man . . .* Then she straightened up and looked at me challengingly. It took me a moment or two to catch on. Then I leant forward and sang, very softly: *If I were the woman/and you were the man . . .*

I sang softly, but not softly enough for Sonia, who was dancing beside us with a red-haired man. You Americans, she said loudly, you really do have a song for every occasion.

Susannah was rather irritated by this remark. Come on, she said, let's stroll over to those trees. I've no objection to people eavesdropping, but they ought to keep their comments to themselves.

We drank a glass of Chardonnay beneath the trees. Almost as good as your South Tyrolean, said Susannah. A bit oaky, but a lot of modern wines spend too long in the cask. Or is it oak shavings that do it?

Earlier on, I said, someone asked me about my vineyard. I had to explain exactly where it was.

I know, said Susannah. Then, very abruptly: Is it like that with Ellen too?

What?

Your molecular balance.

I've never thought about it. There's probably no such thing as molecular balance. Only molecular weight.

Maybe not in science, said Susannah. In love there certainly is. And there are people like you and me. We aren't entirely men or entirely women, but something in between. I went through a bad patch a few years ago. I was feeling completely drained, burned out. The analyst I consulted was scared of me. I guess he'd never come across anyone like me before. At one stage he said: You must dismantle the masculine aspects of your personality, Susannah. I really did scare him stiff. He was always wanting to try out this primal scream therapy on me. He kept suggesting it, but we never did it. I think he was apprehensive of my primal scream – scared it might simply blow him off the face of the earth.

We laughed.

When we were dancing again she said suddenly: You aren't scared of me. You aren't afraid I may blow you off the face of the earth. You're made for love. You are.

I've lived alone for over twenty years, Susannah. I'm not made for love. I destroyed all that in an instant, and our child is dead.

Yes, she said. You did something terrible, but that doesn't alter the fact that you're made for love. That's something indestructible.

Nothing's indestructible, I said.

We danced and talked to other people and ate and drank, and Sonia chatted to the red-head she danced with most of the time.

I organized this party just for you, Fritz. I wanted my friends and everyone to see you. You may be going into a Buddhist monastery, but they all think you're my latest lover – and you're just the opposite. I want to dance with you tonight, only with you. But it isn't our last dance. I'm going to get you out of this. The United States still has the edge on the Russian Mafia, even though it's common knowledge that they've been operating here for ages. At all levels.

Later, when we were sitting side by side on a couch, she said softly: *I am a woman of heart and mind. With time on her hands. No child to raise. You come to me like a little boy. And I give you my scorn and my praise.* Do you know it?

Of course I do.

239

That song didn't exist in our day. It only came out around ten years later, by which time I already had a child of my own to raise. But now I'm back the way I was – time on my hands and no child to raise. Carey turned thirty this year, and there's no daddy or mummy to wrest me away from you. As for the German–Jewish dialogue, let's leave that to the professional philosemites and the professional Jews, okay?

Susannah, I've ceased to be the kind of man who ought to live with a woman. It's just not on where I'm concerned, not any more.

What about Sonia?

Sonia and I can't help ourselves. We've been shackled together by force of circumstance.

So have we. What's more, it's not too late to do something about it. Anything *but* too late!

We didn't speak for a long time. Then Susannah asked: How would you say "woman of heart and mind" in German?

It's untranslatable.

What was Ellen like, Fritz? What *is* she like? How would you describe her?

I've never described Ellen to anyone, I said. I've never ventured to. It's never occurred to me to do so.

You mean she's taboo? Is it forbidden to describe her?

Yes. Maybe. "Woman of heart and mind" is a pretty fair description. But I've never tried to describe someone called Susannah Timmerman either. I've only ever told a few stories about her.

That's good. So in Germany there's someone who can't be described in German.

Ellen lives in Scotland these days.

Oh yes, I'd forgotten.

She's registered at the department of "Aliens & Firearms" section.

Susannah laughed, and the room and the house around us disappeared. Suddenly we were sitting on the couch with the night sky overhead. Life without Susannah was unimaginable. Without her laugh, her eyes, her hair. Without her this and that. Without her voice.

Talking of what is and what isn't translatable, she said, I read a lot of German literature while I was learning the language. Much of it is, well ... peculiar. I won't say boring, but it's often unsociable. You often get the feeling that some spindle-shanked little gnome has been sitting at his desk, scribbling grandiose ideas in solitude. Then again, it can be wonderful. I learned a lot of German poems by heart.

She hauled me up off the couch and out into the garden to dance. Here and now, Fritz, she said, time is standing still for us. I feel quite dizzy, and at the same time very remote, like a dark blue sky. I'm nothing but dark blue air.

We danced, but she still hadn't finished with German literature. There's a story she said, a really touching story, one of the best short stories I know, I can't remember the author's name, Hebel or Hebbel, which describes how a miner at Falun in Sweden –

It's Hebel.

What?

The author's name.

Yes, of course it is. Anyway, this miner and his girlfriend intend to get married, and it's all arranged, but a rockfall buries the miner in his mine, leaving the young woman on her own, and time goes by, maybe fifty years go by, and she grows old and grey and wizened and walks with a stick, and one day – in 1809, I think it was – the miners excavate a new shaft and come across a young man's body that has been completely permeated with ferrous sulphate, so it's quite undecayed and unchanged, and the old woman sees the dead body of her sweetheart looking as young as he did fifty years earlier.

Susannah looked at me. I didn't tell the story properly, but you seem to know it anyway. I cried my eyes out when I read it. And now, today, I feel it's like that with us. It hasn't been fifty years but thirty-five or thereabouts, and I don't walk with a stick and I'm not old and grey and wizened, far from it, but we're like the two people in that story. You're back here with me, my young miner, but you aren't dead and you aren't a *young* miner any more. You've been alive the whole time. And you've lost your innocence. But now let's dance.

*　　*　　*

Sonia and I got back to the hotel at three in the morning. When I said goodbye to Susannah she put her arms round my neck. I've got time, Fritz, she said. I've got plenty of time. The rest of my life.

Later, when Sonia and I were in bed, she suddenly punched the wall.

What's the matter?

I'm so furious, Harry. I'm so confused. You're against the witness protection programme because you won't be able to see Susannah any more, right? It's not because of me. You're against it because you'll be parted again, the two of you. And the protection programme is far more final than German history. There'll be no reunion because a reunion could prove fatal.

242

I laid my hand on her forehead. I'm against the programme because I can't leave Susannah any more. I mean, I don't want to live in a world where I can never see her again. And I'm against it because *we* can't leave each other, you and I. If they separate us we'll both be all alone in the world. There'll be no one left. No one we know – no one we're *allowed* to know. It's as simple as that. And as terrible.

Saturday

It's Saturday again. Two weeks later. We've changed hotels twice, and the passing days have brought an alternation of mist and sunshine, Sonia and Susannah, hope and emptiness. There's been no news from Washington, and then there was that frightful night beside the sea. Friday of last week. We've been staying at Susannah's since then because the San Francisco police are looking for us now too. Or rather, for me.

On Friday, on Friday of last week, on that god-damned Friday, I'd gone jogging with Susannah in Golden Gate Park. The evening was rather cool, and we ran a bit faster than usual. Susannah was telling me about a new software programme, but I wasn't listening. That's to say, I wasn't listening with my ears and didn't understand a word, but my entire body was listening. As before, her voice was like a gentle, pleasant breeze that caressed my cheeks and every part of me. Her voice was in my hair and my blood and everywhere, and I could have spent the rest of my life running through Golden Gate Park at her side, nothing more. I kept looking at her face. Her forehead. Her nose. Her mouth. It was a long fascination, a song without end, a gentle shock I never wanted to get over. I looked at her forehead, her nose and her mouth, and suddenly there was a recurrence of another shock I'd had not long ago.

A few weeks before I met Sonia I was standing in a Munich bookshop with a book in my hand. It was going cheap, *Bavaria in the Aftermath of World War II,* or some such title, a volume of photographs dated 1945–50, around the time I was born. I was leafing through it and looking at the pictures: bomb damage, children that looked the way I did in photos of the period, the American Library, GIs, demos, vaudeville dancers with plump upper thighs, and then, all at once, a picture of my mother. My head started spinning as I stood there in that bookshop. My mother stood in a classroom full of schoolboys, pointing to a blackboard with her left hand. The photo had been taken in 1946, when Tess had just turned twenty-four. She was smiling the way she always smiled when she'd asked a question. Then I looked at the writing on the blackboard. The characters were unfamiliar, and I wouldn't immediately have recognized them as Hebrew but for the caption below the photograph: "A Hebrew lesson in the primary school of Munich's Central Committee of Liberated Jews." The photograph was in a chapter headed "Displaced Persons". That's just what I myself have been for a long time, a displaced person. An expellee. Someone with no place to go, but someone who has expelled himself.

I was disappointed when I saw the Hebrew characters. It couldn't be Tess after all. The face, the smile, the outstretched hand, the bare arms – everything was like her. But it couldn't be her. Besides, she wasn't living in Munich at that time, two years before my birth. Nor, of course, did she know Hebrew. Yet the person in that bookshop a few months ago, the person in that classroom in June 1946, was Tess. It was her and it wasn't.

Susannah doesn't resemble Tess in the least, and yet, as we ran along side by side, I'd been reminded of that picture. Someone I'd lost had suddenly reappeared. I told her about the photograph.

She stared at me in surprise, stared at me for a long

time. Then she laughed. That would be great, she said. All my family's hatred would have been in vain. All my mother's hatred, and all my brother's. Michael always shared my mother's sentiments, and she treated him like the Messiah. Her own personal Messiah. He was her first-born son, after all. Josh wasn't as important to her. Better than a girl, but not as important. A supernumerary. Michael used to leave the room whenever you came to see us. He never looked at you, remember? My mother never left the room. She merely waited for you to say something stupid, some monstrous enormity she could reproach me for afterwards. But you aren't stupid, and you very seldom say anything monstrous. No more often than me and Albert Einstein, at least. Yes, it's true: my mother and Michael would have obliterated you. She and her Messiah. Josh would have made a far better Messiah. He's so emotional, he never allows himself to be ruled by his emotions. Like my father. He uses his head, whereas people like Michael are happy to be able to feel anything at all. For them, hatred is a sign of progress. My mother was utterly beside herself when Michael got married. She sobbed as if it were a funeral. She didn't cry when Josh got married, and when my turn came she was delighted to be rid of me ... Hey, would you like to know what Josh and Michael do for a living?

Tell me what Josh does.

He's a psychologist. What else could he have done? He would never advise anyone to dismantle the masculine aspects of their personality. Josh has never been scared of me. Just like you.

We were already sitting in her car in the parking lot, ready to drive off, when she added: Aside from Josh, I was the only member of the family who liked you even a little bit.

At least that made two of you, I said.

She kissed me. When we drew apart I saw a cyclist standing in front of the car. He must have been riding past and had come to a stop. He was standing some six or seven yards away, dressed in a black cyclist's outfit – one of those skintight, streamlined jobs. His face was invisible beneath a black helmet and sunglasses. Taking a pad and pencil from his little rucksack, he looked over at us, or at the car, and jotted something down. It looked as if he'd made a note of Susannah's licence number. He tore the sheet off the pad and replaced the pad and pencil in his rucksack. Then he removed his sunglasses. It was Pancho, the Mexican I'd kneed in the guts that night!

He grinned and waved the slip of paper.

I'll have to have a word with him, I told Susannah. I may be some time. Go home. If you don't hear from me within the next three hours, call the police.

Mafia? she asked.

No, I said, just someone I had a run-in with a while back. Now he's got your licence number. If you call the police, tell them you're being harassed by a Mexican. Threatened, even. He may be called Pancho, but that could be a false name. You mustn't tell them anything about me. My name mustn't be mentioned or I'll be done for. So will Sonia.

Okay, she said. Be careful.

I got out and walked towards Pancho, who hadn't stopped grinning at me. Then, when I'd almost reached him, he pedalled off. He started circling me in the almost deserted car park, maintaining enough of a gap between us for me not to be able to catch him. He kept his eyes on me the whole time. Susannah drove slowly out of the parking lot and into the street.

I tried to explain to Pancho that it had all been a

misunderstanding. That I'd thought he meant to mug me. That I'd panicked.

He kept riding around me in a circle, still grinning. I offered him money, but he just grinned even more.

Ha, you and your beautiful lady friend! he said. He spoke with a strong Latino accent – a fake accent. He hadn't had a trace of one when we'd first met. It was his way of taunting me, presumably.

Leave her out of this, I said. She's just someone I go jogging with.

Jogging? Is that what they call it now, he said, smooching in a car?

I offered him money again.

I could certainly use some of your money, he said, but my *cojones* wouldn't approve. My *cojones* very proud and very offended. My *cojones* want their revenge. You hurt them bad and they want their revenge.

I'm sorry, Pancho. I'm really sorry. It was a misunderstanding, that's all.

Not for my balls. Not for my proud Mexican balls. My balls don't misunderstand. I'll get your money anyway, but first I'll get you. The money I'll get from your lady friend.

He continued to circle me, chanting derisively, over and over: Pretty baby! Pretty, pretty baby!

Give me that piece of paper, I said, knowing that it wouldn't do me any good. Susannah's licence number is very memorable. It's "BLUBOY" followed by some numerals that are just as easy to remember.

Pancho crumpled the slip of paper, put it in his mouth and spat it out in my direction. Pretty, pretty baby, he parroted, tapping his forehead repeatedly. I supposed this meant he wouldn't forget the licence plate in a hurry.

Then he rode slowly off, heading north.

Pretty baby! Pretty, pretty baby!
Bluboy! Bluboy!
Jogging lady!
Fucking lady!
Bluboy! Bluboy!
Run, lover boy! Run, run, run!
Pretty baby! Pretty, pretty baby!

I ran after him. I didn't know what he had in mind. Perhaps he had been shadowing us for a long time and planned to lead me into a trap in some side street, where his friends would be waiting for me. Or perhaps he meant to humiliate me – to wait until I was too exhausted to defend myself, then attack me. But I continued to run in his wake.

Run, lover boy! Run, run, run!

I ran and ran.

Pretty baby! Pretty, pretty baby!

I ran and ran, further and further to the north.

I won't touch you! I called after him. I simply want you to leave us alone!

Run, lover boy! Run, run, run!

Pretty baby! Pretty, pretty baby!

Sometimes he allowed the gap between us to close, only to put on speed again. We crossed Lincoln Park and kept on going in the direction of the sea. I felt an agonizing pain in my lungs and came to a halt, barely able to stand.

I'll give you money! I shouted. But it wasn't a shout, it was a croak I could barely hear myself.

I ran on. On and on I ran, and on and on he pedalled, but the truth was, he was really chasing *me*. He was just waiting for me to exhaust myself and collapse. Through the trees we went, heading in the direction of South Bay. At one stage he stopped and waited for me to catch up.

Come on, lover boy!

Run, lover boy! Run, run, run!

Then, very slowly, he recited Susannah's licence number. That was when I grasped what I'd known all the time: Pancho couldn't be allowed to survive. He was totally uninvolved. He was innocent. It was all just a terrible coincidence, but Pancho couldn't be allowed to survive. He had that licence number in his head. He would never forget it, and he would never leave Susannah in peace. That number in his head was his death warrant. Or mine. It occurs to me as I write this – not that I thought of it while I was chasing him – that Susannah would also have been in the clear if *he* had killed *me*. He would have been a murderer, and she had seen him, and he would never have dared approach her. On the other hand, the guests at her party had seen me. They would have recognized my picture in the paper, and then nothing in the world could have saved Susannah and Sonia. But that's just hindsight. When I was chasing Pancho my one desire was to beat the number out of his body and out of his head.

All at once I felt immensely calm, immensely strong. I ran on as fast as I could. The pain in my lungs and legs had gone. I had only one ambition: to overtake Pancho and kill him.

He must have sensed the sudden change in me, because he pedalled harder. It was almost dark by now, and then came the moment when he made a mistake. He looked round at me for just too long and collided with a tree or a root, I couldn't see exactly.

He got up at once and retrieved his bicycle, but the front wheel was buckled. No one was going anywhere on that machine. I drew nearer and nearer. By the time I was almost on top of him he had a knife in his hand. I lunged at him and felt a sharp pain in my left forearm. The pain lasted only an instant, but that was long enough for Pancho. He kicked me in the stomach and ran off.

Come on, lover boy!

Run, lover boy! Run, run, run!

I sprinted after him. The path dropped away and ran steeply downhill towards the sea. I felt branches whipping my cheeks, then nothing more, as if my body had ceased to exist. I was all hatred and strength and violence.

When I reached the shore I saw a big expanse of boulders and Pancho's shadowy figure clambering over them.

He scrambled on to a rock higher up and waited there for me. Perhaps he still had his knife. I looked up at him when I was only a few yards away. Pretty baby! he began to chant, but the mockery had left his voice. He was out of breath.

Come down, I said.

He didn't budge.

Not letting him out of my sight, I knelt down and groped around for a stone until I found one the size of my fist. Then I slowly straightened up. All I could see was the outline of Pancho's head, and all I wanted was to hurl the stone at that head whose only sin was a licence number it would never forget.

I missed. Pancho laughed, and all I felt within me was cold hatred. Icy calm.

He was still laughing as I bent down, picked up another stone, and hurled it in his direction. He tried to dodge it but slipped and fell headlong on to the rocks below.

Silence fell. A terrible silence.

I picked up another stone and slowly made my way

to the spot where he had to be lying. Or waiting for me, perhaps with a knife in his hand.

But Pancho wasn't waiting for me. He was simply lying there, waiting for no one. Cautiously I bent down, laid my hand on his forehead, and said: Pancho. He didn't stir. I put two fingers on his carotid artery. Nothing. I couldn't feel a thing.

That was the last I remember. I must have passed out. I don't know how long for, but when I came to I was lying on the rocks beside Pancho. I felt his throat once more. Then I ran back up the path. I ran and kept on running, without any idea where I was going. I simply ran on and on.

I had reached a road when the headlights of a car came up behind me. The car was slowing, I noticed. It drew level with me, but I ran on. It kept pace with me, and I heard the driver's window being lowered.

Fritz!

It was Susannah.

Fritz, stop! Please stop and get in.

My God, what a sight you are, she said when I was sitting beside her.

Why didn't you go home and stay there? I said.

I couldn't just sit around, not knowing what had happened to you. What's with Pancho?

Pretty baby! I shouted hysterically. Pretty, pretty baby!

What's the matter with you?

Pancho's dead.

My God! Did you kill him?

No, I didn't. Not directly, at least. He fell.

I could see how relieved she was.

Come on, she said, we're going home. It's not far. You could use a hot bath, You're bleeding, and your face is all scratched.

252

Sunday

Some tourists found him down on the rocks the next day. His bicycle was also found. Pancho's real name was Garcia Sanchez. He'd left Los Angeles for San Francisco two years ago. The police suspected an act of revenge by some gang from LA.

I should really have got a doctor to look at the knife wound in my arm, but we couldn't take the risk. Susannah suggested driving down to Tijuana – a Mexican doctor wouldn't ask any questions – but I found that an obscene idea. I was responsible for the death of that unfortunate Mexican. How could I get a Mexican doctor to treat me? We had to risk letting the wound get infected. I had the shivers and ran a temperature for a few days, partly because of hypothermia, but my arm looks pretty good now. The scar will never disappear.

Two days later the police abandoned their act-of-revenge theory. All the suspects in LA had an alibi. Besides, the bloodstains found on Pancho's clothing hadn't come from him. Blood group A1. Mine, of course.

The police now believed that Pancho might have lost his life after mixing it with a tourist. He had once or twice been arrested on suspicion of mugging tourists in the San Francisco parks, but nothing had ever been proved against him. This was not so far from the truth.

Sonia has to leave the hotel, said Susannah. They'll be checking all the hotels.

Sonia took a taxi to the airport so that superficial investigations would suggest that she had left. Susannah picked her up at the airport and drove her home. This is precisely what shouldn't have happened, I told Susannah. Now you're landed with both of us. You're in as much danger as we are.

She simply laughed. Then she looked grave. That poor guy. I doubt if they'll trouble to run a match on your blood. He was just an anonymous Mexican, after all. Even if his name was Pancho or Garcia, he was still an anonymous Mexican, so why bother? Awful, isn't it? He died because, far away in Europe, the Russian Mafia wouldn't let a woman go, and because of all that's happened since. A terrible series of coincidences.

The series gets longer and longer, Susannah. And now I've killed the guy.

You didn't kill him. He fell.

He fell because of me. Anyway, I *would* have killed him because he'd have involved you in my problems. Because Sonia and I would have been blown.

I became involved in your problems long ago, Fritz. And I don't believe you'd have killed him. What would you have done, grabbed a rock and smashed his skull in?

I *did* kill him. Or as good as.

* * *

One or two more brief reports appeared in the papers. That, it seemed, was the most that could be done for Garcia Sanchez. But the police are bound to be checking the hotels for me. For a tourist who may have been involved in his death.

Thursday

At first I thought I was dreaming when I heard the door creak. It was dark, and I'd been fast asleep, and then I didn't think I was dreaming any more. The door really had creaked. The door of my room in Susannah's house! In the middle of the night! Fear shot through me once more – a long, violent jolt of fear. Then I gave up. Let them come for me, I thought. Let them kill me. I can't go on.

I can't go on and I won't, that's what I thought as I lay there in bed, and I let myself go. I subsided once more into sleep, or into my dream. So it was just a dream after all, and the room and time and my fear disappeared, and I was back in our Munich flat with Ellen and Jessie. The happy time. What was it Luigi had said, more than once? Life here is almost the way it was meant to be.

The door had creaked as it did then. Our kitchen door had always creaked in the days when life was the way it was meant to be. We never oiled it. And when I was cooking in the kitchen on my own and Ellen came in, the door always creaked. I could hear her before I saw her. And when the door creaked later on, it would be either Jessie or Sally, our cat.

We had found Sally on a compost heap in a public park. She was very small and utterly forlorn, just a tiny handful of cat, so to speak. Ellen picked her up and said: Poor little poppet. She was known as Poppet right from the start. We only called her Sally when we had visitors, because Poppet would have sounded a bit odd.

When everything ended and I was alone, the cat was still there. She lived on for quite some time. Her food and water bowls were in the kitchen, and at night, whenever she went for a snack, I would hear the kitchen door emit that long, wonderful creak, and for a moment it was Jessie going into the kitchen. For one brief, blissful moment.

This went on for a long time. Until Sally died. The door never creaked at night after that. And now, for the first time in all these years, a door had creaked again. Jessie came into the kitchen and nestled her head against my leg, and I said: You're welcome to come for me, you're welcome to kill me. You won't get me anyway. And then I was in another kitchen. I was lying beside my mother in that huge white cocoon, but I wasn't screaming now, nor weeping as I had when a child. My grandmother and grandfather came in and looked at us. Quite calmly. Quite serenely. Without agitation. And then, quite suddenly, Jessie was there in that huge kitchen, and we were all there together. I was with the dead, and they weren't dead at all, and I put out my hand to stroke Jessie's head, and a voice said softly: Harry! Don't be scared, it's only me.

It was Sonia, sitting on the edge of my bed.

* * *

Ellen called. Just now, while I was writing this. I pressed the button on my mobile and there was Ellen's voice: Harry, my flat has been searched. No, not ransacked, but obviously searched. Could it have been the police?

No, the police would have come with a search warrant.

I know, she said. I know.

Can you leave the building without being seen?

Yes, probably. Perhaps.

Then leave. At once. Don't let anyone see you. Hide. Go somewhere, anywhere, and don't speak to anyone. And take your mobile. I'm coming. By the next plane. Tomorrow.

Harry? Come as fast as you can.

I'm coming, Ellen, I said. I'm coming.

After the End

Harry flew to Europe the next day. He left at eight a.m., on a United Airlines flight to Amsterdam. That was three weeks ago. He used Aliosha's American passport. The passport of the man he had shot. *We* had shot.

We haven't heard from him up to now, Susannah and I. We left San Francisco two days later and are staying in a safe place. If he and Ellen fail to escape the Mafia, they'll torture him until he tells them where I am. And until he gives them Susannah's name. I can't imagine anyone not cracking under torture, so he'll tell them. And what if they do something to Ellen? I know those people, they'll do something to her if they can. If it'll make Harry talk.

I made a printout of this book, this account of our journey into fear, and read it. Then I gave it to Susannah, but Susannah felt it belonged to me. I don't know who it belongs to, but it seems I'm the only one who wants it. I shall dedicate it to Susannah.

Harry never talked to me about Ellen or Jessie. I knew nothing about them. He mentioned their names only once. It was all news to me. Not to Susannah. Susannah knows the whole story.

If they escape the Mafia they'll need protection. There's bound to be a witness protection programme in Great Britain. Perhaps they've gone to the police in Scotland and already have new identities. Except that Harry would have called us by now. Perhaps they won't let him, but we've got to find out somehow or other.

Susannah is trying to discover something through her contacts in Washington, not that they'll get anywhere if the British programme is any good. She wants to get the British and Americans to cooperate, but I don't know if she'll manage it.

Perhaps Ellen joined Harry in Amsterdam and they went to the police and turned themselves in. I've no idea.

* * *

I pray for him and Ellen. Yes, I'm a praying mafiosa. Harry was right. Some idiotic voice inside me says: Praying mantis – she gobbles him up while they're making love. But that's silly. It isn't like that. It *wasn't* like that. I'm simply praying, I don't know to what or to whom.

It's not true that Harry didn't possess a photo of Ellen. I went through his wallet once. Yes, I do things like that. I'm mistrustful. A mistrustful Russian. In his wallet was a coloured postcard of a railway station, I forget which. The station square was deserted save for a girl, a young woman, holding a bicycle and looking at the camera. She was wearing a white blouse and a red skirt with white polka dots. I couldn't make out her face because she was just a tiny figure in that vast square outside the station. Unidentifiable, though someone who knew her would probably have recognized her. There were some words written on the back of the postcard: "I didn't know you then." No signature, no name. Nothing. It was a wholly anonymous photograph. A postcard of a railway station, in fact. What else could one expect?

No, the girl was unrecognizable, but I know now that it must have been Ellen. Who else could it have been? She was sixteen or seventeen at the time. You could tell she was roughly that age from the way she held herself. That must have been when Harry was in California – when he and Susannah were together. Strange, that. I was two or three years old at the time. A general's daughter. The little daughter of Anna and Vladimir Kovalevsky. I can't understand why that girl outside the station was the only person on the postcard. Perhaps the photographer was her father, and she was the personal trace he left on it.

* * *

I wish Harry would come back to America. I'd like to see him, that's all. I want to make sure he's still alive. I wouldn't even speak to him. I'd simply like to know that he still exists. I wouldn't even have to see him again. All I ask for is his continued survival. A postcard would be enough. A view of San Francisco for tourists. A crowded cable car, perhaps, and on a nearby sidewalk it two little figures walking down the street. Ellen and Harry. Unrecognizable unless you knew them, but I'd know Harry anywhere.

That's all I ask. All I pray for. I don't know who it is I ask and pray to, but I often think, often say quietly to myself: Don't be frightened, we all have to die in the end.

But not now. Not now. Not yet.

America, autumn 2000   *Sonia Kovalevskaya*